DROP TROOPER BOOK ONE
CONTACT
FRONT

ALSO IN SERIES

DROP TROOPER BOOK ONE

CONTACT FRONT

RICK PARTLOW

DROP TROOPER BOOK ONE

CONTACT FRONT

1

THE BILLBOARD SPEWED GOVERNMENT LIES FAR ABOVE US, AND I pretended to listen while I watched the crowd in the Zocalo.

"Final casualty estimates from what has already become known colloquially as The Battle for Mars have yet to come in, but Commonwealth Fleet Admiral Sato has announced that the cruiser *Midway*, which was set to launch from the shipyards there, has been destroyed, along with several other ships in the docks for repairs and refitting. The Tahni attack was beaten back at great cost and Fleet sources say it may be some time before the cruisers lost in the strike can be rebuilt."

The talking head was narrow-faced, short-haired, and androgynous, a computer simulation meant to come across as pleasant and non-threatening while it told the masses the official story about an alien attack on the Solar System that had taken out a good portion of the Commonwealth's military arsenal. Did the government think we were stupid? Did they think if they sugar-coated the news enough that we wouldn't get scared?

Watching the cattle shuffling along obediently through the shops of the Trans-Angeles Underground, heads down over their scansheets, reading the latest celebrity gossip, I decided the government was probably right. A billion people were crammed into the Trans-Angeles Metro Center, most of them chawners on the dole in the Underground, living on free soy paste and spirulina powder and free virtual reality entertainment, in boxes ten meters on a side. Sometimes it seemed not one of them cared about anything past the end of their nose.

"Hostilities with the Tahni erupted again decades after the Truce ended the First Interstellar War," the announcer continued, "when the Tahni attacked squatter colonies in the Neutral Zone with a ruthless nuclear bombardment."

The inoffensive face was replaced by images of a planet from orbit, pinprick flares of light rising over one of the continents. *Who took the video?* I wondered. Or was it another simulation, like the announcer, like most everything about life down here in the Underground?

"Commonwealth President Gregory Jameson responded by launching targeted conventional strikes against Tahni observation posts on their side of the Neutral Zone, and it was assumed things would return to the status quo before the Tahni launched a vicious sneak attack on our military shipyards in Martian orbit."

There he was. I tuned out the billboard stream and the hawkers at their kiosks trying their best to drown it out with advertisements of their wares, and locked my focus on the man in the green and yellow jacket. It was cheap and flashy, made on the public fabricators from free patterns on recycled material, typical for the chawners in the Housing Blocks, but in this case, it was camouflage. This guy wasn't a chawner on the public dole, and he didn't live in a ten-by-ten box. The edge of a holographic tattoo crawled up the side of his neck, an expensive extravagance most people down here couldn't afford.

The backpack was what I was interested in. He tried to wear it casually, as if it was a change of clothes or his virtual reality gaming headset, but the fingers of his right hand were curled around one of the shoulder straps, gripping it like his life depended on it. I knew his face, knew his route, knew where he liked to stop for lunch. I'd been watching him for two weeks, from the minute he got off the train at Whitlow Station until he reached the far end of the Zocalo and emerged from a particular shop without his backpack.

And the very next day, if you knew the right way to ask, that shop suddenly had plenty of Kick to sell you. Synthetic endorphins were popular, incredibly addictive and illegal as hell, which meant they were big business for the people who really ran the Underground: the gangs. The Kibera 1087s, in this case. Nasty fuckers who liked to hurt people just to make a point. They manufactured the Kick in labs deep inside their territory, where the cops were afraid to go, but there was no money in the Housing Blocks and the working class who would come to the Zocalo to buy drugs wouldn't risk going down into the Kibera. So, they used couriers. Like Mr. Ugly Jacket here.

He passed by my position without giving me a glance and I fell in behind him, blending into the crowd. It was a diverse group, like all the Zocalos in the mega-city, mixing the typical Underground dwellers with the more upwardly-mobile working poor from slightly higher in the food chain. There were even a few of the ground-level surface-dwellers who worked hard enough to see the towers where the Corporate Council bigwigs lived, even if they'd never set foot in them. That sort of envy might even make me want to slap a drug patch on my neck and feel like a king for a couple hours.

But I'd settle for the money I'd get from stealing their drugs and selling them myself. It was still addictive, but I can quit anytime I want. I touched a control on my datalink and it posted a pre-arranged ad on a public personals site, where anyone could see it. No direct connection between me and anyone else. Ten meters away, a slender, leggie girl with bobbed pink hair and calf-high boots shifted her course just a step or two, her eyes down like everyone else's, a public scansheet in her hand playing a video only she could hear on her ear bud.

I slipped a hand into my jacket pocket and felt the cold ceramic and plastic of the stun wand, and flicked off the safety with my thumb. The pink-haired girl gasped an apology as she bumped into the courier and he cursed at her in a patois of Spanish, English and Tagalog. He'd pay for it two seconds later. I jammed the business end of the stun wand into his side and held down the trigger.

Ugly Jacket Man stiffened, every muscle in his body tensing up as the shock coursed through him. This close, I could smell the cheap cologne he used way too much of, the sickeningly sweet stench filling the air between us and making me want to gag. I grabbed the right shoulder strap of the jacket just as I let off the trigger, stripping it off him with practiced smoothness as he collapsed to the tile floor, slipping it onto my own back and stepping past him as if nothing had happened.

Pris didn't slow down, didn't look back, her pink bob merging into the crowd as she headed off away from the Zocalo toward the train station. I arced around the edge of the kiosks, not wanting to look as if I were following her, but needing to get to the same place as quick as possible. I tried to stick to the spots where the crowd was the thickest, but the group I'd fallen in with was heading for an entrance to the Zocalo, and when I split off from them, I was suddenly alone and very, very obvious.

I'd known there would be security. An outfit like the 1087s wouldn't send a shipment of Kick worth thousands of Trade-notes to the Zocalo without having someone around to watch the courier's back. I'd been counting on speed and confusion to shield us from them, but I locked eyes with a tall, dark-eyed, raven-haired man thirty meters away and I had a suspicion I was screwed. When he pulled a gun, I was certain of it.

The hair rose on the back of my neck. Guns were incredibly easy to fabricate and cheap to buy, but hard to get past the security on the trains, which meant this guy had either bribed the right person or managed to get the patterns for an undetectable pistol. Either possibility meant he was someone good enough with a gun for the 1087s to go to this much trouble.

I ducked right, then cut left just as he fired his first shot. It wasn't loud, the sound of someone clapping their hands, and I wasn't sure if anyone except me noticed it. If it hit anything, the noise of the crowd covered the sound of the ricochet and before he could fire again, I was running.

Pris turned from her casual stride across the square and her eyes went wide.

"Cam?" she blurted, and I was too scared to be mad at her for using my name.

"Go!" I urged her.

It was probably the wrong decision. If she'd stayed put and pretended she didn't know me, the shooter might have ignored her. But I didn't have time to sit around and debate, and the image of her standing there like a statue while some gangbanger shitbag put a bullet through her head seemed more pressing than second-guessing myself. She ran, and I pushed her ahead of me, heading for the train station.

There were detectors there, and even if the gun could beat those, there were live cops. The shooter wouldn't want to chance a run-in with the Transit Authority Police. Not even the 1087s fucked with the TAPs.

Another hand-clap somewhere behind me and someone screamed. I knew screams, knew their subtleties and varieties very well, and this one was pain, not fear. I grabbed Pris by the hand and ran faster, knowing how hard it would be for her to keep up in those damned boots. I'd told her not to wear the boots, but she never listened.

"Have you got the bag?" I asked her, yelling breathlessly. She nodded, not speaking, either because she was already tired or too scared to talk. "We're going to duck into the bathroom and make the transfer. Get ready."

She fumbled at her waist, unbuckling an expandable pack and pulling it open. Getting the pack had been the hardest part of the whole job. Not that it was impossible to find a signal jamming container, but most of the sources for them were the gangs, and the whole purpose of this was to pull it off without letting the gangs know who did it. That way, they'd all want to blame each other for it.

We dodged behind a cluster of people who were finally looking up at the world, just noticing the screaming and the commotion around whoever had caught the bullets meant for us, and used the concealment to duck into the restroom. The first half a dozen stalls were occupied and panic surged in my gut at the idea the gunman would walk in on us as we circled the curve of the restroom corridor searching for an open toilet and kill us here in the bathrooms.

A young woman with a little boy in tow was camped outside one of the doors, waiting for it to open and I groaned at the thought they must all be in use, but then a door popped open and a doughy-faced older man dressed in clothes two sizes too large for him stumbled out, waving a hand across his face.

"Might not want to go in there right away," he cautioned me, but I ignored him and pulled Pris inside, pushing the door shut.

"Oh, Jesus!" Pris exclaimed, covering her mouth with her hand at the smell. "Hurry up, Cam!"

I held my breath as I pulled the backpack off and ripped it open. The drug patches were sealed in individual plastic cases, and the whole thing was sealed a second time in a large bag. The tracker would be planted somewhere in all that shit, and there was no time to dig it out right now. I stuffed the plastic bag into the waist pack and shoved it at Pris, then slipped the backpack onto my shoulders.

"Wait thirty seconds," I told her, "then get on the train and head back to the Favela. If I don't show up in two hours, your best bet is to dump it and run."

She nodded, but I knew she wouldn't do it. If I didn't show up, she'd take it to the broker herself and try to sell it. Pris was nothing if not self-sufficient, which was why I was with her. I didn't like needy girls. She braved the smell in the toilet to kiss me, and then I was out the door again.

The bathroom corridor curved in a half-circle and I followed it out the other entrance, walking fast rather than running, not wanting to rush into the path of a bullet. I saw him almost immediately, towering over most of the crowd only twenty meters away, his right hand and the gun I presumed he still held concealed under his jacket. He hadn't seen me, but I needed him to, so I ran.

The walkway between the Zocalo and the train station was packed with pedestrians, but I didn't try to weave through them, pushing them out of the way instead. Yells, curses, and obscene gestures followed me, a signpost for the 1087 gunman. He'd be coming after me, which was just what I wanted, but I needed to get inside the train station. I didn't think he'd follow me in there, not with the TAPs ready to swarm all over him. That was what I kept telling myself.

The entrance to the station was a broad archway, made from cheap buildfoam like everything else down here but with a façade of fake brick, as if it were a leftover from the old world. What bullshit. I knew the old world and I didn't want to be reminded of it, but I was happy as hell to make it through that arch, because it was where the weapons detectors were housed.

Come on, just stay out there. It's not worth the risk for you to come in here.

I slowed my pace and risked a look behind me.

"Shit," I muttered.

The tall man hadn't even hesitated, just followed me right through the detectors. Maybe he'd ditched the gun, but I couldn't take that chance. I didn't have time to wait for a train and if he followed me onto one, I'd be just as dead. I took off for the north terminal at a jog. There were four tracks running parallel from south to north, each reachable by a series of escalators arcing over the intervening trains.

These weren't evacuated bullet trains running on magnetic suspension like I'd heard they had between the cities, thank God, just regular monorails. If the tracks had been sealed, there would have been no way I could get away with this.

I ran up the escalator three steps at a time, wriggling around other travelers where I could, pushing them out of the way when I had to, and not sticking around to hear them curse me out. I slid down the handrail on the other side, earning a few dirty looks and nearly falling off the edge and busting my ass, then I was up the next one to do it all over again.

I didn't see the TAPs and damn it, for once I wanted to. If the TAPs were running a patrol, they'd stop me or the gangbanger, and either one would work. I wasn't carrying any contraband and I wasn't wanted for anything at the moment. Sliding down the escalator might get me a ticket, or a three-day ban from the station, but I could live with that.

There's never a cop around when you need one.

I stopped at the bottom of the last escalator, panting in exhaustion, my adrenalin running low, sweat soaking the small of my back and dripping down into my face. I wiped it away, deciding I needed a haircut, and checked behind me.

Son of a bitch. The black-haired man was coming over the top of the last arch and didn't even seem out of breath...and his gun was in his hand.

I bolted for the tracks. Some places, they had polycarbonate shields in place to keep people from doing just what I was about to do, but if there'd ever been any here, they'd taken them out years ago and left us peons to Darwin's mercy. The yellow lights were flashing that a train was coming, but I wasn't going to wait for it. I vaulted the railing, bending my knees to absorb the impact of the two-meter drop and still twisting my ankle a little.

The lights were flashing red now, and an alarm was sounding, but the train was going too fast to stop this close. I ignored the flare of agony in my ankle and hopped over the rail assembly in the center of the tunnel, trying to get up a running start before I hit the opposite wall. I could see the maintenance door, just fifteen meters or so down the tunnel along the walkway. It was locked, but I'd paid a worker in Kick to get the universal code key a couple months ago.

I jumped and snagged the edge of the walkway with my fingertips, the worn buildfoam way too smooth and slick from decades of use. The toes of my work boots scraped against the surface of the wall as I pulled up straight, trying to use the big muscles of my back. My forearms burned and I kicked my legs like I was running in mid-air, putting every last bit of desperate energy I had into getting my center of gravity over that wall.

There was a roaring in my ears, and as much as I wanted to think it was my adrenalin rush hitting again, I knew it was the train coming. A bullet smacked into the wall beside me and I rolled over the top of the walkway and fell flat. The tall man had climbed over the railing on the other side and jumped down after me, and he was vaulting over the monorail assembly, still shooting one-handed as he came, the rounds hitting the wall behind me.

He was a meter from clearing the track when the train hit him.

Blood sprayed across the wall a few centimeters over my head and I closed my eyes out of instinct, even though it was too late. The train rumbled past, slowing to a gradual halt with a screech of brakes as the first cars reached the other end of the station, a hundred meters away. I was drained, empty, lacking the energy to even roll over, but I had to move. I pushed myself up onto my knees and struggled to my feet, sucking in a long breath.

The door. Had to get to the door. What was the code?

Damn it, I couldn't remember.

I pulled my datalink off my belt and pulled up the note I'd made myself, my fingers clumsy and fumbling. There it was. I tapped it into the keyboard on the door's security plate and was rewarded with a solid green light across top of the plate and a welcoming click of an electromagnetic lock releasing.

I laughed and pulled the door open.

A Transit Authority Police trooper waited on the other side in grey body armor and a dark-visored helmet, the bell-shaped muzzle of his sonic stunner pointed right at my head. I didn't even have time to curse before he shot me.

2

"CAMERON ALVAREZ?"

I looked up from the scansheet at the speaker set in the cell door.

"You know it's me," I grunted, not bothering to get up from where I squatted on the floor of the little three-meter by three-meter chamber.

The scansheet gave me the choice of streaming the latest news from the war or celebrity gossip, and I couldn't figure out which was more irrelevant to my life. Since most of my last three weeks had involved staring at the walls of this damned Transit Authority holding cell, it was *all* pretty much irrelevant. I'd woken up here with a headache, a brand-new yellow jumpsuit, a flimsy scansheet, and not a damned thing else.

"I need positive acknowledgement of your identity," the voice went on, patiently, "for your scheduled meeting with your court-appointed advocate."

My eyes rolled so hard I thought they might stick in that position. No use arguing. This was an automated system.

"Yeah, I am Cameron Alvarez," I said. I pushed my back against the smooth, white wall and slid up to my feet, tossing the scansheet on the bunk.

"Turn and face the wall with your hands behind your back," the faceless voice instructed. "If you attempt to resist, you will be stunned."

"I've heard it all before," I muttered, turning away from the door like a good little peon and obeying the machine.

It rolled in on plastic casters and slipped plastic restraint straps around my wrists, tightening them just to the point of being uncomfortable before it backed away.

"Turn around and follow the security bot. If you attempt to run, you will be stunned."

"Yeah, I know."

The halls were narrow and grey, and unoccupied. That was probably by design. I imagined they timed things like this so there wouldn't be multiple prisoners in the hallways at once. Probably a lot of gang beefs that could erupt into something violent otherwise. If the 1087s knew who I was, I could be on the receiving end of one of those beefs.

The bot led me to an unmarked doorway. None of the doorways had any markings, again probably by design. Hard to make an escape when you didn't have any idea where you were. The door opened automatically onto a tiny booth with a single chair, the walls a shining silver concave. Holographic projection screens.

"Fucking virtual meeting," I sighed, stepping inside anyway. I should have known.

"I am removing your restraints," the automated voice informed me. "Do not attempt to run or…"

"Or I'll be stunned," I finished for the thing. I cocked an eyebrow at it. "Right?"

"That is correct."

Thing wasn't sophisticated enough to have a sense of humor.

The plastic straps fell off my wrists at the machine's metal manipulation, and before I could turn around, it was gone and the door closed.

"Please sit down so the meeting with your court-appointed advocate can begin," the voice advised me. Damned thing got around.

The moment my butt hit the plastic, I was somewhere else.

The room was full of leather upholstered furniture and real, hardback books in real wooden shelves and all bright with real sunlight and just screamed at me that yes, this was all a simulation. Across the mahogany desk from me was a handsome, blond-haired man with skin too smooth and teeth too bright to be real, dressed in what looked like a vat-grown business suit that would have cost more than I could make in my whole life.

"Good morning, Mr. Alvarez," he said with the false cheer of a salesman or a lawyer. "I'm Neville Bickerton, your court-appointed advocate."

"You're a fucking AI subroutine," I corrected him. "Let's skip the play-acting and just tell me how bad it is."

"As you wish." The smile didn't waver, but the simulated lawyer sorted through a stack of simulated papers from a simulated file folder until he found the one he wanted. "Mr. Alvarez, you're being charged with felony battery, possession of illegal narcotics, reckless endangerment and felony homicide."

"Felony homicide?" I repeated, disbelieving. "Of who?"

"Whom," he corrected me. "Of one Mr. Ivan Jaropillo." He held up a still photo of the raven-haired gunman, except this one was a file photo taken from the man's police record.

"He jumped in front of a Goddamned train!" I protested, throwing my hands up. "While trying to kill me! How the hell is that my fault?"

"Technically," my AI lawyer explained with the patience of a computer simulation, "if you are in the act of committing a felony and anyone in any way connected to that felony is killed, by accident or even by the police, you're culpable for felony murder." He smiled again. "In all likelihood, this charge would be dropped in a plea bargain were we to threaten to take the case to trial."

"Well, let's fucking threaten then!" I said. "I didn't kill anyone!"

"That's one option, but there are others, if you'd care to hear them."

"Fire away, Neville." I sank down in my chair, head in my hands. Murder. They wanted to charge me with murder.

"The main problem, Mr. Alvarez, is that you're nineteen years old and a legal adult now. Your previous offenses were as a juvenile, your sentences of professional counseling were completed, and your records sealed. This is different. If you're convicted of felony murder, you'll be looking at a century of punitive hibernation, minimum."

"That's as good as a death sentence," I said. "Even if the Tahni don't kill us all, some asshole judge or politician could decide it would be popular with the voters to leave the murderers in hibernation forever."

"Possibly. Even if, as I've theorized, the prosecution dropped this charge, the cumulative sentence for the rest of them, which are undeniable and inarguable, would most likely come to either fifty years hibernation or twenty years of restitutive labor with compulsory vocational training in one of the colonies."

Working for room and board for twenty years on some shithole colony world, learning how to be a fabricator repair tech or an algae farmer. If there was a fate *worse* than death, that might be it.

"And what else?" I pressed him. "You said there were other options, so what are they?"

"There are two." Bickerton steepled his fingers, elbows resting on the desk. "If you were willing to give up your partner, Priscilla Young, and tell us where she took the synthetic endorphins to sell them, your sentence would be reduced to five years restitutive labor on a colony of your choice from an approved list."

"No." My voice was flat, the firmness of the instantaneous decision surprising me.

"The police know she was involved," Bickerton assured me. "She was observed on security cameras accompanying you into the bathroom area and her social media accounts show a relationship with you lasting for the previous ninety-four days." His eyebrow went up. "Although two weeks ago, she attempted to wipe you from her streams and is now in a relationship with a man named Nazir."

I grunted. That didn't take long.

"It doesn't matter," I insisted, staring at the grain of the simulated mahogany. I felt as if I could see patterns in it if I looked close enough. "I'm not a rat. Put me in fucking deep sleep if that's what they want. Not like I have anyone that would care."

"There is one other possibility," Bickerton reminded me. I met his eyes, far too blue to be natural. "You'll receive a full pardon for all crimes committed up to this point if you agree to enlist in the Commonwealth Fleet Marine Corps."

I blinked, stared at him for a long second, then blinked again, wondering if I'd heard him right.

"What?"

"If you agree to enlist in the Marines," he reiterated, "and make it successfully through training, you'll receive a full pardon and have your record expunged. When your enlistment is up, you'll be eligible to emigrate to a colony of your choice at the government's expense."

"Shit." I breathed the word out like a prayer. "Are things really going that bad?"

"Badly."

"Are you a lawyer or a grammarbot?" I snapped, getting irritated with the AI.

"The official reports," the Bickerton-bot told me, ignoring my comment, "are that the war is going well, that Commonwealth Fleet forces are striking deep into the heart of the enemy." The corner of the simulacrum's mouth turned up. "As I am your advocate, I am obligated to tell you everything my sources have heard, and the rumors are that we're getting our asses kicked."

I snorted, not at the bad news but the turn of phrase from the strait-laced AI.

"The military settled into a defensive stance after the Truce and was totally unprepared for a shooting war. The Marines, in particular, had nowhere near the personnel they need for any sort of ground war and they're desperate for warm bodies." Bickerton hesitated just like a real person might have. He was, if nothing else, well written. "I have to warn you, rumors are that casualties have been high. They wouldn't be making this offer if the odds weren't against most of their recruits surviving."

I said nothing, closing my eyes, shutting out the illusion and trying to think.

It didn't work.

"Yeah, okay. Sign me up. Get me the hell out of here."

"Tell me something, Mr. Alvarez," Bickerton said, and I thought I detected a very human-like curiosity in his tone, "why would you risk this to protect Ms. Young? Every indication is she merely used you and discarded you."

"That's who she is," I admitted, maybe to him, or maybe to myself. "But it's not who I am."

Twelve Years Old:

The foster care facility was like all the others, like every group home I'd been in since I'd come to Trans-Angeles: crowded, tense, tiered like a wolf pack. Curtis was the Alpha. Taller than anyone else by a head, fourteen years old, past any hope of adoption. No one wanted a violent teenager, not even when the government would pay extra for him.

I wasn't sure why the people who ran the place put up with him, but maybe they needed that extra cash…and maybe he was a good actor when he was around them. Most sociopaths are. I'd looked up shit like that on the scansheets, just to figure out what particular kind of crazy

Curtis was. Well, maybe it was just to get some cool-sounding names to call him when he was being a dick.

Like now.

"Get out of my fucking way, Alvarez," he said, trying to make it a growl. His voice broke just a bit at the end, spoiling the effect. "I won't tell you again."

I snuck a look over my shoulder at the girl. Her name was Natalia and she had about a year on me, but looked older than that, with curly red hair down to her back, which was what had attracted Curtis to her when she'd arrived a few days ago. I'd been a bit googly-eyed at her myself, until Mr. Matvienko had introduced her, telling us in his own, incredibly awkward and cringy way that she was "developmentally challenged," which I'm sure made her feel great about herself.

She looked even more helpless and scared now than she had slinking in behind Matvienko. Her shirt was pulled open and there were red marks on her arm from where Curtis had grabbed her. If it had been one of the other girls in the home, I might not have worried about it. They were tough, nearly as tough as Curtis, and there were lines even he wouldn't cross with them.

"Leave her alone," I said. It was a lot of words. I didn't say much, especially not to Curtis.

His shove was hard, harder than I remembered from the last time. He might have gained some weight, probably from eating other kids' share of the food. I went back a step but set my feet and squared off again. I wasn't sure why. What did I care about this weird girl I'd only met a few days ago? But I couldn't stop thinking about Mom, and what she'd say.

"You don't learn, do you, you little shit?" He liked to swear a lot. He thought it made him sound more like an adult. "I run this place, not Old Man Matvienko. Me."

"Sure." I shrugged. I didn't care. "Just leave her alone." My jaw clenched. "It's not right."

His fist came out of nowhere and I didn't have time to block, just jerked back instinctively. His knuckles grazed my cheek, a dull pain spreading out through my sinuses in contrast to the sharp spike of fear in my chest. I wanted very badly to run, but the girl wouldn't move, just sat huddled against the wall, knees drawn up to her chest, eyes hidden behind an arm. And I couldn't leave her there, not with Curtis worked up like this. I raised my fists up to guard my face and bounced on the balls of my feet the way I'd seen the fighters do it on the net. Mr. Matvienko said those fights were virtual reality, but they were based on how people really used to box.

Curtis snorted a laugh and swung at me again, a hard punch, putting all his weight behind it. I wanted to duck away again, but that wasn't what the guys in the videos had done, so I went forward, past his fist, inside the swing. The bone of his forearm stung when it connected with the back of my head, but not as much as the punch would have. I planted a fist into his gut, almost surprised when it connected. His breath was stale in my face as it whooshed out of him, distracting me, but I had the thought I should hit him again while I had the chance.

It wasn't a great punch, clumsy and lacking the force I'd hoped for, and it probably cut my knuckles worse than it hurt his teeth. But when he stumbled back, I saw blood on his lip and felt a momentary elation... until he spat the blood on the floor and snarled.

The blows rained down so close together I couldn't hope to block them all, and I just covered my face as best I could. My ear was ringing, my ribs aching, and blood was dripping from my nose when someone finally pulled Curtis off me.

I squinted up from a fetal position on the ground and saw Mr. Matvienko scowling down at me through bushy, black eyebrows.

"What in the hell is going on here?" he roared. "Why are you boys fighting?"

Were we fighting? It had felt more like a beatdown to me, but okay.

"Alvarez started it," Curtis said, pointing an accusing finger at me. "See this cut on my lip?" He pulled his lower lip down to show the old man the blood there. There was a shitload more of it flowing down my shirt from my busted nose, but I guessed that didn't matter. "He sucker-punched me and I got mad and hit him a few times."

"Is that true, Cameron?" Matvienko demanded, hands on his hips

I looked back at Natalia, hoping she'd say something. If I said it, the old man wouldn't believe me, and none of the others would back me up. They were too afraid of Curtis. But if Natalia told the truth, told the old man what Curtis had done, maybe they'd have to get him out of here, put him in a psych evaluation center or something...

She shook her head, said nothing.

"Yeah," I muttered, wiping blood out of my face. I could taste it coppery and sickly-sweet in the back of my throat and I fought to keep from throwing up.

"Let's see if spending the next two days locked in your room will adjust your attitude then, young man."

"No!" I said quickly. If I was locked in my room, Curtis could find a time to get the girl alone. "Please, something else, Mr. Matvienko..."

The old man's face twisted in thought the way it always did.

"All right," he said. "If you apologize to Curtis, then I suppose we could give you another chance."

Oh, that was just fucking great. Apologize to the giant sore on the ass of humanity because I was the only one with the balls to stand up to him. I thought of the fear on Natalia's face and swallowed blood along with pride.

"I'm sorry," I said, putting all the hatred I could summon behind my eyes.

"That's okay, Alvarez," Curtis said, his sneer marred slightly by the cut on his lip. "I know you'll make it up to me."

"There you go!" Matvienko said, as cheerful as if it had never happened. "I knew you two could work it out."

He left the room, but the sneer didn't leave Curtis' face.

"Oh yeah," he assured me, hands tightening again into fists. "We'll work it out."

3

"I'VE BEEN OUT IN SPACE FOR TWO WEEKS," THE GUY NEXT TO ME IN the shuttle complained, "and I haven't seen anything but the inside of a ship."

He was about my age, I thought, maybe a year or two younger, but with one of those lean faces you thought might be older at first. He had his hair buzzed short like he'd already been getting ready for Boot Camp before he even boarded the ship to Inferno. His accent was familiar to me. I'd heard it sometimes in the Zocalo, from the rich kids who came down there to slum. I didn't know what the hell a rich kid would be doing in the Marines, but that wasn't my business.

"You'd rather have been riding outside in a suit?" the girl on the other side of him wondered, chuckling so softly I almost couldn't hear it over the distant bang of the maneuvering thrusters taking us out of the docking bay of the transport.

As the shuttle emerged from the metallic womb of the ship, the light of the system's primary star whited out the image in the passenger cabin's overhead viewscreens for a second until it adjusted the contrast. The ruddy brown and algae green of Inferno came into focus as the merciless glare of 82 Eridani faded in the background and I sighed in anticipation of the misery. They'd warned me it would be hot. The Underground was never hot.

"There's your view, buddy," I said, nudging the guy who'd complained. "Get used to it. We'll be spending a lot of time there."

"Eden's just an orbit over," he mused, eyes fixed on the scorched desert and steaming jungles below us. "Temperate, comfortable, a paradise."

"You been there?" I wondered.

"Me?" He shook his head. "Naw, I've never been off Earth. Just audited it a lot, virtual reality and stuff. That's why I joined. To get away...from Earth, I mean."

"Yeah," I murmured. "I guess most of us joined to get away from something."

"Secure for boost in thirty seconds," the shuttle's crew chief warned us over the intercom. "Things are gonna be uncomfortable for a few minutes."

I made a face, remembering the shuttle I'd taken from the Trans-Angeles spaceport to McAuliffe Station.

"I'm Randall Munroe," the lean-faced kid told me, sticking out a hand.

I stared at it, cocking an eyebrow. Shaking hands was a rich people thing. He seemed to remember that suddenly and reddened, offering me a forearm. I bumped it with mine.

"Cam Alvarez," I returned.

"Maybe I'll see you around down there," he said, grinning.

Rich people sure were talkative. He sounded lonely, though, and he also sounded like a guy who wasn't used to being lonely.

"Yeah." It wasn't likely, but no use bringing him down any more. "Good luck."

Then six gravities of boost kicked us in the ass and we weren't in the mood to talk any more. I don't know why going-down boost hurt more than coming-up boost, but somehow, it did. Or maybe it was just worse because I knew what to expect. It was like a boot on my chest...or maybe more like every boot of every asshole in the Underground who'd ever beaten me down standing on my chest at once.

The crew chief had said a few minutes, but I could have sworn it was hours and I couldn't even keep my eyes open long enough to look at the viewscreen, I just had a vague impression of black turning to blue and white, brown and green, and then black again as we crossed the terminator to the night side of the planet.

Finally, God took his foot off my face and everything was black clouds for long minutes and not one of us said a word. It wasn't like we'd been told not to talk, more like those black clouds had slipped through the fuselage of the shuttle and settled in among us, leaving each of us alone with their thoughts. We'd all said our oaths and signed on the dotted line, but once the shuttle touched down at the base, that was it. Our old lives were over.

Shit.

Now I was doing it to myself. I closed my eyes and tried to clear my head, the same way I'd used to when I was sleeping in the maintenance tunnels because the gangs were looking for me at my apartment…well, at the closet the government had given me and called an apartment. One was as good as the other, except for the roaches and the rats. The tunnels didn't have as many of either. The tunnels didn't have a door I could lock, though, and every noise sounded like someone coming to kill me.

It still worked. When I opened my eyes, we were on the ground and the belly ramp was lowering with a whine of servos.

That was when all hell broke loose.

"Get out of my fucking shuttle, you maggots!"

I hadn't actually seen the man board the craft, but I'd been trying to find the quick-release for my seat restraints and I'd just got my hand on it when the scream echoed off the fuselage like a sledge hammer. I yanked down on it reflexively and the straps parted ways from the hub at my chest, but I was still frozen in place by the shock.

He was short and wide, perhaps wider than any man I'd ever seen. I figured he must have been raised in a higher gravity field than Earth or Inferno because there was no way that was natural. His neck was about as big around as my thigh and he was nearly as broad at the shoulders as he was tall and the green and khaki dress uniform he wore must have been fabricated specially for him, because there was no way anyone stocked that size.

"Are you motherfuckers fucking deaf?" This time, the bellow was so loud it seemed to physically slam into my head, a sonic slap to the face. If you looked up the definition of "furious" on the net, you'd find this guy's face. "I said, get out of my fucking shuttle and do it now!"

Munroe was the first one out of his seat, and after him. It was like someone had uncorked the bottle and we all rushed out in a sea of arms and legs and wide-open eyes. All I had to do was step out of my row and I was pushed along with the flood of humanity almost tumbling down the belly ramp to stumble onto the pavement below. It still radiated heat from the landing jets and between that, the ambient humidity, and the glaring floodlights surrounding the landing pad, I was sweating through my clothes in seconds.

I looked around, wondering where to go, instinctively watching the surrounding darkness for avenues of escape.

"What the fuck is this sorry gaggle of useless pieces of shit?"

It was the short, wide guy again...no, it wasn't. There were more of them, coming in from all sides, dressed alike but shaped differently. A couple of them were women, though any one of them seemed large and mean enough to kill me with their bare hands.

"Get your goddamned feet on the footprints, you worthless maggots!"

"Feet on the footprints! We drew you a fucking picture! Can you not even read pictures?"

What footprints? The thought was desperate, and I looked around in the air like a moron, wondering what the hell they were talking about. But I saw other people looking downward and my face flushed with the heat of embarrassment, realizing there were yellow footprints painted on the ground off to the side of the pad. I scrambled over to the nearest unoccupied set and stood in them, daring to take a breath now that I was doing what they wanted.

That was a mistake. My shoulders had barely had time to sag when one of the human public-address speakers ran up to me as if he was going to tackle me and take me to the ground, though his arms were almost thrown back behind him to get his face closer to mine. I couldn't describe what he looked like, because he was too close for my eyes to focus on him.

"Get your sorry ass in the position of attention, you fucking maggot! That means straight up and down, eyes forward, hands at your sides, chest out, gut in, heels together, don't move and don't say a fucking word! Have you got that?"

"Yes, sir..." I began. Mistake number two.

"I said don't say a fucking word!" I could smell coffee on his breath and spittle hit my cheek like raindrops. "Don't move, don't say a fucking word! Is that clear? And don't fucking call me sir, I work for a living! When you address me, it will be with one of three phrases! 'Yes, Drill Sergeant,' 'No, Drill Sergeant,' or 'No excuse,

Drill Sergeant!' Now you may speak, do you fucking understand me?"

"Yes, Drill Sergeant!" I barked the words as if my life depended on them.

"Out-fucking-standing! Now stay here until someone tells you to move!"

I sure as hell wasn't going to move. My legs were quivering and I was sweating and bugs were flying around my head and landing on my neck. I felt one bite and wanted to swat at it, but I restrained myself. At some point, one of the sergeants yelled at all of us to get on the bus, except with a lot more expletives, and it was taken up like a chorus by the rest of them. This time we all ran for it, not only wanting to obey their orders but also just to get the hell out of there.

We squeezed a good fifty people into a bus meant to hold about thirty-five, and now that I had the time to look around, I could see other buses loading down the line, from other shuttles landing. We weren't the only late-night arrivals, and if this was a typical day…

"Jesus," I muttered. "How many people are they bringing in here?"

What the hell had I gotten myself into?

———

"Get your lazy, filthy asses out of bed!"

The words were punctuated by the crash of a metal trash can on the bare cement floor of the barracks and the flare of sun-bright lights coming on overhead. I nearly fell out of the top bunk before I realized where I was.

"Platoon guide! I better have a platoon guide in front of me by the count of five!" That was one of the female Drill Sergeants. Her name tape read Benitez, but it didn't matter. None of them had names except "Drill Sergeant," as far as we were concerned. "Five, four, three…"

I didn't know the poor son of a bitch who'd been appointed platoon guide, but his name was Williams or something, and he was dressed in a white T-shirt, underwear, and black socks and he looked about as ridiculous as anything I could have imagined and as scared shitless as I would have been.

"Yes, Drill Sergeant!" He screamed the words because if there was one thing we'd been taught in the last couple days, it was that we could never answer the Drill Sergeants loud enough to satisfy them.

"Get this pig-sty cleaned up, get your filthy bodies cleaned up, and get into your fatigues! I want everyone out in front of the barracks and ready to march in exactly one hour, and for every minute you're late after that, you'll spend ten minutes in the PT pit! Do I make myself clear, Private Williams?"

"Yes, Drill Sergeant!" was the only acceptable answer.

Williams turned on the rest of us with wide eyes and a look of abject desperation on his hollow-cheeked face, his mouth working for a moment but nothing coming out.

"Assign one squad to clean the floor," I murmured, "one to make the beds and two to go shower, and then swap them out and have the last two clean the toilets." It was pretty fucking obvious.

He didn't hear me, but I think the Drill Sergeant did. Her eyes narrowed as they fell on me, her mouth a thin line, and I thought she was going to light into me, but she said nothing.

"First squad!" Williams squeaked. "Get on the bathrooms! Everyone else get dressed and then make your bunks!" He squeezed his eyes shut and spluttered a correction. "I mean, everyone else get showered and dressed and then make your bunks!"

Oh, good God, he was screwing this up already. Oh well, it wasn't my problem. I mean, it *was*, in that I was going to wind up doing push-ups and sit-ups and a bunch of other different exercises I had never heard of until two days ago out in the sand pit, in the brutal heat and humidity of mid-day on this half of Inferno. But I knew interfering with Williams' pathetic attempt at organization would only get me stuck in his position, because that was exactly how he had wound up in charge.

If everyone was going to be blamed for the platoon guide's screw-ups, I'd rather be hot and sweaty and anonymous than hot and sweaty, desperate and hated. I grabbed my shower kit and waited for the upcoming disaster.

It didn't go as badly as I thought. We managed to make it outside before the hour was up, despite the fact that Williams' screw-up meant we had to clean the bathroom twice. Of course, we'd probably fail the inspection the same way we had yesterday. That guy Munroe had told me on the flight from Earth that the Drill Sergeants *always* found a reason to fail you during inspections, no matter how hard you worked. He'd said the whole purpose of Basic Training was to tear down what you had been as a civilian and rebuild you into a Marine.

I wasn't sure how well that was going to work with me. There wasn't much there to tear down.

We marched to breakfast in the dark, ate it under the anemic lights of the dining facility, sitting at attention the whole time, then lined up again just as 82 Eridani was peeking over the horizon and marched back to the in-processing center. That was why they'd given us so much time to get ready, why they'd woken us up before reveille, why they hadn't put us straight into the PT pit. Because we had yet another day of in-processing.

I'd been through a full medical and psychological exam before I'd left Earth, and I knew those records were attached to my profile, but for some reason, I had to do everything again here, just in case I'd developed a genetic disorder between Earth and Inferno. They scanned every centimeter of my body with lasers, MRIs, CAT scans, ultrasounds, alpha wave detectors, and other shit I couldn't remember even though the techs had cheerfully informed me of each and every procedure. They took enough blood and genetic samples to clone bits of me if they had to, which I supposed made sense.

Then there were even more psychological tests. They put a neural halo on my temples and flashed pictures at me while the machine read my responses. I just sat there, helpless to fake anything because I didn't even know what they were looking for. I don't know that I would have tried to cheat even if I could have. If my artificial attorney had been telling the truth, they were desperate enough to take street criminals, so a little personality disorder probably wouldn't get me shipped back to Earth for punitive hibernation.

We marched back to the chow hall for lunch, only getting screamed at three times for being out of step, though one of those times was my fault.

"Your other left, Private Alvarez! Do they not teach you Earther dumbasses your right from your left?"

It was hot by then. I mean, it's almost always hot on Inferno. Half of the damned planet is uninhabitable most of the year, and the half the Commonwealth Space Fleet had taken possession of during the first War with the Tahni ranged from uncomfortably warm in a winter I'd only heard rumors of, to the oh-my-God-it's-hot we were experiencing currently. But at mid-day, the too-close primary star added its convection-oven best to the Godawful humidity and beat the worst day I remembered from Tijuana. Of course, I had been a little kid then, and the heat didn't seem as bad.

Nothing seemed as bad.

I couldn't remember what lunch had been about two minutes after eating it. I mean, it was soy paste and spirulina powder, but I didn't even notice what artistic representation of real food they'd tried to mold it into with the food processors. Something like pasta and maybe faux chicken? I had to keep my eyes straight ahead the whole time so I couldn't even look at it, and we had about five minutes to get through the line and shovel down the food before we were back at in-processing again.

This time, the tests were different. They popped me into a Virtual Reality pod with a neural halo hugging my temples, controls in my hands and under my feet, and projected spheres of various colors in the haze of grey surrounding me, with an aiming reticle in the center like I'd seen in virtual reality games I'd played a few times. On other people's game sets. I couldn't afford one and didn't have an account. I moved the controls in my hands experimentally and the reticle split into two, one for each hand, then I moved my legs and the view changed, the spheres growing closer or drawing farther away. I wondered if I was supposed to just keep trying to figure out the controls on my own, but the question was answered by what I assumed was an automated voice in my earphones.

"Place the left-hand reticle over the purple sphere and keep it there as long as possible, or until told to move it."

It seemed simple enough, but when I tried it, the purple sphere began moving away and dodging to the right. I remembered what the foot controls had done and worked my heels up and down, gaining on the violet ball of light until I was able to put the left reticle into the center of it. It moved again but I moved with it, smiling through clenched teeth with a sort of childish satisfaction at the accomplishment.

"Now place the right-hand reticle over the green sphere, but try not to lose target-lock on the purple sphere."

"Easy for you to say," I muttered.

The green sphere was bobbing and weaving and Mr. Purple was still trying to evade as well, and I wound up with both arms extended, seeing a hazy vision of the different targets out of the corners of my peripheral vision. My feet were moving as if of their own accord, keeping my view moving, twisting the virtual world around to keep both spheres just in the edge of vision.

"Disengage with the purple target and lock onto the yellow target while maintaining your lock on the green target…"

And so it went, getting harder and harder, for what felt like hours. It probably wasn't hours because I would have keeled over from dehydration if they'd kept me in the pod that long, but it was enough that I really had to go to the bathroom by the end. About halfway through, I would have been willing to swear the computer-generated voice was replaced by a live human. There was something qualitatively different about the tone of the instructions, and it almost seemed as if whoever was guiding me was doing their best to get me to screw up. I didn't though. I never lost target lock for more than a few seconds.

When the pod opened and I stepped out into the blissfully cool climate control of the simulator room, there was an officer standing in front of me. The techs who'd sealed me and the rest of my squad in had all been enlisted Fleet personnel, but this was a Marine major, dressed in utility fatigues. He had one of those pinched faces that looked as if all the features had been crammed into the center, and his too-broad forehead was wrinkled in thought as he stared at me.

"Alvarez, right?" he asked me as I accepted a squeeze-bottle of electrolyte mix from one of the techs. I braced to attention and answered with the bellow we'd been instructed to use when addressed by officers or trainers.

"Sir, yes, sir!"

"Oh, stow that shit, Private," he said, waving it away as if it were an insect buzzing around his face. "Where are you from?"

"Trans-Angeles, sir," I told him, my voice closer to normal volume.

"Yes, yes, your file says that." He seemed impatient but not annoyed. "It also says you were a transient orphan. Where were you from originally?"

"Tijuana, sir."

He raised an eyebrow, sniffing in what might have been surprise. "People still live there?"

"Only if they can't get away, sir." I was probably pushing my luck, but there were no Drill Sergeants around and this guy seemed like he wanted an honest answer.

"So, no possibility anyone tinkered with your genes, optimized for anything?"

I wanted to laugh at the suggestion, but I managed to control myself. Barely.

"No, sir. My parents raised goats." And chickens, but no use complicating things. Over a decade of soy hadn't driven out the memory of what real chicken tasted like.

The major grunted and made a note on his tablet.

"May I ask a question, sir?"

He looked up almost as if he'd forgotten I was there and nodded absently.

"What is this test for?"

Now he smiled, and it seemed to stretch his too-close features into something almost normal. "Don't worry about it right now, son," he replied. "If it was important, you'll find out soon enough."

4

I WAS BARELY AWAKE WHEN THEY STUFFED US ON THE BIRD. IT WAS the first time I'd flown in anything other than the shuttles to and from the transport, and the VTOL troop carrier had a much different feel than the hundred-meter-long, fusion-powered aero-spacecraft. It grabbed at the air and rode its coattails rather than brute-forcing its way into the sky like a shuttle, and I could feel the constraining hand of the thick air around us, even if I couldn't see it. I couldn't see anything. The troop compartment wasn't lit except for the faint glow of instruments at the crew chief's status terminal, and it was pitch black outside, the constant overcast even thicker than usual and the planet's lone moon nowhere to be seen.

Me and the rest of my platoon were jammed cheek-by-jowl into the passenger compartment, all of us shifting as one with every sway and bank of the aircraft. And no one had told us a damned thing. The Drill Sergeants hadn't thrown any trash cans, had barely yelled. They'd just switched on the lights at somewhere around oh-dark-thirty and instructed poor Private Williams to have us in our utility fatigues, helmets and tactical vests with full water bladders in half an hour. No cleaning, no running around, just get everyone out to the busses.

The busses had gone to the landing field and once we'd arrived, an armorer's truck had pulled up and issued us training rifles. We'd had a short familiarization briefing on them right after in-processing and I struggled through the haze of sleep deprivation to remember what the sergeant had told us. They were modeled after the Gauss rifles the Force Recon Marines and other dismounted units used, but were only capable of shooting a targeting laser. There were photoreceptors built into our tactical vests, helmets and fatigues that would register a hit from one of the lasers and flash into the helmet HUD whether we were dead or wounded.

"What do you think we're supposed to be doing out here?" Williams asked. He was sitting right beside me by a coincidence of our loading order, but it took me a second to realize he was talking to me. "I mean," he went on, holding up the rifle that had been nestled between his knees, "they haven't even taught us how to use these things, or anything about fighting."

"Maybe that's why we're out here," I suggested.

He might have shrugged. I couldn't see well enough to be sure. I frowned. The helmets had pull-down visors and I figured they must have night vision built into them, but they hadn't told us how to use it. I felt around on mine for the knob I remembered seeing near the crown and used it to slide the visor into place.

Nothing. No power. I shrugged and raised the visor again. Maybe there was a trick to it. They'd probably tell us once we were on the ground. Or would they? There was no Drill Sergeant on the aircraft, just the crew chief and the pilots. I thought that was weird. We hadn't been left to ourselves for more than a minute unless we were in bed, lights-out, and even then there was a Drill Sergeant sleeping in an office in the same barracks.

"On the ground in two minutes!" the crew chief told us, holding up two fingers. "Two minutes!"

Nerves ate at the inside of my stomach and I wondered why I was scared. I closed my eyes and counted the seconds for two minutes, timing my breath with the count. I had very nearly gotten my pulse back down to something reasonable when the landing gear slammed into the ground with enough force to throw me forward against my restraints.

"Go! Go! Go!" The crew chief was yelling, motioning out the open side hatch into the outer darkness.

I threw off my safety harness and shuffled off the airplane somewhere in the middle of the platoon. I tried to stay with my squad, but that was nearly impossible in the darkness. The engines were still idling with a high-pitched whine, the airflow through the reactors a hot wind against my face and hands. We stood in a gaggle in the circle of the plane's landing lights, waiting, wondering what the hell we were supposed to do.

"Attention!"

The call was loud, amplified by a public address speaker. I turned in the direction of the voice and saw a tall man made taller by infantry body armor and a full-visor helmet. The helmet's external speakers carried his voice over the plane's turbines and the gabble of forty wannabe Marines standing around in the dark with our proverbial dicks in our hands.

"This is not training," he declared. I couldn't see his face through his visor, but his voice was as sharp as a bayonet point and I pictured a face chiseled from hardwood like a recruiting ad. "This is a test. Not of skills you've been taught, because we haven't taught you anything yet. Not a test to see how good a Marine you can be, but more to determine which of you has a certain killer instinct, a will to survive."

Shit. Was I going to have to kill someone?

"When this aircraft takes off, you have exactly ten minutes before the next one lands. If you're not at least a kilometer away from here by then, your casualty identification software will declare you dead and you're to sit down wherever you are and await pickup. If you make it far enough away...well, the next plane in will be carrying your Op-For. That's short for Opposing Force. The enemy whose job it will be to hunt you down."

He raised a finger and, for a half a second, I thought he was pointing it directly at me, but then he traversed it back and forth across all of us.

"Your job will be to use your training weapon to shoot the Op-For if you can, while avoiding being spotted and killed yourself. It's that simple. The operation will be over when either the last of you has been killed or captured, or when the last Op-For has been killed." There was what I thought was the hint of a chuckle in his voice at the idea.

"Can we work together?" Williams asked.

It was a good question, but one I hadn't even considered. I didn't trust any of these people well enough to count on them.

"You could try," the faceless Marine allowed. "Given that none of you has ever worked with the others, though, and also given that the Op-For will have full enhanced optics, including thermal and infrared, as well as sonic sensors, the odds are that all staying together will do is make you a bigger target."

That sent warning bells going off in the back of my head. If this guy was discouraging us from working together, it probably meant it would screw with their test, not that it would hurt us. We should try to do it, but the problem was, something like that would require a leader to take charge of this bunch of half-panicked kids in the dark, yelling his or her head off the whole time, and probably getting themselves taken out early. No thanks.

"Good luck," the armored man told us, then stepped up into the VTOL transport just as the hatch began to ascend.

The turbines whined and screamed in protest as they came up to speed, and all of us scattered from the plane before the hot breath of its jets could knock us off our feet.

"Alvarez!" Williams called, but I was already running. "Alvarez, we should stick together!"

Yeah, good luck with that, man.

The ground was fairly flat, and I took advantage of the brief wash of light from the transport's running lights to get an idea of the surrounding terrain. It rose up into the hills north of our landing zone and a spike of apprehension that threatened to turn into panic reminded me I'd never seen hills before except in pictures and video streams. I didn't know why it scared me, but it did, even though I barely caught a glimpse of them.

I pushed down the constricting feeling in my gut and concentrated on the trees. There was a stand of them nearby, short and twisted and gnarled, unnatural looking. I didn't know if they were genetically-engineered transplants or native to this world. It was hard to tell sometimes. Either way, they'd be damned easy to run right into with the light gone and I angled away from them, heading for a shadowed section of ground between the valley and the hills. It was a draw or a ditch or maybe a creek bed, but it was cover and I needed cover.

Cover and concealment. The guy from the shuttle, Munroe, had talked about it and what he said had made sense. Cover blocked bullets, concealment kept people from seeing you, and not knowing the difference could get you killed. The trees would be concealment, and not even good concealment if the guys they sent after us had thermal sights, while the ditch would be cover *and* concealment.

Something nagged at me, maybe my conscience, telling me I should get some of the others and take them there with me. But the more people hiding in the same place the bigger the chance they'd get found out. I didn't need the rich boy to tell me that, I'd found out the hard way when four or five of us had tried to jam into a maintenance tunnel to get away from the TAPs when I was ten years old. They'd read our heartbeats on their sonic sensors and I'd wound up with yet another psych rehab assignment. It had worked about as well as the first three.

The last flicker of light from the ascending transport died away and I slowed down immediately, going from a dead sprint to a shuffling, flat-footed jog. It was as if someone had dropped a black curtain over everything, like I was back in the tunnels. I wasn't scared by the darkness, it was as comfortable as an old, familiar blanket.

Gradually, with painful, glacial slowness, my eyes adjusted. I couldn't make out much, just a darker shade of blackness against the dark grey of the clouded sky, but it was enough to see the outline of the hills, enough to keep me going the right direction. I had less than ten minutes and I had no way of estimating how far away the ditch was. It could have been kilometers, but distance was my friend whether I reached it or not. When the bad guys came, they'd catch the low-hanging fruit first, the ones who'd ducked into the trees or hid behind bushes.

Man, what I wouldn't have given for thermal sights like those guys had...

Hold up. I *did* have a thermal sight. My helmet's targeting system might not be hooked up, but the sights on the rifle had to be. They wouldn't have sent us out without working sights on our rifles. At least I hoped not. I slowed to a walk and brought the rifle up to my shoulder, putting my cheek against the stock. Nothing. Blackness.

Shit.

I touched the trigger... and the view in front of my right eye lit up. There were numbers and symbols all around the central image and I didn't know what any of them meant, but the picture itself was all I needed. The hills were lit up like daylight, every tree and rock visible, and the ditch was straight ahead. I still had no idea how far, but at least I was going the right direction.

I lowered the gun and cursed my own stupidity. Now my night vision was shot. I started walking anyway, figuring the ground was even enough to walk blind, and I immediately tripped over something, a root or a clump of plants or a rock, I couldn't tell, and fell flat on my stomach.

At least no one had seen me. I nearly waited there until I regained my night vision, but every second passing was one closer to the Op-For plane coming in. I crawled. If I'd had full body armor like the guy who had briefed us, it would have been painless and quick. With just my utility fatigues, every bramble, thicket, and rock dug into my knees and elbows, but still I crawled.

I don't know why I felt so desperate. It was a test, but I'd failed tests before. If I just let them find me, they'd take me back to base and I'd probably sleep in a bed tonight, but I couldn't make myself do it. After a few minutes, I didn't even consider it. I'd made the decision and going back on it seemed harder than whatever lay ahead.

The darkness began to take shape again and I used the butt of my training rifle to push myself up to my feet. It felt like it had been more than ten minutes, but the Op-For plane was nowhere in sight.

But then, it wouldn't be in *sight*. They would be coming in like they were at war, not with their running lights on the way we had. I tried to listen for engines, but I was breathing too hard to hear anything, and when I tried to hold my breath, my pulse pounding in my ears still drowned out everything but the sound of my own footsteps.

No, wait. There it was. A sound like a wind rushing in, but there was no wind, not a single breeze to carry away the sweat coating my body. It had to be jet turbines. They were coming in the same way we had.

I ran. Knowing I might trip at any second, knowing I might fall right into the ditch before I saw it, but I ran anyway. The distant roar of wind had become thunder rolling across the plain. And something else was coming with it, something even more frightening. Dawn. It was just a line of lighter grey on the horizon right now, just a slight brightening of the darkness, but it was coming. The safety of the darkness might have been illusory, but it was all I had.

The incremental increase in the light helped me spot the ditch before I fell into it. Only it wasn't just a ditch, it was a dry river bed. Those I *had* seen before, as a kid, though this one seemed wetter than the ones back in the Sonoran Desert on Earth. Probably seasonal, but I hadn't seen any rain since I'd arrived and I hoped we were in the dry season. I clambered down into the river bed and flopped into a grooved slide, a notch between two higher outcroppings, and brought the rifle to my shoulder again.

It took a few seconds of scanning back and forth before I found the aircraft. I was looking too high and too far away. It had landed already and it was damn close, maybe three hundred meters from where I was concealed. The side hatches were open and Marines in infantry body armor and visored helmets were pouring out, rifles at their shoulders, falling into a prone position a couple dozen meters away from the plane, in a semi-circle around it.

It was a long shot, particularly when I'd never fired anything but a zip gun in my whole life, but I figured the laser training system wouldn't be affected by wind or distance. If I could see it, I could hit it. I pushed the trigger just a little harder and a circular aiming reticle popped up in the center of the image. I didn't need to be too well trained to know what that meant; I'd played video games, after all, even the banned, violent kind. *Especially* the banned, violent kind.

I put the circle over one of the Marines who was still standing, just coming down the ramp, and I pulled the trigger. Nothing happened outside the gun-sight. I was fairly sure of that as I had kept both eyes open. But inside the targeting optics, a red line connected the rifle to the Marine's torso for a fraction of a second and he stopped in his tracks. I'd hit him, I knew it.

I laughed and slewed the gun to the right, trying to find another target. There was one other still upright. He might have been a sergeant or an officer, but he was running towards the semi-circle where everyone else was already lying down flat and I had to put the reticle just ahead of him, trying to get him to run into the shot. I squeezed the trigger and the red line appeared in the optics once more, but this time I had missed off to the right, leading him too far. I shifted my aim and tried again. He stumbled, not falling over because this wasn't a real weapon, but stopping and obeying the orders of his system, taking a knee. I could almost hear him cursing.

That was when I found out the gun's optic also detected *incoming* targeting lasers and simulated them with bright white flashes like horizontal lightning. The only reason I didn't get my ass virtually killed right then was the little outcropping of rock at the left side of my helmet. It absorbed the laser enough that the helmet's HUD, suddenly very willing to operate when *they* told it to, informed me I'd only received minor flash-burns and could still walk, see and fight normally.

Well thanks very much, but I've learned my lesson just the same.

The dry riverbed was cover and concealment and, more importantly to me right now, it was also a highway. I slid down the bank and my boots sank a few centimeters into the sloppy, muddy soil in the bed. It was narrow, maybe a meter across at its widest, and strewn with rocks and pebbles and gravel where it wasn't slick with mud, and I moved down it with a side-to-side, flat-footed motion, the same way I did back in the maintenance tunnels when they were wet from a drainage pipe leak.

The Op-For troops were probably shooting at me, I figured. If I'd taken the time to look through the rifle's optic, maybe I would have seen it. They might even send some people up to check out the riverbed, and if they found me, I'd be totally screwed, with no choice but to take down as many of them as I could before they got me. But they only had one plane-full, and there was all of us to track down. I liked my odds enough to keep moving.

The blacks were grey now, and the greys were becoming brown and white and even a little blue, which made me feel horribly exposed but also let me see my footing. With every slick patch exposed, I could pick out the bits of gravel and flat rock and turn my slide-skating into a run. I was exhausted, soaked with sweat, my helmet was a lead weight on my neck and the training rifle seemed to mass a hundred kilos, but stopping to rest just didn't even occur to me as an option. To stop was to die. I could have ran that riverbed forever, but the problem was, I was running toward the source, uphill, and as it ascended, the bed began to get narrower and deeper and wetter, until there was barely room for me to walk heel-toe and every step sank into the mud centimeters at a time.

I was going to have to get out.

I grabbed at the bank on my right-hand side and it collapsed when I tried to dig into it, sand, mud and muck giving way until I thought I might be burying myself in it. The emotional inertia that had carried me this far waned in the space of an instant and I settled back against the bank of the dry creek bed and sucked in air. Every shuddering breath was an effort and I felt more exhausted and drained than I had running through the train terminal, more afraid now than I'd been when that guy Ivan Jaropillo had been chasing me with a real gun that could really kill me.

I wondered what Pris was doing now. Had she made enough off the score to get out of the tunnels, get out of the Underground even? Probably not. She was tough and smart but she didn't have the kind of connections to get that much money from one shipment of Kick. She'd probably try to use the profit to buy more Kick, or Spindle, or Zero, or maybe some illegal ViRware, try to sell it on her own. Eventually, she'd either get snapped up by the cops or killed by the gangs. There wasn't a third option for people like us.

Unless I was ready to consider this a third option. Maybe it was, but it amounted to being snapped up by the cops for an opportunity to get killed, which sort of made it the worst of all possible worlds. At least it was something new.

I sucked in a breath and tried to draw energy into my body along with the thick, humid air. The only tool I had was the rifle, so I used it like a shovel, digging the stock into the mud and dirt and sand of the bank until it went in far enough to stick, then levering myself up out of the hole. I nearly slipped back in getting the rifle free of the dirt, but finally collapsed at the top, resting on my back for another few seconds.

The sky was still grey above me, but it was a light, morning shade of grey, with thick clouds promising the possibility of rain later on. I hadn't felt rain in over a decade. Rolling over onto my side, I used the rifle again, this time as a stick to force myself to my feet. A copse of trees boxed me in, taller than the ones down in the valley but still twisted and warped, their bark black and scaly, their leaves dagger-sharp. They looked mutated, warped, and they fit in just right in this place, on this world.

I stumbled through the trees, out of the enclosure, needing to get a better idea of where I was and how far I'd come from the Op-For. Underbrush tried to trip me up, pulled my attention downward, making me watch each step. Multiple twisted columns branched out into winding spirals, each with spiked leaves and five-centimeter thorns, reaching out as if they were trying to trap me. The tip of one of the leaves brushed against my neck and I bit down on a curse, slapping a hand against the sudden pain. My palm came away with a speck of blood, and I began to suspect the trees on Inferno were carnivorous, planted here by the military to sort the wheat from the chaff.

There was light past the trees, an open area somewhere, but it seemed hazy and nebulous past the much closer and more immediate maze of thorns. I twisted and ducked and sidled through what seemed like an intentionally designed barrier, using the rifle to smack the thinner, more malleable tendrils away. The tangle seemed to be thicker as I went and I thought I'd either have to try crawling beneath them or turning back when one last contortion through one last layer put me out into the open at the base of the hill.

The valley stretched out in front of me in the full light of dawn, open and broad and mottled in dead brown and insistent green and yellow. It was empty of people, empty of anything, nothing at all to be afraid of.

And yet I was petrified. I couldn't move, couldn't breathe. I didn't remember falling yet I was on the ground, curled into a ball, eyes squeezed shut. The blackness was a comfort, but not enough of one. I couldn't see the terrible nothing, the vast emptiness, yet somehow its presence was wriggling through my closed eyelids, penetrating my attempts to shut it out. I *knew* it was there and I couldn't un-know it.

I grabbed at sanity with both hands, but it slipped through my fingers like smoke and all rational thought was gone.

———————

Seven Years Old:

Heat mirages wavered at the horizon, turning saguaro cactuses into the silhouettes of silent giants, watching him suffer and not offering their aid. He had no words for the heat and the thirst tormenting him, no way to describe the pain and longing, no concept of the grief. He had no water, no food, no shelter, no idea where he was or where he was going, just a conviction he had to keep going, that sitting still meant death.

That was what Anton had told him before they'd left Tijuana in the old car, before hours of rattling and shaking and bumping through the night, before its inevitable breakdown and the cursing and pounding on the old, rusty hood of the ancient vehicle. He'd been scared then. His father never cursed, never raised his voice, not since Momma had died.

And then they'd seen the truck in the distance and Anton had told him to hide in the trunk where it was close and dark and hot, and not to come out no matter what he heard until he heard nothing. And when he did come out, he should run and not stop running until he couldn't run anymore.

He couldn't run anymore. He could barely walk. Everywhere he looked was nothing but more of nothing, sand and cactuses and rocks and hills that never, ever seemed to get closer no matter how long he walked toward them. He wanted to sit down, wanted to cry, but he had no tears left. There was no one around to see them, no one around anywhere. Poppa and Anton were gone, just like Momma, and they were never coming back. Poppa had told him people didn't come back from dying, not until you saw them in Heaven.

This place was not Heaven. It felt more like Hell, the place where the bad people went, the people who had killed his father and brother. Like the people who'd killed his mother. They would all go to Hell one day, he was sure…but what had he done? He'd been a good boy. His father had always told him he was such a good boy. Why had God sent him to this Hell?

He thought he saw something glinting in the sky just past the hills, but it was hard to tell through the shimmering heat. There was a city across the desert, his father had said. A place he'd called Trans-Angeles, a shining paradise where they would all be safe. He'd promised them that the city would take them in if they could only reach it, that the people there would give them a place to live and food, and it would be so much better than things had been back home, without the bad people trying to hurt them and each other. He had to reach the city. He headed for the glimmer of light...

5

"I GUESS YOU WON, ALVAREZ."

I blinked as if I were only now waking. I was in the head at the barracks, staring at my own face in the bathroom mirror. The scratches still seemed raw, red, though they would be gone in a day or so after the treatment, but one of them bisected my chin, the other slanted across my nose. I must have run blindly through the thorns back to the riverbed where they'd found me.

I turned and looked at Williams as if he'd grown another head.

"What?"

It was almost lights-out and he was dressed in the ridiculous undershirt-tucked-into-shorts outfit they forced us to wear to bed, though somehow it looked even goofier on him. He was a toothpick with google-eyes pasted to one end and oversized feet at the other.

"You were the last," he clarified, and I couldn't miss the bitter anger behind the words now, though I certainly tried. "Took them ten solid hours to find you hiding in a fucking ditch,"

"I didn't know," I admitted, shrugging it off. I couldn't even remember them finding me. The first thing I recalled after freezing up on the hillside was the motion of the VTOL transport.

"I suppose you think you're some hotshot now, huh? You think you're special because you abandoned everyone else and did it all on your own?"

I stared at him the way I might have an aggressive rat warning me away from scraps of garbage in the tunnels. Did he think he sounded tough or intimidating? I didn't even consider telling him the truth. It was none of his business.

"What do you want, Williams?" I asked. "Did you think this bunch of stupid kids…." I waved a hand back at the platoon bay on the other side of the wall. "…was gonna form up into some sort of commando unit with you in the lead? Did you think we were going to ambush a bunch of trained Force Recon Marines and then come back and get steak dinner from the Drill Sergeants?"

"We should have tried to work together!" he snapped, taking a step closer to me. I could smell the issue teeth-cleaner on his breath. "I asked you for help!"

"You heard what the man said when we got dropped off. It was a test, and one we were supposed to take on our own. I don't know you well enough to trust you."

"Then why the hell did you join the Marines, Alvarez?" He nearly yelled the words and I wanted to tell him to shut up, that he was going to bring the Drill Sergeants down on us, but maybe getting smoked for a few hundred pushups would shut him up, if nothing else.

"For the same reason everyone else does," I told him. "I didn't have any other choice."

I turned back to the mirror and ignored him until he went away. I hesitated at the door to the bathroom. No, shit, I decided I'd better start using the terminology they'd taught us. I hesitated at the *hatchway* to the *head*. Straight ahead was the platoon bay, rows of bunk beds and work I still needed to do before lights-out. To the left was a narrow passageway leading to the office of the platoon's training officer, a First Lieutenant named Harrell. I'd barely seen her since we'd arrived, but I knew she stayed in her office until lights-out.

I also knew if I bothered her without going through the Drill Sergeants, I was asking to get my ass dragged out to the PT pit. But I needed an answer to this question. I knocked on the door, then braced to attention. I expected her to yell at me, either to come in or go the hell away. Instead, she opened the door and looked me up and down. My eyes were straight ahead, but I saw short brown hair and clear blue eyes and a spotless uniform, its edges pressed sharp and straight.

"Alvarez," she said, her voice firm and authoritative but not bellowing like the Drill Sergeants'. "I was wondering when you'd come by. At ease, come on in."

Her office was small, the walls white and bare, the only furniture a metal desk and two folding chairs, one behind the desk and one in front of it. They looked uncomfortable and, when she invited me to sit with an offhand motion, I found out they felt just as uncomfortable as they looked. If I had to spend as much time in an office as she did, I'd have tried to make it more comfortable. Maybe she thought that would make her look soft to us, or the Drill Sergeants or maybe senior officers, I didn't know.

The only personal item I could see in the whole room was a picture cube sitting on the desk, images and video clips cycling over all the visible sides of the thing. One I noticed was Lt. Harrell in civilian clothes but with her military haircut, standing beside a tall, good-looking man with skin the color of café-au-lait and long, flowing black hair. Husband maybe? Boyfriend? Hell, if her family was rich enough, it could be her father. The people who lived on the surface in Trans-Angeles never got old.

"All right, Alvarez," she said, falling into her own chair, elbows resting on her desk in a casual posture I wished I could imitate. "You want to ask the question or should I just save us both the time and give you the answer?"

I opened my mouth, closed it again. She'd given me the choice between saying something or not, and silence had always seemed safer to me. She sighed, and I thought maybe she was disappointed with my choice.

"You want to know why you aren't on the first available ship back to Earth," she said, "waiting to get stuck into punitive hibernation." The corner of her mouth quirked up, a smile she wouldn't quite let herself show. "You aren't the first recruit we've found huddling in a ditch, babbling and incoherent. You aren't even the first one this month."

I frowned, confused.

"We get most of our recruits from the mega-cities," she explained, her tone patient, almost gentle. "From the underclasses, people who live their whole lives without ever seeing the sky, without ever seeing an open field or a square meter of ground without humans on it. The biggest miracle is that more of you aren't agoraphobic."

"Agoraphobic?" I repeated, forehead wrinkling with confusion.

"An unreasoning fear of open spaces. We get it a lot." She shrugged. "Some people have it worse than you, although I've rarely seen someone go into the sort of fugue you did today. It's treatable.

I can't promise there'll be time for you to get it in Basic Training or even Advanced Occupational Training, but if you don't wash out, they'll treat you for it eventually."

"How am I going to be a Marine if I can't even walk outside without passing out, ma'am?" I blurted.

"This test was a bit of drama," Harrell admitted, "partially meant to impress on young people who've never been in this sort of situation just how unprepared for it they are. But partially to pick out candidates for Force Recon." She cocked an eyebrow. "And although we don't usually share this sort of information, I will tell you that if you hadn't fallen apart at the sight of an open horizon, you would be on the track for Force Recon. You took out two of them without getting killed yourself, with no training or experience. But you can't handle the wide-open spaces, so…" She waved a hand demonstratively.

An emptiness filled my gut, a hole big enough to pull me down inside myself like a popping balloon collapsing inside-out. I sucked in a breath and nodded acknowledgement.

It is what it is. Pris always said that, and I'd always hated it, but it seemed to apply here.

"Does that mean I get to clean toilets on Inferno for the rest of the war then? Ma'am," I remembered to add a beat too late.

"No, it doesn't. If you make it through Basic Training without washing out, you'll be sent for AOT at Battlesuit Operator School. If you make it through, you'll be a battlesuit Marine, what they call a Drop Trooper."

She picked a tablet as thin as a scansheet off the desk and touched the screen. An image appeared on it of what looked like a metal giant, an oversized caricature of a human form, bulky and broad and imposing.

"Wow," I murmured. I was impressed by the thing, which surprised me. I looked between it and her. "Have you ever been inside one of those, ma'am?"

That almost-a-smile again. She pulled back the hair from the sides of her head and turned it slightly in either direction to show me the metal and ceramic implant jacks there. I'd seen them before, but only on netdivers working for the gangs, cracking security systems.

"You need these," she explained, "because neural halos are too slow. A microsecond, but it counts when you're talking about trying to control something that big in combat." She snorted, less amusement than disgust. "In the first models, they tried to use motion feedback from actually moving your arms and legs, but the reaction time was for shit. Thank God the Tahni didn't have anything better."

She tossed the tablet back on the desk, frowning in what might have been regret, or maybe resentment.

"I'd still be running a suit if they hadn't decided they wanted me for training duty. God willing, I'll be back in one when I make captain."

"What's it like, ma'am?" I hated the way my voice sounded, too young and eager, too much like the teenagers from the surface I used to see in the Zocalo.

Her eyes were far away, the way Poppa's used to get when he talked about Momma.

"It can be," she told me, "like lying in your mother's arms. Or it can feel like a coffin, if you've ever heard of those, Alvarez."

"I'm from Tijuana, ma'am," I told her, and the too-young feeling passed as quickly as it had come. "I know all about coffins."

"Well, then," she said, pushing herself to her feet, her chair legs scraping across the floor like a signal that the talking was done. I leapt to my feet, coming to attention. "Get back and get ready for lights-out, Recruit. Before you become a Drop Trooper, you need to learn how to be a Marine."

6

I RAN THE PAD OF MY RIGHT THUMB OVER THE INTERFACE JACKS ON my temple and behind my ear. They felt cold, unnatural. In the mirror over the sink, they seemed huge and obtrusive against my freshly-shaven scalp. They were hooked up, so I was told, directly to my cerebellum, the part of my brain that controlled movement and balance. With the jacks, I could control the battlesuit without even thinking about it, as if it were my own body.

Did they make me less human? And did I care?

Something hammered against the bathroom door and I abandoned the self-examination.

"Dude!" Trent's voice was muffled by the door, but not much. It was cheap, thin plastic. "Get your ass out of the toilet or we're gonna be late for the fitting."

I rolled my eyes at the tall, gawking teenager on the other side of the door. He looked as young and green as I did, but Trent Garner had been part of one of the roughest gangs in Capital City out on the east coast. It wasn't as large or as densely populated or nearly as violent as Trans-Angeles, but you could die just as dead on the east coast as you could the west. I didn't ask him what he'd done to wind up with the same choice I'd had, but it probably wasn't something small.

"Didn't you learn anything in Basic Training, man?" I asked. "This is a head, not a toilet. And it's a battlesuit synchronization and calibration, not a fitting."

"Oh Jesus, give me a break!" Trent raised his hands palms-up in surrender. "We're still gonna be late!"

"We'll be fine." I sealed my collar and checked my gig line. At Advance Occupational Training, it wasn't as likely some random sergeant would rip me a new one for having my rank and branch slightly off-center, but it was a habit I'd learned in three long months of Basic. "Let's go."

At least we didn't have to go outside. Inferno was still hot as shit, whether you were in Basic or AOT. Staying in the shaded, climate-controlled passageways of the Battlesuit Operator's School was infinitely preferable to heading out into the afternoon glare of 82 Eridani and sweating our asses off waiting for the busses to take us somewhere else we could wait around and sweat our asses off some more. Plus, we wouldn't have to gaggle up in some pansy-ass formation and come to attention and march and all that shit. We were all so over that after Basic, and the trainers didn't care, either. We were here to learn how to do our job.

We still walked fast and made sure we saluted any officers who passed us, because the main thoroughfare through the school was considered fair game for saluting, unlike offices or classrooms. But there was no more screaming, no more PT pit, no more Drill Sergeants watching our every move. All that counted now was paying attention in the classes and passing the tests.

And being on time. That was still important. I'd timed it right, though. We didn't even have to run to make it to Hangar 13 Bravo five minutes early...which, in military terms, meant right on time. The rest of Second Platoon, Alpha Company, 3rd Battalion of the 85th Training Regiment was already gathered in the cavernous expanse of the hangar, and our platoon guide, Edith Rogan, gave us a dirty look for being the last ones to show up.

Trent made apologetic noises, but I ignored her. There were no brownie points for showing up twenty minutes early instead of five and I didn't give a shit if we made things inconvenient for her. She strode over to one of the techs hovering around banks of computer readouts hooked to the battlesuits and came to attention.

"Warrant Hancock," she snapped off smartly, "Second platoon is all present!"

"Cool," he murmured, waving back at her. "Chill for a bit, it's gonna be another ten minutes."

The only reason I didn't laugh at Rogan was my attention was on the suits.

Battlesuit wasn't a good word for them, I thought, not for the first time. It makes it sound like they're small, like something you put on over your clothes, like the early powered exoskeletons they'd shown us in classes we'd had on the history of the Marines. A battlesuit was something you climbed into like an airplane; it just happened to be shaped like a man.

Three meters tall and nearly as wide across the shoulders, they were hunched over like a gorilla, the head just a dome-like protrusion, the arms reaching down past the knees. Stretching back from the heavily-armored shoulders was a boxy, angular structure, what might have been a backpack if the armor had been a human but built into the suit rather than hanging from it. Centimeters of BiPhase Carbide armor shielded the isotope reactor at its core, and the turbines flanking it, powering the suit's byomer musculature and the jump-jets that made it so mobile and versatile.

These weren't armed, but the hardpoints were there on the arms and shoulders for attaching plasma guns, Gatling lasers, missile launchers or a half a dozen other weapons systems I'd read about, watched videos of, and seen live-fire demonstrations of, but longed to use myself. Staring up at the monstrous, metal titans, I felt a lust that made anything I'd felt for Pris, or a dozen other girls before her, pale by comparison.

"Okay then!" Warrant Officer Hancock said finally, clapping his hands like a teacher trying to get his class' attention. He actually reminded me of the instructors at my Primary School classes, soft around the edges and self-consciously chill. "We're all set. Ladies and gentlemen, I give you the WF-4100 Vigilante Amplified Personal Armor Suit, your next of skin for the foreseeable future. We can run you guys a squad at a time, so who's up first?"

"First squad!" Private Rogan barked, far too involved in her brief authority for me to ever like her. "Move it up!"

"That's us," Trent reminded me, as if I'd somehow forgotten what squad we were in.

One of the enlisted techs under the warrant officer waved me forward to one of the faceless machines. She was short and skinny, light enough she might have blown away in one of the monsoons this part of Inferno was going through periodically this season, but her fingers moved without hesitation across the control board hooked up to the battlesuit via fiber-optic cables and there was a bored professionalism in her expression.

"Let's bust this pig open," she said, slapping a glowing green symbol on the readout.

The chest plastron of the battlesuit swung downward with a hum of servomotors, low enough for the grooves built into the inner surface to serve as steps and hand-holds as I scrambled inside. It didn't move beneath my weight, as solid and unyielding as a mountain, and when I settled into the padded indentation designed for the human pilot, it seemed to embrace me, sheltering me from everything outside.

"Plug the interface cables in," the woman said, nodding at something beside me.

I glanced from side to side and finally caught sight of the spooled cables just as the tech edged forward as if she'd have to do it for me. It was, perhaps, the strangest feeling of my life sliding the jacks into the sockets implanted into my skull, and a twist of nausea wrenched at my stomach as they clicked home. I swallowed hard and nodded to the woman.

"We won't bother to strap you in," she went on, as casual as if this were something I did every day, "since you're not going anywhere yet. I'm gonna seal you in and start the synchronization. I'll warn you ahead of time, it's gonna be weird. The system is going to be adjusting itself to your brain activity and, to some extent, adjusting your brain activity to match the controls. It's gonna cause some feedback. Could be some funky hallucinations, could be lucid memories." She chuckled. "Don't worry though, you won't be able to go on a rampage or any shit like that. We're freezing the suit's motivators from out here, and you'll be frozen out of your own body by the interface so you won't claw your own eyes out or anything. We good?"

If she was trying to make me nervous, it was working. I dealt drugs, but I didn't do them and I didn't want any alternative states of consciousness or whatever other bullshit people talk about who don't want to admit they took Kick to feel like someone better for a couple hours. But I wasn't going to back out now.

"We're good," I assured her, flashing a thumbs up. The cables tugged at my head when I moved it to meet her eyes, and I tried not to grimace at the sensation.

"The bright side," she assured me, eyes on the controls again, "is you don't have to do this again unless they come out with a newer model."

The servos were much louder from inside the suit, echoing off the interior of the chest plastron as it swung upward, the door to a prison, closing in on me. It shut with a pneumatic hiss and I was in total darkness, the interior of a casket. I could understand Lt. Harrell's warning now. They probably lost a lot of recruits right about this point. I knew a lot of guys were nervous about being shut up inside the suit, but I wasn't surprised at all when it didn't bother me. I knew my fear now, and enclosed spaces weren't among them.

I found the darkness comforting, the isolation a relief. They were reminders of old hiding places. Then light returned and with it, memory.

———

Five Years Old:

"Have you been fighting again, mi Corazon?"

The words were chiding but the tone was gentle. I couldn't remember Momma ever yelling at me, but she didn't have to. Just the slightest hint of disapproval in her eyes was enough to make me want to cry. Especially when I knew I'd done something wrong.

"Yes, Momma," I admitted. I rubbed at the bruise on my cheek and wished I could melt into the rich, black earth of her garden.

"Oh, Cameron," she sighed, planting her spade into the soil point-first. She had a black streak of dirt on her face and she wiped at it with her forearm, smearing it with sweat without actually wiping any of it off. "Not at school again?"

I shook my head.

"On the way home. The Gomez boys were picking on Camilla again, calling her names because she can't walk right. They wouldn't stop, so I pushed Elian and then Roberto hit me."

"Your heart is so big, Cameron." She pulled off her gloves and pulled me into a hug. She was warmer than the sunshine of the spring

afternoon. "But you can't fight the world by yourself. The world is bigger and it will always win."

"But Momma," I protested, feeling the sort of righteous indignation only a five-year-old who's sure he's right can experience, "there wasn't anyone else! Camilla was all alone!"

"She will be all alone sometimes," Momma told me. "And even when she is not, you can't always fight your way past the cruel and ignorant. The best you can do for her is to be there, support her, let her know she has friends."

I scowled, pulling back from her to make sure she saw it.

"She's not my friend!" I planted my feet, suddenly indignant again but for the opposite reason. "She's a girl! Girls are yucky!"

She laughed then. I loved Momma's laugh. It was like music. It didn't last long, because then we both heard the shouting. It came from the usual place, up the street from our house, at the corner where the bad men would hang out during the night. Poppa called it a bar, and Momma called it the Bad Place. I'd heard her say to my older brother, Anton, to stay away from it, that cartel thugs came there. I wasn't sure what a cartel was, but "thug" sounded like a good word for the men who would stand around the building at night and drink from bottles or cups. They weren't usually loud this early, not before sunset.

They were cursing, words I'd heard before but Momma told me never to say. And they were close, halfway between us and the bar. No one else lived in the houses between, and Poppa had said it was because they were afraid. I understood. I was afraid now.

"You said you would have the money by today, mericon!" one of them screamed at the other, pointing in his face.

He was a fat man, which meant he was rich. Only rich people were fat in Tijuana. His shirt was nice, the kind I'd been told was made from silk. Poppa had told me it came from a worm's butt, but I thought he might have been teasing me.

"And you said you would give me another week!" the other one yelled back. He was taller and very skinny, and he was wearing a funny hat, the sides turned up. He pointed his own finger. I had always been told pointing was impolite. "You're a fucking liar!"

"Cameron," Momma said, coming to her feet, "you need to get inside. Go tell your brother..."

I heard the gunshots and flinched. I'd heard them before. Some of the bad men would shoot their guns in the air at night after they'd drunk for a long time. But this one sounded different, so much closer. I could see it in the fat man's hand, shiny and polished on the flat parts, twinkling in the sun. It moved in his hand and there was a flash from the end of it, the muzzle. One after another and the skinny man was falling to his knees.

And so was Momma. She was gasping for breath like she'd been running hard, but she wasn't running, she was kneeling. There was blood on her chest, spreading out from a rip in her work shirt and her hands went to cover it, as if they could hold it all inside.

"Momma!" I said, even more afraid now. "Momma, are you okay?"

She didn't answer. Her mouth was moving like she was trying to talk, but blood was coming from her mouth too, and only a gurgle came out.

"Momma!" I grabbed her, hugged her to me, sensing she was going away from me and not wanting to let her. Wet warmth soaked my shirt, and I could feel her ragged attempts at breathing, felt her heart thudding in a strange, irregular beat.

And then it stopped and she fell away from me, collapsing in the garden soil, crushing the seedlings she'd planted that day.

I wanted to scream but I couldn't. I looked down at my hands, at the blood dripping off of them and couldn't seem to catch my breath even enough to call out. Poppa was there, but I didn't remember him coming out, and he was screaming. I could tell by the way his mouth was open, his chest heaving, but I couldn't hear him. I couldn't hear anything, couldn't feel anything.

Momma was gone.

———

Light flooded through the open chest plastron and Warrant Hancock's frowning face followed it.

"Hey man," he said, sounding concerned, "your heart rate and BP are kinda spiking here. I think we should pull you and maybe try again later."

"No," I said, shaking my head. Sweat spattered away from it, and I felt the cables tugging once again. "I'm okay. Just hit a bad memory."

"Yeah, that can happen," he acknowledged, sounding relieved. "Pro tip, it helps if you concentrate on something positive before the system grabs your cerebellum. Kind of starts the train running."

"Sure, will do. Thanks."

A positive memory. Could I think of one? Sex? It was positive, but damned if I could grab onto a specific memory, barely even a face.

I found something just as the plastron closed again. It wasn't much, but it was all I had.

———

Ten years old:

The closet was dark, tight, packed with boxes and old clothes. It smelled of dust and age, and I wondered what was in the boxes. What did the people who ran this group home think was worth saving? Maybe arts and craft projects from the kids who'd used to live here? Maybe hardcopy printouts of old records? He'd seen those, but he didn't know why the staff here would want them. They didn't seem to care enough to know anything about the kids now, much less worry about ones who didn't even live here anymore.

But it seemed to me as if the memories of those other kids were shielding me here, guarding me like Momma used to. The bruises on my arms still ached from the one they called Tito. He punched me in the arm whenever I got within reach of him, like it was a game, trying to hit the same spot each time. He was half a meter tall than me, at least twenty kilos heavier, so fighting back wasn't an option, and neither was telling the staff. I'd been warned about that from day one by the other younger kids. All the adults would do is take you to confront whoever you'd accused of bullying and try to force the two of you to "talk it out." Tito wasn't stupid, he would make all the right noises to not get in trouble, then make you pay later.

And no one would stand up for me, no one who could. This was the safe way, the easy way. I could stay here all through lunch, and no one would care. In here, I would be safe until I got too hungry, or thirsty, or had to pee. Hours. I could even sleep in here, so I wouldn't have to sleep at night, when Tito could get to me. I could sit up in bed and watch. But now, I would rest.

I closed my eyes and just breathed.

7

THE WORLD DROPPED OUT FROM BENEATH ME AND I FELL INTO THE darkness wrapped in two tons of metal. I'd simulated it a dozen times in virtual reality, which seemed even more real than virtual through the interface jacks, real enough I'd wondered why we'd bothered training for it in actual suits at all.

Now I knew. The interface could duplicate the physical feelings, the sensations, but not the emotions, the gut-deep conviction I could really die. Warrant Hancock had told us in his own, colorful way that the Vigilantes were military hardware, built by a Corporate Council fabricator, shielded from monopoly regulations and product-safety lawsuits by the necessities of war. All it would take was one slip-up, one bad batch of circuit boards getting by the scanners and the inspections and the jump-jet turbines wouldn't catch in time and the suit would fall the whole four hundred meters and probably look intact afterward. I, of course, would have to be poured out of the suit through a strainer.

The turbines did ignite, though, as a push of command from my thoughts translated through the interface more swiftly and certainly than any hand or foot control could have managed. Their abrupt boost pushed upward through my feet, into my spine, compressing me by a centimeter with the added gravities of deceleration and my vision narrowed into a tunnel for just a moment before the thrust evened out and everything flickered back to light.

It was the dead of night outside, past midnight, but it meant nothing inside the suit. The infrared, thermal, lidar, radar and sonic sensors were all meshed together into an image brighter than daylight and projected in 180 degrees around me. Actually, it gave me 360 degrees of coverage, but my brain could only handle optical input in 180 degrees. The rest was fed to me via the interface as something I can only describe as instinct. The way I knew down in the Zocalo if someone was watching me, the way I could sense even in the darkness of the maintenance tunnels if someone was nearby.

And someone *was* nearby. Identification Friend or Foe transponders glowed blue in the sensor display, showing me the positions of the rest of the squad, *my* squad today. I don't know how the hell I had wound up as squad leader on the first live mission, but that was how it had fallen out. I didn't like it much. I had no ambition to be an NCO and would have been happy not to worry about anyone but myself.

"Garner!" I snapped to Trent. "You're drifting west, man! Pull it back in. You, too, Rogan," I added, not bothering to hide a bit of malicious glee. The only good thing about being in any sort of leadership position was the self-important Private Rogan being subordinate to me. They had call signs, of course, and they were even displayed helpfully beside their IFF transponder avatar, but what was the point? The damned Tahni weren't going to be searching for us on the net if we used names, even if they were somehow capable of intercepting a laser line-of-sight signal, which they weren't. I was sure I'd get gigged for it later, but I didn't care. I had enough other shit to think about.

"Tighten it up!" I added on the general net to the whole squad. "The terrain down there's rough and our landing zone is tiny!"

There were six of us, a typical Drop squad, in a platoon of sixteen and we were supposed to touch down in a canyon and approach the target from the west, and I'll be damned if that canyon didn't look barely wide enough to fit a suit's shoulders on the map. It didn't seem any bigger in person. We were dropping onto it fast, faster than I would have thought was survivable if my suit systems weren't swearing to me I was right on the beam. I would have felt better if I could have watched another unit touching down first, but I could barely see the rest of the platoon on the map overlay.

First squad was the westernmost unit in the platoon and we were supposed to provide that end of a pincer movement to cut off an enemy convoy. Well, a notional enemy convoy. In reality, it would be a bunch of Marines, probably dismounted Drop Troops pulling duty as Op-For, driving cargo trucks down a dirt road and waiting to get attacked.

Maybe. I had my doubts it would be that easy. The Virtual Reality training pod programs had thrown in hiccups every now and again, but nothing too hard. They'd been trying to get us familiar with the control systems and didn't make things too complicated, but I knew it was coming. I figured it would be something small at first. Maybe the convoy would have mounted Gauss guns or Gatling lasers or even air support, and I was looking forward to it. I wanted to see what I could do with this thing.

The altimeter was down to a hundred meters and the terrain below was coming into focus, rough and rocky and nearly bare of vegetation here in the more arid northern half of the Gehenna subcontinent. The canyon had once held a river, back when Inferno had been in a wetter stage, or at least that's what our operations order had said. I wasn't sure why it was important, but I got the sense the junior officers who wrote that kind of thing threw in esoteric details like that just to pad the length and make themselves look smarter. All I knew was I wished the river had been wider.

The jets gave me one last kick in the ass, a braking burn harsh enough that my vision clouded up and all the displays seemed blurry and faded for a moment. Dust billowed up around me and the suit touched down with a flexing of mechanical knees and hips, a jolt that ran through my body and bounced my forehead off the padding around it.

My first drop. I took a moment to savor it, just to try to remember the way the ground felt under the feet of the suit, the way the weight settled into the sand, the sound of the pinging of the cooling metal after the jets shut down. The rest of the squad fell into what our instructors had called a Ranger file behind me, about fifty meters between us, the last of them around a curve in the canyon, so far back I couldn't even see them on the sensors.

"First squad, sound off," I barked, counting on the laser LOS relay to take the command back to the last of them. "Status report."

"Bravo Two, down and ready," Rogan said, her reply sharp and loud, insisting on going by the book, as usual. She set the pattern and the rest of them answered the same way, like cattle.

"Bravo Three, down and ready," Trent said.

"Bravo Four…"

And so it went, through Said, Dominguez and Calvey. I didn't know them very well. With all the training crammed into an abbreviated schedule designed to get us out on the line as quick as possible, there wasn't much time left for bullshitting, and the only reason Trent and I were halfway friendly was because we shared a compartment.

"All right, move out," I ordered. "We need to be on target in twenty minutes, so keep a quick pace, but everyone stays on the ground, no jumping. They'll pick us up on thermal if we jump this close."

I was just repeating what the op order had said, what the training officer had repeated and the training NCO had reiterated, but I needed to sound sure of myself, and since I didn't know a damned thing about armored combat, the only things I was sure of was what the trainers had told me.

"The canyon runs another four kilometers before it widens out into the valley floor," I went on, still running through the briefing from memory, "and when it does, we'll be in position to interdict the convoy from the west. When it opens up, we switch to a wedge formation with me and Alpha Team on point."

Technically, I should have let someone else walk point. That was the way I saw it in the training videos, but they hadn't said I *had* to do it that way and I didn't trust any of the others not to fuck up.

The canyon was maybe four meters across, which would have been plenty wide if I'd been walking through it on foot, but seemed tight enough to scrape the paint off the shoulders of my suit at the moment. I lumbered forward, the footsteps of the suit drumbeats against the old riverbed, but I kept an eye on the sensor readings from up ahead, wondering if this was the first curve the planners would throw at us, trying to send us down a passage too narrow for our suits and making me decide whether to risk being spotted by hopping up out of the canyon and walking on the plateau above it.

The old riverbed snaked to my right ahead, so sharply I couldn't see around it, and I muttered a curse as I leaned around the curve, sure this was where we would get stuck.

The figures were so still, they could have passed for statues left behind in this dry, winding labyrinth by some mysterious alien culture, stone guardians to keep intruders at bay. But I knew what they were on an instinctive level and acted before the thought had echoed from one side of my brain to the other.

Battlesuits. No IFF transponders on them. Enemy. Ambush.

We didn't have live weapons, of course. We'd fired them on the range, but for this exercise, laser designators were our only tool, and our armor's detection systems would tell us how effective our notional shot had been. The weapons were manually controlled, the only thing that was. I suppose they didn't want a Drop Trooper getting their lather up and firing off a shot through sheer bloody-mindedness, and requiring a finger to pull a trigger added a layer of intent.

My right thumb was already hovering over the trigger for what should have been a plasma gun, and I jammed it down reflexively before I'd even managed to process what I'd seen through my conscious mind.

"Contact front!" I yelled, fumbling over the phrase we'd been taught. It meant I had enemy to the front, but even as I said it, they were already hitting the jets and arcing over my head to attack the rest of my squad behind me. "Enemy armor!"

The one I'd shot didn't move, and the simulated image projected over the suit by the targeting program told the story of why. I'd hit him with a virtual plasma blast right in the center of the chest. There were centimeters of BiPhase Carbide plating there, but I was less than thirty meters away, point-blank range for a weapon that delivered gigajoules of energy in the form of a coherent packet of hyper-ionized gas the temperature of a star. It would have burned right through the armor and the pilot behind it and that was just what the targeting screen image showed, a ragged, blackened hole surrounded by white-hot metal.

Which was one down, and a shitload to go, and I was facing the wrong direction. There was a whole squad of battlesuits, and five of the six had jumped the second I'd made contact, leaving the lead one to deal with me. I went with my first instinct. They'd gone airborne, so I jumped right after them, the crush of the jets a comfort, a signal I was doing something, even if it turned out to be the wrong thing.

Triggering the jets with my nerve impulses was easy, one of the first things we'd learned in the simulators. Twisting the body of the suit around in mid-air to turn myself around and angle the jets the opposite direction wasn't quite as easy and definitely not intuitive. Controlling the jump-jets through the interface wasn't a matter of thinking "fly!" or picturing the motion in my thoughts. If the Commonwealth military could read thoughts through the interface, they hadn't let us in on the secret. Instead, the interface read the impulses my cerebellum was sending to my body, intercepting them and using them as control keys for the suit.

To jump, all I had to do was...jump. How high and how far depended on how hard I tried to jump, just as if I was doing it with my physical body. Unfortunately, that meant I couldn't really maneuver the suit unless I knew how I'd maneuver my body the same way, and I wasn't any sort of acrobat. The Vigilante flailed awkwardly in mid-air, over-turning and over-correcting just the way my brain told it to, but I finally got it and myself pointed in the right direction.

"I'm hit!" someone screamed into the net, but I couldn't tell who from the voice and didn't have the attention to spare to read it off the IFF transponder.

"There's too many of them!" Rogan was yelling, and then Trent's transmission was stepping over hers and I couldn't make out what anyone was saying and I was already tired of their shit.

"Get off the fucking net!" I bellowed, coming down almost on top of Rogan's position, only meters behind her. "Get out of the damned canyon! Jump!"

Even in mid-air, I was being bombarded by data, and even a system designed to break it down into something easy to understand and control was having trouble making it coherent for me. Rogan was behind me, still yelling something despite what I'd told them all, a warning that there was an enemy trooper right in front of me, as if I couldn't see the big, three-meter hunk of man-shaped metal only ten meters away. It was damaged, Rogan was damaged, there were eight other battlesuits somewhere in front of me, with IFF transponder warnings flashing at me not to shoot them by accident and other flashing warnings basically saying "hey dude! You got enemies here, better shoot 'em!" at the same time.

"Oh, fuck it," I murmured and gave one last burst on the jets. Instead of coming down between Rogan and the enemy suit, I landed right on top of the damned thing. I don't know how much I expected it to hurt, but it was worse. The impact shook me like a bone in a dog's teeth and metal rang and screamed and shrieked as if it were about to give way, and I felt like Ivan Jaropillo getting smacked with the front end of a train. I could only console myself with how much worse the other guy must feel.

The Op-For trooper collapsed under the weight of my Vigilante, and I somehow kept my feet, triggering a stabilizing burst kick of the jump-jets when I thought I might stumble backwards. My head was floating somewhere ten meters over my body, or at least that was how it felt, and I was too out of it to even remember to shoot the guy. Rogan took care of it for me, her suit moving stiffly from the simulated damage, reminding me of old Mrs. Martijena creaking through the streets of Tijuana on her wooden cane. She blasted the downed Op-For with her training laser and the suit went still, its damage sensors freezing its servos as they sensed its destruction.

I was already moving, spurred by a massive adrenaline dump, my senses overloaded by the eye-searing flashes of simulated electron beams scorching the air up and down the canyon in the display. In the moment, I forgot we were playing a war game, forgot the worst that could happen was embarrassment and failure, and really expected to die at any second. IFF transponders were flashing distress and I couldn't tell exactly how bad it was or even who was getting hit because the system was doing its best to distract me.

I had to focus on one thing. It was the only clear thought hammering its way past the confusion, the noise, and blinking lights. I had to do one thing and do it fast, and I had to keep it simple. Kill the enemy. That seemed simple enough, and it had the added benefit of protecting whoever in my squad was left alive.

"Get out of the canyon!" I yelled again. It was the only order I could think to give, the only thing that made sense, but I wasn't sure if anyone was listening.

The enemy certainly wasn't. They liked it down here, where everything was close and we were trapped in a shooting gallery. I wasn't much of a shooter, not before the Marines. I'd fired a gun before Basic, which put me one up on most of the other recruits, but I didn't like them. Nothing philosophical about it, it was just too easy to get caught when you had a gun. A stun wand was a battery with some wire leads encased in plastic. It could have been anything, and wasn't even illegal most places. I'd taken a couple of long-distance shots at the Op-For during Basic, but I'd had time to think. I wasn't doing much thinking at the moment and I forgot about my missiles, barely remembered the plasma gun and waded in like a brawler.

Battlesuits were wedged into the canyon ahead and thank God the sensor array lit up my people with blue haloes, because all the grey metal looked the same even with the enhanced optics and I wasn't exactly a surgical weapon. I swung fists half a meter across in wild hammer-blows, ignoring the flash of simulated energy weapons, ignoring the alarmed shouts of my own squad members and ignoring the damage warnings on the array projected in front of my face.

I hit the right target almost by chance, pushing aside a Vigilante suit I thought might have been Trent with a hip-check and slamming my suit's armored fist into the shoulder joint of the enemy. I think the impact surprised the Op-For trooper more than it damaged them, but it was enough of a blow to throw off their aim and the computer-generated flare of a simulated Tahni electron beamer passed a meter off to the right of my head.

I shoved my right arm where the Op-For Vigilante's chin would be if it had an articulated head and triggered the plasma gun. Damage indicators screamed at me and I was sure I would have blown my suit's right arm off, and maybe my own, if I'd tried it for real, but number three bad guy was down.

And that was enough for them. Jets glowed white and red and the surviving enemy troopers were gone just as quickly as they'd arrived, leaving me standing in a cloud of smoke and holding my proverbial dick.

What the hell was I supposed to do now? I hesitated a moment then keyed the squad net.

"Status." I scowled. Maybe now wasn't a bad time to start sounding professional. "This is Bravo One. Sound off with your status, First squad."

"Bravo Two," Rogan answered, not sounding quite as full of enthusiasm as before. "I'm mobile but my missile launch tube is down and my main weapon is damaged."

"Bravo Three here." Trent's voice sounded shaky. "I'm…I'm down, I got no reactor feed, dude. You guys are gonna have to go on without me."

"Bravo Four, I'm up," Said told me. He was curt, quiet, to the point, which I appreciated at that moment.

There was a silence and I checked the IFF. Bravo Five, Dominguez, was completely off the board. No telemetry, no biological readings, no reactor output. He was dead…or at least his armor wasn't letting him move or respond, which was close enough for the exercise.

"Bravo Six, status?" I snapped, irritated with Dominguez for getting himself killed and Bravo Six for wasting our time. "Calvey, are you awake in there?"

"Uh, yeah, I'm here," she stammered. "My reactor took a hit, getting a lot of thermal blooming and interference from a gap in the shielding, but I can still move."

"Everyone hold up here," I ordered, hoping they'd listen better now that no one was shooting at them.

I jumped out of the canyon, twenty meters straight up and then arcing out another thirty onto the plateau above. We weren't supposed to break comms silence, but the enemy already knew we were here.

Hell, they're Op-For. They probably saw the assault plan before we did.

"Alpha One," I called for the acting platoon leader, a guy named Marcus, "this is Bravo One, come in. We've been hit by enemy armor; we have one KIA and one immobile. Do you read?" I paused, got nothing, saw no IFF in the sensor display or any readings on long-range thermal towards the planned attack. "Alpha One, do you read?"

"Index, index, index."

I groaned, sagging against the padding inside the armor. The voice belonged to Major Bullough, the lead Armor trainer, and "index" meant the end of the exercise.

"All units are loose from damage holds. Report to the main Collection Area for the AAR."

AAR was the After-Action Review. That was where we could sit around and listen while the trainers told us how badly we'd fucked up.

"All right, First squad," I sighed. "Everyone out of the hole and follow me back."

This wasn't going to be pretty.

"OKAY, WHO HERE CAN TELL ME WHERE YOU FUCKED UP?"

Captain Charles reminded me of the nasty, trained dogs the gang-bangers used to keep down in Tijuana. He was thick through the chest and shoulders, with jowls that hung down in an expression of perpetual disapproval, eyes dark, beady and dangerous. And that's exactly what he was, Major Bullough's attack dog, sent to chew us up and spit us out while Bullough waited and watched, tall and lean and nearly skeletal in the shadows, silently observing.

Charles scanned back and forth from where he stood on the isolated boulder at the center of the formation, as if he was a street preacher and us trainees were his flock, clustered around him, butts on the dry, dusty ground. The immobile Vigilante battlesuits were lined up behind him, backlit by the temporary camp the Op-For had set up, an accusatory choir waiting to echo his message.

"No one?" He shook his head, hands raised in invitation. "Come on, someone has to have an idea."

"We joined the Marines," someone murmured behind me, too low and quiet for me to figure out who'd said it, probably too low for Charles to hear, though I thought I saw his eyes narrow.

Finally, someone raised their hand. It was the platoon leader for the exercise, Private Marcus. He was quiet and unassuming, dark enough he nearly blended into the night.

"They knew we were coming," he suggested. "They were ready for us."

"They were," Charles agreed, "and some of you may think that's not fair, that the Op-For cheated. But that's going to happen out there, too." He gestured up at the night sky to demonstrate where "out there" was. "The enemy is going to know you're coming and you're going to have to change your plans on the fly. Still, this was your first live mission and it wasn't designed to be unwinnable. Your problem was your plan. It required too much coordination with limited communication." He pointed at me. "Your First squad was sent on a pincer movement ten kilometers away from the rest of your platoon in a situation where you didn't have secure comms and couldn't coordinate if something went wrong."

His grin was broad and unfriendly.

"And there's the lesson, boys and girls, the reason for this exercise. Something *always* goes wrong. You all heard of Murphy's Law? Anything that can go wrong will go wrong. I think Murphy must have been a Second Lieutenant or a Corporal, because they're the best ones for finding out what can go wrong with a plan."

A few chuckles at that.

"So, given that things *will* go wrong and we can't always anticipate them, we have to be ready to improvise, adapt and overcome. But we can't do that if we've split our forces and can't even talk to each other because we're out of line-of-sight. That's what you did wrong, Private Marcus." His eyes settled on me. "As for you, Private Alvarez, you fucked up in a totally different way." The smile again, a canine smile that was more a baring of teeth than any good humor. "Don't get me wrong, you gave the Op-For boys a black eye."

"Literally, in one case." That was Bullough, commenting from his position off to the side, and I glanced over at him in surprise.

"Yes, sir," Charles agreed, chuckling. "But the problem is, their job was to stop you linking up with your platoon and, losses aside, they accomplished that mission and you failed in yours."

"What could I have done differently?" I blurted. Then added, "Sir." Not that I thought things had gone well, but…

"Just one thing, Alvarez, but it's a damn important thing. You could've carried out the mission. There's no way you could have known the enemy battlesuits were there, and there's no way you could have beaten them all, but once the ambush was tripped, your priority should have been to get your ass out of that canyon and alert Marcus here that you were blown."

"I should have just left them there, sir?"

"The mission, the men, and you." Charles shrugged. "It's an old saying, older than spaceflight, and my apologies to the females here, from a time when women were not allowed in combat. It still applies, though. The mission always comes first, before your people, before yourself. Notifying your command that they were heading into an ambush should have been your priority over blasting bad guys."

I said nothing more, sinking back onto the ground in a sullen funk.

If the idiots in my squad would have listened to what I said, it wouldn't have been a problem.

"Which is not to say there wasn't plenty of blame to go around," Charles added, as though he'd read my thoughts. "None of you really know how to lead yet, which is expected, but too damned many of you don't know how to follow, either. Following orders isn't just something you do when a trainer yells at you, it's what you do when the guns are firing and lives are on the line. That's when it's the *most* important. Tonight, I heard your squad leaders, your platoon leader, and a platoon sergeant yelling orders, and no one was listening."

He shrugged, hopping down off the rock platform and pacing through the sand.

"Maybe they weren't the best orders, maybe they were *stupid* orders, but part of the oath you swore when you signed up was to carry out the lawful orders of your superiors. Not just the convenient ones, not just the ones you think you'll get in trouble if you ignore, but all the lawful orders. So, before any of you start blaming the leaders we appointed for this mission, think about what you did and whether you did everything you could to support them."

Captain Charles checked the datalink on his wrist.

"All right, that's it for tonight. We'll go over the nuts and bolts of the mission later, but for now, get organized into your squads and get back in your suits. The shuttle will be landing right out here...." He pointed behind us at the expanse of flat rock stretching off into the darkness of the cloud-wreathed night. "...in about forty-five minutes to take you back to Tartarus. Dismissed."

I was about to call First squad together when a hand touched my arm. I looked around, and then upward. Major Bullough was nearly two meters tall and I wondered if they had to configure his suit to accommodate his height. His eyes were buried under thick brows, nearly invisible in the darkness.

"Sir?" I asked, stiffening to attention. It wasn't required in the field, but I wasn't that long out of Basic Training.

"Relax, Alvarez." He jerked his head off toward the flat rock landing zone. "Walk with me a moment."

He strode out into the darkness, his long legs eating up the meters with little effort, and I had to fast-walk just to keep up, nearly running into him when he stopped abruptly. His hands were clasped behind his back as he stared out into the darkness as if he could see the sky through the low-hanging clouds. I tried not to focus on the distance, knowing how petrified with fear I would be if it were daylight and I was standing out here on the edge of nothing. It was bad enough at night.

"I am not overly fond of this planet, Alvarez," he confessed. He was smiling thinly when he turned back to me. "I don't know anyone who is, if they're being honest. But the one thing I like about my job, despite being stationed here, is the opportunity to find men and women with the potential to be great Marines. They don't come very often." He shrugged, a motion of shoulders and hands, more fluid and expressive than I would have expected, as if he were an actor on stage. "Oh, most of the recruits who come through here are passable, useful for the war effort, but so few have what it takes to be great."

I said nothing, not sure where this was leading...or maybe, having a wild guess and not wanting to indulge it.

"Private Alvarez, you handle a battlesuit with an incredible instinct. We don't see it often. Most Drop-troops take months, if not years to really feel at home with the interface, to move the suit as if it's their own body. I was impressed with the instinctive way you reacted in combat, even with very little experience. So was the Op-For NCO who you beat the shit out of." There was a hint of amusement in his tone. "He wanted me to tell you no recruit has ever killed three Op-For suits in one mission, particularly not their first."

That felt good to hear, and I wanted to revel in it, but I knew better. I kept my mouth shut because when someone like Major Bullough says shit like that, there's always a "but" coming.

"But," he went on, "every Marine, from the lowest recruit to the Chief of Staff of the Marine Corps not only has to be ready to be an infantry troop on demand, they have to be ready to be a *leader*."

I thought about lying, telling him what he wanted to hear, that I was doing my best and I'd get it right any day now. But I had a sense I should be honest with the man, that he knew more about me than he was letting on.

"I've never really wanted to lead anyone," I admitted. "I've pretty much always been on my own."

"And that's fine, for now." He waved a hand expansively. "We need warm bodies, and as good as you are in a suit, we'd take you if you were a narcoleptic necrophiliac. But if you ever want to be more, Cameron, if you ever want to be *great*, either as a Marine or as a man, then you're going to have to be more than just a talented killer. You're going to have to become a leader. You're going to have to decide you're in the Corps for more than just a ticket out of the Underground, or to avoid prosecution for one crime or another."

He'd struck pretty close to home and twinges of paranoia crawled up my spine as I wondered just how much he knew about me. Bullough glanced sidelong at me, something canny in his expression, as if he could tell what I was thinking.

"Don't worry, no one cares what you were before. Everyone here has a past, even Academy graduates like me. That's the choice you're going to have to make. At some point, there'll come a time when you have to move beyond what you were, or what you think you still are, and become a Marine."

"Yes, sir." I wasn't agreeing so much as acknowledging I'd heard what he said, but he didn't push it.

"Get back to your squad," he told me. "Tomorrow's the fun part of a field exercise."

"What's that, sir?" I wondered.

"PMCS, Private Alvarez. An acronym you'll come to hate as much as you hate this planet. Preventative Maintenance Checks and Service." His grin was as cruel as the one Captain Charles had shown us earlier. "You get to clean every damn bit of sand and dust off your suits...even if it takes all day."

9

Major Bullough was right about two things. I did learn to hate PMCS and I was already getting damned tired of Inferno by the time I got through AOT. And I wouldn't be getting away from either of them any time soon.

82 Eridani beat down, as merciless at mid-afternoon than any of the bullies I'd faced in group homes as a child, though more equanimous in its brutality. Poppa used to say "it rains on the just and the unjust" but it hadn't rained on anyone here in a month and wouldn't again for the rest of the dry season. The monsoons had hit about a quarter of the way through AOT and turned the dirt to muck across the continent, then ended about three days before our graduation ceremony, as if God Himself had some sort of deal with the Corps to make things as miserable as possible in the field.

And Goddamn, that mud was hard to get out of the joints of a Vigilante.

I only hoped that the armorers at Third Platoon, Delta Company, Fourth Battalion of the 187th Marine Expeditionary Force (Armored) were less picky than the ones at AOT.

I wiped sweat out of my eyes with my free hand, pulled my duffle bag higher on my shoulder and double-checked the sign on the rough, unfinished buildfoam wall of the company headquarters building to make sure I didn't wander around the wrong offices for half an hour, because once I stepped into the air conditioning, I wasn't going to want to come back out.

Sucking in a deep breath and trying to steady myself, I stepped through the doors. The cool, dry air inside hit me in a wave, drying the perspiration coating my scalp, and it felt as if ten kilograms lifted off my shoulders in an instant. There was a desk a few meters inside the front entrance, crewed by an actual, human clerk on the theory that privates are cheaper to maintain than automated systems and needed to be kept busy. The one at the desk looked even younger than me and not nearly as happy to be working inside as I would have been. He squinted at the rank displayed on my chest and collar and decided I didn't rate any sort of formality.

"You need anything?" he asked, sounding supremely bored.

"I'm looking for the Platoon Sergeant for Third," I told him.

"That'd be Gunny Guerrero, but he's at an NCO meeting right now."

Shit. An NCO meeting meant no First Sergeant either.

"Should I wait?" I wondered. "I need to report to the platoon. I'm just arriving from AOT."

"Oh, you're that guy Alvarez?" He scrolled through screens on his scansheet, then nodded. "Okay, yeah, Gunny Guerrero left a note, said you were supposed to go ahead and report to your platoon leader, Lt. Ackley." He pointed down the hallway to his right. "She's the second door down on your...." He seemed to a do a mental calculation, trying to figure out my directions from his. "...on your left." He waved behind his desk. "You can leave your bag here if you want."

I took him up on it, throwing the duffle against the inside of the desk, glad to be rid of it after hauling it across the length of Tartarus on three different busses. There was nothing in it I gave a shit about, nothing personal because I had nothing personal. It was my issue uniforms, boots and the one set of civvies I'd had fabricated after Basic. It could have been replaced in an hour if I needed it.

I looked around for a speaker or a buzzer or a security panel or *something* at Ackley's door, but this was a no-frills military base and I knocked on the door with my bare knuckles like I was back in Tijuana.

"Come." It was a female voice, firm but young. Young and inexperienced *could* mean someone insecure enough to expect spit and polish, and I decided I'd better toe the line until I found out different.

I opened the door and stepped through into an immediate position of attention.

"Ma'am, Private Alvarez reporting for duty!"

The words were sharp and parade-ground loud and I followed them with a salute to match, eyes frozen on the wall straight ahead, landing on a still picture hanging there of a smiling couple in civilian clothes. They had the ageless look of surface-dwellers, not just in Trans-Angeles but anywhere in the Commonwealth, people who weren't necessarily rich but comfortable enough that their parents and probably their parents before them had been able to afford anti-aging treatments. They didn't look over thirty, but were likely decades older than that.

Lt. Joyce Ackley looked a lot like her father, I saw when she stood up to return my salute. She was tall for a woman, assuming she was from Earth and not somewhere with lighter gravity, as tall as I was, though probably fifteen or twenty kilos lighter. Her face was long, her nose straight and her jaw strong, with a set of determination to it.

"At ease, Alvarez," she said. "Close the door and grab a seat."

Not quite as stiff and by-the-book as I'd feared, then. The chair wasn't particularly comfortable, just folding plastic, and it threatened to collapse under my weight, so I sat up straight and tried not to move around much.

"Gunny Guerrero will meet up with you tomorrow," she told me, leaning back in her office chair. "He's trying to hash out the details of our new training schedule with the rest of the battalion senior NCOs. We're going to be deploying soon on the *Iwo Jima* and we have a limited time to get some final requirements down before we ship out."

"How long do we have, ma'am?" I wondered. Something tingled in my gut and it might have been eagerness to get into the fight, but I had to admit it might also have been fear.

"Three weeks." Her voice was quiet and I wasn't sure if I was imagining the slight break in her voice. "Then another two weeks on the ship to reach our target."

Less than two months till I saw combat. Maybe less than two months to live.

"You're replacing a casualty," she informed me. "Training accident, not combat. None of us have been in combat yet except Top." Top would be the Company First Sergeant, though we'd all been cautioned in AOT that not all First Sergeants liked the term. "And Captain Covington," she added, as if that part was obvious. "The Company Commander. He's prior service, fought in the Pirate Wars. Re-upped after the Battle for Mars."

My eyes went wide. The Pirate Wars had been twenty-five years ago. That would make the CO at least in his forties, maybe fifties. Not that someone who'd had anti-aging treatments would be physically unsuited for combat, but you didn't usually see people that old joining up.

"Giannelli jumped too early on a practice drop," she went on. "The drop order hadn't been given. He just lost his cool. You know what happens when you drop in a Vigilante at too far over four hundred meters, Alvarez?"

"They told us in Armor school," I said, remembering the lecture very well, and the video and pictures that had gone with it, "if you drop from over four hundred meters, that usually means the shuttle hasn't decelerated enough for it to be survivable."

"For a normal drop. It varies for atmospheric density and local gravity," she allowed, "but at anything near standard one gee, you'll be looking at multiple broken bones between four to six hundred meters. Giannelli dropped at a thousand meters."

I gulped, trying not to imagine how high that was.

"Did he…?"

"He's alive." Ackley shrugged. "They're growing him a new spine at the Tartarus Medical Center but it'll be three months before he walks again."

She was trying to be nonchalant about it, but I'd learned to read people a long time ago, in the group homes and on the streets. It bothered the lieutenant, and I guessed it would bother me, too.

"I don't need to see something like that happen twice, Alvarez," she said, a gruff hoarseness in her voice. She cleared her throat and went on with a firmer tone. "I've seen from your training records that you're a natural in a suit. Don't let it go to your head. If you get sloppy once, ignore one safety protocol because you think you're just that good, you'll wind up dead before the Tahni get a chance to take a shot at you."

"Aye, ma'am," I acknowledged. I hadn't honestly considered it a possibility. If there was anything more important than me not getting killed, I hadn't discovered it yet.

There was a knock on the door.

"Come," Ackley said, not bothering to rise.

"You called, El-Tee?"

The man was the type I'd come to think of as a generic Marine drop-troop. Medium height, medium build, hair buzzed on the sides to bare the jacks and regulation short on top, pale even in this sun-drenched hell-hole because he spent all his time outdoors in a battlesuit. There was something different about this man, though, just a hint of irreverence in the set of his eyes, in the shadow of a grin that wouldn't quite leave his face.

"Sgt. Hayes," Ackley said, "this is Alvarez, your new trooper. I want you to get him settled in the barracks and show him around the squad bay, then take him down to the armorer and get him checked out in a Vigilante."

"Aye, ma'am, will do," Hayes said with a nod. From his rank, E-5, I had to assume he was my squad leader. "You ready to head out, Alvarez?"

"Yes, sergeant," I said, snapping up to my feet smartly. I turned back to Ackley and saluted. "If you'll excuse me, ma'am?"

Technically, she was supposed to stand to return my salute, but she didn't bother, just threw her hand up from her seat. I wasn't sure if she was dissing me or just trying to give me a hint. I didn't need the parade-ground spit and polish, but either way, she didn't sit right with me. I hoped to hell she knew how to do her job, because the whole not getting killed thing would be a lot harder with an incompetent platoon leader.

"Grab your shit and let's find you a bunk," Hayes said once we were out of the office. "We keep two to a room here, but I think we have an empty if you want one to yourself for the next couple weeks. Unless you'd rather have the company. Giannelli's old roommate is Corporal Kurita, but I'm not sure if he's ready for a new roommate after what happened to Gia. They were pretty tight and even though

Gia's not dead, he's not coming back to the Drop Troops, at least not in time for us to head out."

His perpetual grin grew wider as we got out of the offices into the sun, as if he was vitamin D deficient and needed to be outdoors to thrive, like a plant. Me, I just felt annoyed at being back in the heat.

"I'm Scotty, by the way, but not in front of Top. You prefer Cam, Cameron, Alvarez?"

"Cam," I said, a bit overwhelmed by the rush of words from the man. I hadn't met that many NCOs, and none of them had been as garrulous as Scotty Hayes, nor as friendly. "Cam is fine."

"File said you were from Trans-Angeles, right? Damn, that's sure as hell the big city. Me, I've never even been to Earth. I'm from Hermes, out at Proxima Centauri. You know where that is?"

"I've heard of it." Everyone had heard of Hermes. It was the first interstellar colony, though all I knew was what I'd audited on the free nets back in Trans-Angeles.

"It's a great place," he enthused. "Lot nicer than this shithole, I can tell you that."

We both saluted a passing lieutenant, but Scotty barely paused in his monologue.

"We actually get a winter there, for one thing, not just a rainy season. Where I lived, just outside Sanctuary—that's the capital— we would even get a little snow, though not as much as up in the Edge Mountains. You could see them from where we lived and there would always be snow up there in winter."

"Why'd you join the Marines?" I asked. It slipped out in disbelief that anyone would give up someplace like that for Inferno, but Hayes took it for a philosophical question.

"I figured I had to do my part," he said. "I mean, the Tahni are a threat to all of us, right? Isn't that why you joined?"

"I sort of didn't have a choice."

I could tell he wanted to ask more about that, but we'd arrived at the barracks and nearly stumbled over a group of four Marines sitting on the floor just inside the entrance to the squad bay. They were playing dice and it might have been a scene in the vestibule of any housing block in the Underground except for the uniforms and the haircuts.

"At ease!" one of them, a short, wiry corporal with dark hair and closely-grouped features snapped, coming to his feet at Hayes' approach.

"As you were, guys," Hayes waved it away as if he didn't have time for that sort of thing.

It was interesting, though. If he really didn't care about military courtesies, why would they bother to keep doing it? Either the guys respected him enough to do it anyway, or else Top or maybe Gunny Guerrero insisted on it and they were too afraid not to do it.

"This is PFC Alvarez," Hayes went on, clapping me on the shoulder. "He's our new guy for your fire team, Tommy." He nodded to the guy who'd jumped up at his approach. "Cam, this is Lance Corporal Tommy Kurita, your new team leader."

"Howdy, Alvarez," Kurita held out a hand and I shook it, hesitating slightly. In the Underground, shaking hands was considered pretentious, something the Surface Dwellers did. We bumped forearms or sometimes had more elaborate rituals depending on your neighborhood and possibly gang affiliation. "This is the rest of the team, Taylor and Rodriguez." Taylor was as generic as Hayes, but less talkative and bumped forearms wordlessly, while Rodriguez was shorter than Kurita but broader through the shoulders.

"Where you from, Alvarez?" she asked me, not offering her hand or forearm.

"Trans-Angeles."

She nodded, her expression telling me she was familiar with the city.

"Which Block?"

I chuckled and she frowned in a confusion I understood. Your Housing Block was your nation, your fealty, your religion to anyone from the Trans Angeles Underground.

"None of them. I grew up in group homes and lived in the tunnels."

"Damn," she murmured, eyes going wide. "Then this place is like a step up for you, huh?"

"Probably safer," I admitted.

"Kurita," Hayes interrupted the exchange, "you looking for a new roommate or should I put Alvarez in the vacant room?"

"If it's all the same to you, Scotty," Kurita said, "I'm kinda liking having the extra space." I didn't know him, so I couldn't tell whether or not he was bullshitting to hide the fact he was still shaken up about his old roommate.

"No problem, man." Hayes didn't push the matter. "Come on, Alvarez, I'll show you where you can stash your shit."

The rooms were small enough I could understand Kurita not wanting to share one, though they were a hundred times bigger than the ones I'd had as a kid. Two bunks, two footlockers and two wall lockers and about a square meter of bare wall on either side. I threw my duffle bag down on one of the bunks, then cracked my neck and flexed my shoulder.

"So, Scotty, can I ask you something?" I said, checking to make sure none of the others had followed us into the room.

"Sure, what's up?" He laughed. "If it's about where to score chicks, I can tell you to stay away from Banjo's down in the Fifth District." He shrugged. "If you're into guys, I can't help you, but I think there's a guy in Third Squad who could…"

"No, that's okay," I assured him. "I was just wondering what you thought of Lt. Ackley."

"Oh." His eyes narrowed as if he was considering the question carefully. "Well, you know, man, she's a butter-bar and ain't none of them really know what they're doing." He snorted. "By the time they figure out the job, they promote them out of platoon leader and put some new dude in charge. She seems okay, though, not really full of herself the way some of them are, especially Academy grads." He looked at the open door, then leaned over conspiratorially. "I heard her dad was an admiral who got killed in the Battle for Mars, though. Don't know if it's true or not." He frowned. "Or maybe he was a captain, I don't remember. But anyway, she's okay. And even if she fucks up, Gunny Guerrero is there to set her straight. We NCOs are the ones who really run the Corps. Except for the Skipper, of course. He runs everything."

The Skipper was, I knew, Captain Covington, the Company Commander, and if he was indeed a veteran of the Pirate Wars, I could understand Hayes holding him in awe.

"You can put your stuff in the lockers later," Hayes said, heading for the door. "Now we gotta do the important shit." He grinned. "We gotta get you your suit."

10

THERE WAS SOMETHING ABOUT THE VIGILANTES IN THE DELTA Company armory, a qualitative difference from the suits in AOT. Those had been training suits, never destined to see combat. These were weapons, and I stared at them with a sense of awe.

"They're pretty fucking awesome, aren't they?" Hayes said, patting one of the suits with a proprietary pride. "This is mine." He looked around, searching amid the other Marines wandering between the Vigilantes and the maintenance and loading gear clustered around them. "Let me see if I can find Warrant Reese and figure out where yours is. Hang out here for a minute."

I nodded, still staring at the dull grey golems, unable to shake the feeling they were staring back.

"You the new guy?"

He had one of those faces, the kind that warned you just what sort of guy you were dealing with, with the pugnacious set to his jaw and the perpetually narrow eyes. Truth in advertising. His head was shaved to peach fuzz, like he was showing off his jacks.

"I'm PFC Alvarez," I told him, hoping it answered the question.

"Yeah, I heard about you." He nodded, mouth twisting into a sneer as he wiped lubricant off his hands.

"Are you a tech?" I asked, wondering why the guy was talking to me.

"Fuck no," he snorted. "I'm a team leader from Fourth squad."

I saw Lance Corporal's rank on his blouse and "Cunningham" on his name tape and I doubted he'd have volunteered either piece of information.

"I guess you think you're hot shit on a stick," he went on. "I mean, killing off three Op-For all by yourself." Cunningham's laugh was scornful, mocking. "Of course, you totally fucked your mission in the process is what I heard. You some kind of glory hound, Alvarez? Think you're a hero or something?"

I glanced out of the corner of my eye, hoping Hayes would come back and get this asshole off my back, but he was nowhere to be seen. I considered just ignoring him, but he was a bully, I could see it in his eyes. Ignoring them never worked.

"You sound like you really know what you're talking about, Lance Corporal Cunningham," I told him. "You must have seen a lot of combat, right? How many Tahni have you killed?"

"We ain't seen any combat yet," he grumbled. "But it don't matter how many Tahni you kill if you fuck up the mission trying to be some kind of hotshot."

"I guess it's a damn good thing you're going to be there, then." I said, my voice going lower as I took a step closer, nearly nose-to-nose with the man. He was about my height, maybe three or four centimeters taller than me but not much heavier. "I mean, you're the guy who thinks he knows everything about me, right? So, you can make sure I don't fuck things up." I cocked my head to the side so I could get his eyes into focus. "You going to make that your job, Lance Corporal Cunningham? You going to make sure I don't fuck things up for you?"

The words weren't insulting. That was key, that was what you had to do. You had to make them either agree with you, which would mean they could walk away without feeling dissed, or you had to make them ratchet it up to the next level. Because even if you lost the fight, if the bully thought the fight had been their idea, they wouldn't feel like they needed to come back later to save face.

But I also wasn't backing down. Because backing down would be an invitation for him to try to push me around whenever he felt like it. I'd become an expert at dealing with bullies. I wish I knew as much about anyone else.

"You better get the fuck out of my face," Cunningham barked, his breath sour and smelling of some kind of chew, "before I put my Goddamned foot up your ass!"

I didn't move.

"You think you got it in you," I said, not yelling, almost whispering, "then let's get it on."

I tried not to brace myself. The key was to stay loose, to go with it when he pushed me. And he was going to push me. It was always the first move when you were this close, the opening act. He'd push me back and then take a swing, and if I was tensed up, I'd wind up staying just inside his swing. I had to let myself fall back a few steps and make him miss, then I could step in behind the swing and take him down. I hoped.

"What in the living *fuck* is going on here?"

The voice was hoarse and gravelly, the kind that made me want to clear my throat in sympathy, but the words were a bellow echoing off the sheet metal walls of the armory, like every Vigilante in the place was yelling in chorus.

"At ease!" I didn't see who barked the command, but they were enthusiastic about it and both Cunningham and I stepped away from each other and came to attention before going to the at ease position.

The woman who stepped between us was about a head shorter than me, but I wouldn't have tried her on a bet. Her head was shaven so close I could have seen my reflection in it and shaped like an anvil with a neck almost wider than the head curving into shoulders as big as mine. Her rank was on her uniform blouse, the three bars and four rockers of a master gunnery sergeant and I knew that this was Top, the Topkick, the First Shirt, the company first sergeant. The name tape read "Campbell."

"Lance Corporal Cunningham," the woman growled, "I fear you may have misunderstood the orders you were given earlier today. Were you told to perform maintenance checks on your WF-4100 Vigilante battlesuit, or were you instructed to come down here and engage in a Goddamned *dick beating* contest with a fucking newbie?"

"I was told to perform maintenance checks, First Sergeant Campbell!" Cunningham sounded off as if we were back in Basic.

She was centimeters from him, as close as I'd been, but his nose was on a level with the top of her head.

"Since you're having such a difficult time understanding the concept and staying on task, maybe I should have you perform maintenance checks on *every* Goddamned suit in this company then!" Her lips were skinned back from her teeth and I was half-convinced she was about to rip his throat out if he dared to talk back.

"Yes, First Sergeant!" He might have been a bully, but he wasn't a complete dumbass.

She rounded on me, her eyes wide and white and I swallowed hard. She was more intimidating than any of the Drill Sergeants I'd had in Basic, a force of nature crammed into a meter-six of muscle and bone.

"Alvarez, you seem to have taken quite the shine to Lance Corporal Cunningham and we all *know* how good you are *inside* a suit, so let's see how well you do on the outside. You are going to assist Cunningham in performing maintenance checks and he will show you every last detail of how Delta Company takes care of their gear. Since two of you will be on the job, I expect it to be done by the close of business today! Do I make myself clear?"

"Aye-aye, First Sergeant!" I shouted with all the enthusiasm I could muster. It sounded perfectly horrible, but when Top orders a PFC to do something, there's only one correct answer.

She stood between the two of us, eyes scanning back and forth like a security camera.

"Am I going to hear of any more problems between the two of you?" she asked, her words pitched low but still as sharp and serrated as a hunting knife.

"No, First Sergeant!" both of us yelled in antiphonal chorus.

"I'd better fucking not."

She stalked off and Hayes emerged from the shadows, whistling softly, eyes following the stocky woman as she exited the armory.

"Shit, Cam," he said, shaking his head, "you don't waste any time, do you?"

"I guess not." I eyed Cunningham sidelong. "So, you gonna show me how to perform service checks on a suit?"

"Fuck off, noob," the Lance Corporal sneered, giving me the finger as he sauntered away, suddenly fearless again now that Top was gone.

Hayes scowled after him.

"I should go tell his squad leader he's disobeying a direct order from Top. She'll have him cleaning latrines until we lift for our tour."

"Naw, please don't," I begged him. "I don't need to get a rep as a narc already, I just got here."

"All right, man," Hayes said, though he didn't seem happy about it. "Just do the best you can. I'll see you at chow."

I turned and looked across all the suits in the armory. They'd seemed so impressive a couple minutes ago, but now all I could think was how damn many of them there were...

———————

I knew how to perform maintenance checks on a Vigilante, of course. It was probably a third of what we learned in AOT, and probably half of what we did. I found the gear easy enough. There were half a dozen carts full of the scanners and all I had to do was plug them into the data-ports on different sections of the suit, get the readout, then transfer it to the tablet hanging on the rack next to each Vigilante. It was just time-consuming and tedious and I wanted to kill myself after about an hour of it.

"You don't learn a fucking thing about the suits doing that shit, y'know?"

I finished transferring the data from the last reading on Vigilante ARD-227 to its tablet before I turned and found a doughy-faced, beady-eyed little man watching me, his arms crossed, a skeptical frown dragging down his jowls.

"You're probably right," I admitted, checking his rank instinctively and seeing he was a technician, "Warrant. But I gotta finish the checks, anyway or Top'll have my ass."

"Yeah, I heard the little runt running her mouth before," he said with an irreverence I found a bit shocking, even from a WO-3. "She don't know any more about the fucking suits than you do." He worked a wad of chew in the side of his mouth, then spit a dark stream on the stained floor. "You'd think people who count on the fucking things to live or die would want to know more about how they work, but if all you care about are the scanner readings..."

"Hey, Warrant," I protested, holding up my hands, "if you want to..."

"Mutt," he grunted.

"Excuse me?" I blinked.

"Name's Mutterlin," he expounded, "but everyone calls me Mutt."

"Okay, Mutt, if you want to teach me anything about the suits, I'm more than willing to learn, as long as I can keep doing what the Top told me and finish the maintenance checks."

"Oh, son," he said, chuckling as he pulled a cart full of power tools up next to the suit, "we're gonna do so much more than maintenance checks."

We sure as hell did. Mutt and I tore down a full squad's worth of suits from helmet to ankle joint and I became familiar with every single idiosyncrasy and eccentricity of the Vigilante battlesuit.

"There's a lot of shit about these suits the military doesn't want you to know," Mutt assured me as the two of us pulled off the reactor cowling from the rear of one of the Vigilantes. "Take the isotope reactor, for instance. It's got that overheat shutoff, they told you about that, right?"

I nodded. They had stressed that we couldn't use the jets when the heat indicators were in the red, and that we couldn't run too fast for too long if the heat indicators were in the red and yadda yadda yadda, and it all sounded like it would be really inconvenient if someone was shooting at you.

"Well, there's a fudge factor built into that, of course, and what they don't tell you or most people who use the things for a living is that there's a manual override. You gotta go deep into the menus, but once you get to it you can put a shortcut on your display." He barked a laugh. "Of course, you're taking the chance of your reactor melting down and burning right through your shielding and turning you into a black cinder, but you know…"

"Noted." I helped him set the cowling down on a service cart. "I hope I don't have to use that one."

He went silent for a few minutes other than to ask me to hand him tools and lubricants, and then we had to slip the cowling back onto the rear of the suit, which seemed to require so much more effort than taking it off.

"You gonna get that noob to do all your work today, Mutt?" another of the technicians asked him as he passed, cackling loud enough to bounce the sound off the walls.

"You just wish you were smart enough to pull it off, Kenny!" Mutt shot back, laughing just as loud as he walked around to the front of the suit. "Now off with its head!" he enthused, clambering up on the metal steps attached to the maintenance rack and gesturing for me to take the ones on the other side.

The housing for the sensor suite in the suit's head was a lot lighter than the reactor cowling, so Mutt let me take it off all by myself and hold it up while he serviced and calibrated the optical and thermal cameras, the lidar and radar emitters, and the sonic pickups.

"You know, these things can get fucked up easy in combat," he confided as my shoulders began to ache. "They're on top of the armor, not under it, because they wouldn't be much good buried under a couple centimeters of BiPhase Carbide, would they? But if they go down, your targeting system is fucked, too. Your weapons systems won't let you fucking fire without the targeting system, either."

"But...?" I assumed and he grinned, apparently pleased with my intuition.

"But," he agreed, "you go into your targeting menu and toggle all through the submenus until you reach 'admin settings' and you find a choice for 'activate manual targeting.' You choose that and again, set up a shortcut for it in the display and you can use whatever optical or thermal sensors are left. Or hell, just open the damn chest and peek." He pulled out the blower he'd been using to clean the radar emitter and motioned for me to lower the housing.

"Oh, thank God," I moaned, letting the heavy, metal cover slide back into place and letting him reseal it.

"Fuckin' eggheads in design thinking they know better than troops in the field," Mutt spat a brown stream onto the floor again. "Assholes. If they don't trust you hard-shells to aim with your fucking eyes, why do they trust you with guided missiles?"

I nodded in agreement, then thought about Cunningham and wondered if maybe the eggheads were right.

"By the by," Mutt leaned in close, as if he was about to tell me something more forbidden than how to melt down my reactor, "there's also a command override in there to let you take over anyone's suit in the field. Like if they go apeshit crazy and start shooting at us instead of the enemy." He shrugged. "Well, they say the real reason is if you gotta hot-swap suits in the field, but that don't seem too likely to me, you know?"

I didn't argue, but a trooper going apeshit crazy and shooting at their own people seemed even less likely. I let him talk me through the sequence, though, because what the hell? I was a nineteen-year-old kid about to be set loose in a flying, nuclear-powered suit of armor and everything else just seemed gravy.

I probably would have forgotten most of what he told me because I don't have an eidetic memory or an implant recorder, but he didn't just tell me once. We went over it all again and again, with each suit we tore down and put back together, and sometimes the other technicians would stop by and ask him questions that seemed to me to be in another language, though I knew they were just using terms I didn't understand involving nuclear reactions and energy shielding and laser focusing.

The work was hard and we didn't take a break, but I didn't feel tired, even though I was sweating through my fatigues. I didn't think about the time, just concentrated on trying to memorize what he was telling me, details about hot-swapping weapons in the field, rerouting power leads if your guns went down, how to reload weapons in the field that were supposedly designed to be reloaded by dedicated loading crews…things I might never use, but would be damned glad to know if I did.

"Jesus, I need a drink," Mutt said finally, wiping a sleeve across his forehead. "What fucking time is it anyway?"

"Hey, Alvarez!"

It was Scotty again, his face screwed up in confusion or maybe surprise, the entrance doors swinging shut behind him.

"Hey man," he said, hands spread, "I didn't think you'd still be in here! You know it's been six hours, right? Cunningham fucked off like three hours ago and I thought you'd be shamming somewhere."

"Mutt…I mean, Warrant Mutterlin here has been showing me some stuff about the suits," I told him.

Hayes' laugh was sharp and loud.

"You mean Mutt has been getting you to do his grunt work for him. Anyway, it's chow time, man. You need to go clean up and get to the mess hall before they're out of the good stuff."

"The good stuff?" I asked him, cocking an eyebrow. "You mean there's anything except soy paste and spirulina powder rearranged so it doesn't look like something you feed to babies?"

"Well, no," he admitted, his expression rueful. "But there's brownies with real chocolate for dessert if you get there before everyone else eats them all."

"Can't say no to chocolate," I said, grinning. I turned back to Mutt. "Thanks. That was some good shit you told me."

"I was just running my mouth, kid." He waved it away, a glint in his eye. "You were the one doing all the heavy lifting. Good luck." Something clouded over behind his good humor. "Then again, if you had any luck, you wouldn't be fighting in this war at all."

11

THE BROWNIES WERE GONE, BUT I WAS OKAY WITH THAT. I'D LIED TO Hayes. I could take or leave chocolate and only really gave a shit about ice cream. The food was typical military, not a damned bit of difference from AOT, and today the processors gave us the choice of chicken pad Thai or a chicken sandwich on flatbread with fries. I ignored the fact they were all made from the same ingredients and grabbed the pad Thai. At least the peanut sauce was made from real peanuts.

"Here's our platoon," Hayes said, guiding me to a table off to the edge of the mess hall.

I caught sight of Cunningham as we passed another table, and I pretended to rub at something in my eye and shot him a surreptitious bird. He didn't try to hide his own return gesture, and I caught a flare of anger in his eyes and grinned.

Asshole.

"Hey, Alvarez!" Rodriguez said around a mouthful of faux chicken.

I recognized her and Kurita, who nodded without speaking, seemingly a little more sensitive about the whole business of talking with his mouth full. The others...

"Alvarez."

The man was lean and leathery, his face weathered if not exactly old, his hair chopped into a wire-brush cut in a stripe down the center of his skull. He wasn't a tall man, but there was something about the straightness of his posture that made him seem to tower centimeters over me. He said nothing else, as if testing if I was smart enough to guess who he was.

How fucking smart do you have to be to see the rank on his shirt?

"Gunny," I said, nodding respectfully. "Sorry I wasn't able to report directly to you."

"Meetings," Guerrero snorted, looking as if he wanted to spit the word on the floor. "They're the bane of my fucking existence, boy."

He had an accent I recognized as Filipino. Trans-Angeles had a large Filipino population in the Underground, and they usually kept to themselves except to do business. You didn't cross those fuckers twice.

"They give you a heads-up on the training schedule, Gunny?" Hayes asked him, setting his tray down across from the platoon sergeant. I took the seat beside my squad leader and stayed quiet.

"Fuck no." Guerrero punctuated the words by slamming his palm down on the table, shaking my tray and nearly knocking over my water glass. "They told us the requirements and how much time each of them should take, and then they totally flaked on the schedule! Said they had to wait and get back to us after the command and staff meeting! And I asked well, why the hell didn't we wait and have the damn NCO meeting after the command and staff meeting? And nobody had a fucking answer for that!"

I dug into the noodles and tried not to laugh. For a gunnery sergeant, Guerrero was pretty laid back. Of course, my whole experience with gunnies had been them screaming at me.

"We're scheduled for a couple days off next weekend, aren't we?" a woman two seats down from me asked.

She was tall and lithe, with a gentle curve to her jaw that offset her buzzed haircut. I felt a stirring of something I'd managed to keep tamped down since Pris, and I had to warn myself to keep the feelings and everything else in my pants. I had plenty of experience as an outsider, and there was no better way to earn instant hostility than to start macking on some girl you just met in front of her friends. Her name, I noted for future reference, was Sandoval and she was a PFC, the same rank I was, and couldn't have been more than a year or two older.

"Hell, yeah!" the guy next to her crowed, pumping a fist. "We gonna be shipping out in three weeks, I am at least going to spend one last weekend blowing my money on joy-girls and tequila!"

He was my age, maybe, another private first class, but I could already tell we'd grown up in different worlds. He had that kind of face, stretched downward by a perpetual expression of oblivious optimism, the sort that wouldn't have survived two minutes in the Underground. Maybe he was from one of the more developed colony worlds, maybe he was a surface dweller from one of the Earth cities, but I'd have been willing to bet he'd never once been in fear for his life and I wondered what the hell he was doing here.

"You keep talking about joy-girls, Crenshaw," Sandoval scoffed, lips twisted into a wry smile, "but every time we've been out at the rec centers, I've never seen you anywhere but the virtual reality booths."

Crenshaw reddened but shrugged it off.

"Joy-girls are expensive," he whined. "I been trying to save my money. But now we're heading out, there's no reason not to have a blow-out."

"I'm afraid you may have waited a bit too long for the blow-out, Private Crenshaw."

I twisted in my seat, but I recognized Lt. Ackley's voice before I saw her, even though I'd only met her earlier today. She was approaching the table stiffly, awkwardly, and I guessed she didn't make a habit of visiting the platoon in the mess.

"What's the word, ma'am?" Guerrero asked, standing, hands flat on the table as if he thought he might have to dash out of the building on a moment's notice.

"Things have been moved up," she told him. Ackley didn't sit down, just stood beside the table, hands clasped behind her back.

I noticed other officers filtering into the mess hall, each approaching a different platoon.

"How long do we have?" Hayes asked, his normally boisterous and enthusiastic tone now subdued and hesitant.

"The official word's going to come at a company brief tonight at 2000 hours," Ackley said grimly, "but what I'm hearing is forty-eight hours."

"Shit," Crenshaw murmured, sagging in obvious disappointment. "No weekend pass, then."

"Fraid not," the platoon leader confirmed. "Form up in the company area at 1945 hours. Until then…" She smiled wanly. "Enjoy your dinner."

I stared down at the remains of my food as she walked away. It hadn't looked that appetizing to begin with, and was even less so now. Beside me, Hayes tossed his fork down on his plate with a disgusted finality.

"Well, there's some good news, Alvarez," he said to me, grimacing in what I thought was an attempt at a smile. "I guess you don't need to bother to unpack."

────────

I'd been skeptical about this Captain Covington. Everyone seemed to hold him in some sort of awe, to speak of him in hushed tones of respect as if he were a living legend. So, standing at ease in the company area in the humid, barely tolerable Tartarus City night, swatting at mosquitoes, I was curious to finally see the man.

And I was about to get my chance.

First Sergeant Campbell strode out from beneath the eaves of the company office building, tugging on her cover, which I'd learned painfully in Basic was what the Marines called a hat, and coming to attention in front of the gathered troops.

"Company!" she yelled, and Guerrero echoed after it, "Platoon!" along with other platoon sergeants in the formation. "Attention!"

There was the usual business of any company formation where Top got a report from each of the five platoons that all their personnel were present or accounted for, then Campbell stayed at attention and waited as the man walked up from the rear of the formation. I hadn't seen him there before, and I figured he'd circled around the back while the platoons were reporting.

Campbell saluted him with the gusto most Marine NCOs reserved for the presentation of the Commonwealth flag, then turned on her heel and headed to the rear of the formation. Captain Covington turned to face us and suddenly, I believed every word.

There was nothing in particular I could point to, mind. He wasn't a huge man, wasn't massive or muscular or towering. He was lean and rangy, with a fairly normal-looking face, thin and hawkish but not particularly remarkable. But those eyes…

I'd met some dangerous people in my life. I'd come face to face with stone killers who would kill whoever their bosses told them to without question, men and women who tortured people to death as a specialty for the gangs, enforcers who would shoot a bystander without blinking if it meant getting to their target. You could see it in their eyes, the willingness to kill, the familiarity with death, the acceptance of their own impending end and the peace they'd made with it.

Captain Covington had seen death on a scale none of those men and women had ever dreamed of. He'd seen thousands burn, and it had taken away a part of his soul. That was the story his eyes told, and if he was faking it, he was better at it than anyone in the worst streets of Tijuana or the depths of the Underground.

"At ease," he rasped, his voice sounding as if he'd damaged his vocal cords at some point and never had them completely repaired.

I relaxed, hands going behind my back. Most of the time, when officers had addressed us in Basic or AOT, they'd left us at attention or at best, put us at parade rest, I suppose on the theory that enlisted pukes like me would be too tempted to let our attention stray if we could relax too much. But I never even considered it, any more than I would have turned my back on a loaded gun.

"Delta, you've probably heard the news by now," he went on, "that things have been moved up on us. I know you were all counting on the extra time for training, and I'm as disappointed not to have the extra prep as you are. But the war waits for none of us, and the Fleet has its own scheduling issues. And to coin a phrase, no battle plan survives contact with battalion staff."

There was a broken chorus of subdued chuckles, as if some of the troops were half afraid to laugh and half afraid not to.

"Since we'll be doing a shitload of training on the *Iwo Jima* in the virtual reality pods, let's get all the jawing and speechmaking out of the way right now. The Tahni didn't just haul off and hit our Martian shipyards on the spur of the moment. That's not how they operate. The Tahni don't dig a cat-hole without a plan and six months of preparation. They established staging bases between their homeworld and the Solar System a year ahead of time, before they even bombed the human squatter colonies in the Neutral Zone.

"Some of them, the Fleet has hit already to get them out of the way so they don't use them for the next attack. Most of those were on airless moons or asteroids, but our target is different. It's a habitable." He shrugged. "Marginally habitable, but still, the Tahni religion has a thing for habitable worlds. They believe their Spirit Emperor has declared that every living world in the galaxy belongs to them, and anyone who stands in the way, us, for example, are the equivalent of the Antichrist. Which means they won't just set off a nuke and leave it in ashes behind them the way they might a lifeless rock."

He spread his hands. "It also means we don't particularly want to fusion bomb the place from orbit, because we'd like to preserve habitables, too. So, they're all set to defend it, and we want to take it down and neither one of us are keen to blow it to shit. They'll have full deflector screens set up over their base, which makes kinetic bombardment a no-go, so we do this the old-fashioned way.

"We blind their sensors with a proton bombardment, then we send in the dropships and drop right on top of them. It's not going to be neat and clean, boys and girls. We're a sledgehammer, not a scalpel, and they'll know we're coming, so we're going to have to duke it out with them. We root out their armor, take out the air defenses and then the Intel spooks sweep in and get whatever they can before we set charges and collapse the place in on itself. Nothing we can do to make it any easier except train as much as we can, as well as we can, while we can. So, don't spend your off time on board the *Iwo* just plugged into the latest adventure porn, go over the operations order, go over your part of it, your squad leader's part of it, your platoon leader's part of it. Hell, go over *my* part of it." He chuckled, a low, grumbling sound. "I know some of you think I'm immortal, but shit happens."

More muted laughter, this time with a tone of disbelief. He was right, I realized. His people *did* think he was immortal…or, at least, so much better at this than they were that the thought of outliving him seemed absurd.

"All right, follow your superior's instructions and get your shit together because everything is moving double-time from now until we're loaded on the ship. Coffee is your friend, chow will be meal packets eaten while you work, and sleep will be a rumor. If you're going to complain, complain to God, or the Commonwealth Space Fleet, whichever you think is likelier to respond." He took a breath and came to attention. "Company!"

"Platoon!"

"Attention! First Sergeant, post!"

Top returned to the front with the precision of a Vigilante suit striding across a battlefield and exchanged salutes with Covington before turning to face us.

"Platoon sergeants, see me immediately after formation!" she instructed. "Company! Dismissed!"

"You all hang here until I find out what's up," Guerrero cautioned us, heading over to First Sergeant Campbell. I looked around for Lt. Ackley, but she'd already vacated her spot behind us. Probably had her own after-formation meeting to go to.

"What'd you think?" Hayes asked me quietly from beside my shoulder.

"I think I should have made time to get a shower." I still stank from hours breaking down suits with Mutt. Hayes rolled his eyes.

"No, I mean what did you think about the Skipper?"

"Oh." I considered my words. Hayes wanted to be my friend and I didn't want to alienate him. Nothing pisses people off quicker than saying something the wrong way about their heroes. "He's a dangerous motherfucker."

"I've been called worse."

Shit. There was no mistaking that voice and a glance out the corner of my eye told me Hayes was already bracing to attention. I stood straight and still and kept my mouth shut. It was dark out, but I didn't know how I'd missed him circling around behind us.

"Take it easy, Alvarez," Captain Covington said, coming around to the front of me where I could see him. He was taller than he'd seemed out in front of the company. "I'm not the Devil, walking about as a roaring lion, seeking whom I may devour."

"First Peter five, verse eight," I said automatically.

"You read the Bible, Alvarez?" he asked, and I knew I'd surprised him.

"Momma used to read it to us, sir," I told him, "when I was little."

"Not a lot of people around today read anything." He sounded wistful, nostalgic, as if he'd been around when they did. I wondered how old the man really was. He shook his shoulders as if he was shaking off an unwelcome memory. "Welcome to Delta, Alvarez. I usually try to have a meeting with every new recruit eventually, but I'm afraid we won't have the time before we head out."

"It seems like I got here just in time, sir." I laughed softly, despite the man's intimidating presence. It was just too funny not to. "Another couple days, and I'd have missed the boat."

There was something predatory about Covington's return smile.

"Which might have been our loss, Private, but perhaps your gain."

"No, sir," I assured him. "I knew I was going to see combat when I joined up. It's just as well it starts now."

"Like I always say, son," he told me, tossing a wave as he walked away, "you only live once…might as well get it over with."

12

"SEPARATION IN THREE, TWO, ONE...LAUNCHING!"

Acceleration pushed me into the padding of my suit as the words echoed in my earphones and my stomach lurched, wanting to stay on the *Iwo Jima* instead of rocketing free with the dropship. I clenched my teeth against the mouthpiece hanging on a plastic wand from an attachment at the right side of my head, not from the pressure of the launch but mostly from nerves.

I was young still, but I felt old. There were a lot of things I'd experienced that most people never would. I'd had men try to kill me, and I'd tried to kill them back. I'd lived with nothing between me and the street but a stolen blanket. I'd travelled through Transition Space in a starship, twice now, and I'd done a drop in a battlesuit... but I'd never done a Balls-In.

The official term was a Ballistic Insertion, and what it meant in practice was, the troop ship drops out of Transition Space as close to the target planet as hyper-dimensional physics would allow, then starts boosting at about six gravities to build up momentum, not trying for orbit but instead flying as if they meant to plow right into the damned planet. Then, when they'd built up enough velocity, they'd cut their drives and launch the landers.

The math was complicated and even though I'd tried to learn what I could on my own since I hadn't been able to absorb anything in the group homes except how to survive, I'd never been very good at anything more complicated than multiplication and division. But I got the general idea that the landers were traveling fast enough that we could barely survive entry into the atmosphere without burning up, in order to get us drop troops to the ground without giving the enemy too much time to shoot us down.

Oh, and just to make sure we didn't get motion sickness inside our closed suits, someone in Fleet had the brilliant idea of piping the external camera view to our helmet displays. Which meant I could see the *Iwo* disappearing behind us on the half of the screen with the rearward facing view, an armored box with fusion drives at one end and shuttle launch bays at the other, with the living quarters between. We'd spent two long weeks jammed into boxes and oh my God, did I miss that private room I never got to use. Not that I'd spent that much time in my berth, since we'd spent nearly every waking minute running one scenario after another in the virtual reality training pods. Captain Covington's admonition not to spend our off time watching porn had somehow morphed into the officers and NCOs simply making sure we didn't have any free time.

I wouldn't have been that sorry to see the *Iwo Jima* fall away in the rear display if not for the view of what awaited in front of us.

The planet had been designated Bluebonnet by some Fleet planner with a cutesy sense of humor and too much time on their hands. It was a cold place, in the middle of an ice age, and what wasn't brown and dead was buried under a blue-white icecap, with only a thin swathe of green across the equatorial section of the main continent. The seas were blue-green with algae and shallow, and I imagined it wouldn't be a very nice place to live, particularly since the Tahni had constructed their base under the ice at the edge of the northern wall.

The Fleet had gone in first, of course. That was their job and I was more than willing to let them do it. We didn't have too many cruisers left after the debacle the government had tried to rebrand as the Battle for Mars, but two of those we had left were on this mission, That should have been a hint to how important the Commonwealth thought it was, since they could have been back in the Solar System, keeping Earth safe. They hung in high orbit around Bluebonnet, shining silver monoliths connected to the surface at intervals by streaks of coruscating white lightning.

The cruisers alternated fire, cycling their proton cannons as quick as they could, pouring gigajoules of energy into the shields around the base and watching from this distance, I was sure there was no way anything could survive the rain of pure hell. Wishful thinking.

"You're going to look at the proton bombardment," Captain Covington had told us just before we sealed up in the training pods our first full day in T-space, "and you're going to think the fight's over, that the Tahni will be nothing but cinders when we reach the ground. It's been the same since the first time siege cannons laid down fire into a castle in the Middle Ages, but soldiers are good at ducking into any hole they can and digging as deep as they need to, and there's always a fight to be had once the cannons have stopped firing."

His words and Ackley's and Top's and Guerrero's and even Scotty Hayes' bounced around in my head from a dozen briefings starting with the first reading of the operations order right down through the last fragmentary addition, what the military called a "frag-o." There seemed to be a *lot* of frag-o's, like the command structure couldn't wait until the plan was finished before they got it to us, just in case we somehow defied physics and arrived early at the target.

"Their base is underneath an ice shelf," Top had told us, "right at the edge of a wall of the shit a kilometer high, just to make it harder to get to. Their deflector dishes are arrayed around the entrance and, from what we can tell, they've dug out a huge cavern in there, big enough to store all the troops, armor, food, spare parts, assault shuttles, landers, and whatever the hell else they'd need for another attack on the Solar System." She'd been counting off each of the items on a finger and had to go to her other hand at the end. She'd frowned, as if somehow annoyed by the inconvenience.

"Anyway," she'd continued, addressing us all as we'd packed into the cargo bay of the *Iwo*, just after the jump into T-space, "that means that, once the attack commences, we won't have any aerospace support. It's just us down there against whatever troops they got. And we don't know for sure how many that is. They could have left just a token garrison for maintenance, or they could have left enough troops to attack tomorrow. The only way we're gonna find out is by sticking our proverbial dicks into the bear trap."

Well, proverbial in your case, Top. I was kind of worried about my literal dick getting shot off.

"Third platoon," Ackley had told us later, squeezed into our tiny platoon area, "we are the tip of the spear. We're going in first once we touch ground and our job is to tie up any enemy armor until the rest of the company can get inside and support us."

And then, finally, the rest of the wonderful news I hadn't wanted to hear, this time from Hayes.

"First squad," he'd said, with all eight of us barely able to pack into his and Kurita's shared compartment, "we are going to be running point for the platoon."

At least he hadn't seemed any happier about it than I was. Sure, we were going into combat, and yes, I expected to get shot at, but I'd have been more than happy for someone else to soak up the attention and enemy fire before I went in. I'd clenched my teeth and consoled myself that at least I wouldn't be the first trooper in…and then I'd noticed Hayes looking at me.

Oh, shit.

"Kurita, your team is up front, and Cam is going to be out of the gate first."

That I didn't actually blurt out "what the fuck?" was a small miracle, because it had built up in the back of my throat like a tidal wave. I just stared back at Hayes, my jaw hurting from keeping it shut.

"Yeah, I know," he'd admitted, a bit apologetically. "You're just out of training. But you've got the reflexes and I want someone up front who'll shoot first."

"Don't fucking worry about that," I'd assured him. "I may be shooting before I get out of the fucking dropship."

Everyone had laughed like they'd thought I was joking.

"Don't worry," Kurita told me, "I'll be your battle buddy. I'll be next out and I'll stay right behind you."

Which would have made me feel so much better if they weren't in the process of growing his last battle buddy a new spine.

Bluebonnet was growing larger in the front view, the curve of the planet no longer visible, just a solid swathe of white. I didn't start to get really, down-to-my-toes scared until I couldn't see the cruisers anymore, just the actinic lightning-flashes of their massive proton cannons. I fully expected the dropship to fly right into the path of the beam and blow up, and for everything to end for me abruptly and ridiculously, killed by friendly fire before I got the chance to even see the enemy.

But the Fleet knew what it was doing, much as I hated to admit it. The dropship shuddered at the atmospheric turbulence from the incredible energies crackling through it, but the blasts were dozens of kilometers away and we slipped past them unscathed. We followed them down, descending low enough to see the incandescent glow of the deflector shields even before the detail of the ground became clear. Blue and white haloes expanded upward, the shields of the angels my mother had always told me about, guarding the gates of Eden after Adam and Eve were expelled.

They grew with each orbital strike, seeming to draw strength from the power projected against them. That was an illusion, and even a Marine grunt like me knew it. The deflectors were straining, every erg of the fusion reactor under the base being poured into them in a desperate attempt to keep the proton beams away, to diffuse them in sprays of static electricity.

And it was all a ruse, a gigantic, incredibly expensive distraction, designed to keep the enemy's attention focused above, to keep their deflector dishes pointed upward, while the real threat came in from ground level. From us.

I'd thought the turbulence coming through the upper atmosphere had been bad, but it was a gentle breeze compared to the hurricane-force gusts swirling closer to the ground, closer to the massive thermal blooming spewing up from the deflector shields. St. Elmo's fire crackled off the hull of the dropship and the image being projected in the interior display of my suit helmet shook and jerked and tilted wildly and I wondered if I was going to throw up. I'd seen the inside of a suit helmet covered with vomit before, at AOT. They'd forced my whole squad to clean it out when one of our guys had puked during a nap-of-the-earth run in a dropship. We'd all looked at Greene a little differently after that, as if he were something less than a Marine, and I clenched my jaws shut, wanting to avoid that fate.

"Drop in thirty seconds." That was Ackley. There was only room for a single platoon per dropship, and the Skipper and Top would be on the second and fourth bird, respectively. I wasn't even worried about Lt. Ackley anymore, because I honestly didn't believe I'd ever reach the ground. With her announcement, the video feed from the dropship cut out and the view from the suit's exterior cameras showed me the metal struts of the chute and the bare surface of the bulkhead in front of me. Everyone else had a suit in their front view, proof someone else would be going in first. Not me.

"Ten seconds." Whoa. Where had the other twenty seconds gone? I shook myself and concentrated on making sure the suit's systems were all active and I hadn't missed any yellow or red warning lights.

Nothing. All green.

"Five...four...three...two...one! Drop! Drop! Drop!"

All drops were manual. I'd asked in training why they didn't have automated ejection to make sure everyone dropped at just the right time. The explanation by the training NCO had been that there had to be manual controls because there was always the possibility of a suit malfunction, a dropship getting hit at the last minute and going off-course, unforeseen enemy aircraft or a dozen other things that might require a manual control. Me, I'd put it down to the gut-deep stubbornness and resistance to change that seemed to characterize the military. But now, slamming my right heel into the drop control, I thought I knew. They just didn't want anyone falling out of the dropship who didn't have the will to go and fight.

Yeah, I was probably wrong, but it made me feel better.

I dropped into the storm, battered and tossed like a rag doll, and hit the jets immediately. We'd been going fast, right at the limit of the suit's braking abilities, and I'd need every second of boost to stick the landing. My spine compressed with the sudden, violent deceleration and I silently thanked whoever had come up with the idea of the mouthpiece for the helmet, because I would have cracked my teeth without it.

The ground was rushing up to meet me and I reminded myself of the fact that the gravity here was nearly Earth-normal, so there'd be no fudge factor when I hit. I tried to get a sense of my surroundings, but everything was a kaleidoscope of crackling static electricity and rutted, boulder-strewn, glacier-shaped dirt filled with meltwater puddles and cracking ice and it was all I could do not to close my eyes and pray to a God I hadn't trusted in ten years.

The jets roared with all their might, sending clouds of steam billowing up around me and blinding most of my sensors for a moment. I was sure I was about to break my neck but then I touched down light as a feather.

I cut the jets automatically, on instinct built from hundreds of hours of training in the simulators and dozens more in real suits. I was alive, and on the ground, and the enemy was ahead of me.

I ran to meet them.

13

THE SCENE WOULD HAVE BEEN BEAUTIFUL IF I'D HAD THE TIME TO appreciate it. The ice wall was incredible, like something I'd seen in virtual reality fantasy games, and I half-expected a dragon to fly off the ledge, but instead only a stream of meltwater coursed over it. The deflectors were shedding heat in every direction and, according to the Vigilante's exterior thermometer, the temperature out there was heading quickly into the twenties, probably the warmest this planet had seen in a thousand years.

The deflector dishes were a tempting target, but they weren't *my* target, or Third Platoon's. We were here to smoke out the High Guard, the Tahni version of our drop troops, sort of. They were in battlesuits similar to ours, but they didn't generally do Ballistic Insertions, preferring to land their troopers the more conventional way. I knew more about their suits than I did the aliens inside, but I guess they don't waste enemy psychology courses on junior enlisted.

And they'd be spun up, waiting for us. The base was dug into the wall a kilometer ahead, an artificial cave probably carved with a high-powered construction laser, or maybe enlarged from a network of natural caverns. The opening was huge, two hundred meters across and fifty high, and even a kilometer away, the shuttles stored under the overhang were already visible, their vertical stabilizers nearly scraping against the ceiling. Rows of them, at least a dozen, and behind them stacks of cylindrical cargo crates in racks stacked just as high. This place was serious and I had a bad feeling they hadn't just left it with a crew of janitors to watch over things.

The suit was sinking half a meter into the mud with each step and I knew I was going painfully slow, but the concrete pad the Tahni had poured into a ramp and landing pad at the end of the overhang was only a few dozen meters ahead, tantalizing. The anti-aircraft turrets at the edge of the pad were scanning back and forth in aggravated futility, searching for targets they couldn't see past the interference of the angry, swollen deflector shields, their missiles and lasers couched in hungry restlessness.

I took the last step out of the mud up onto the pad, boosting myself with just a microsecond burst of jump-jets, and there they were. They'd come out sooner than we'd hoped, but that was how this sort of shit went down. The enemy had their own plans. I'd seen them in simulators, but they were uglier in person, subtly different than our Vigilantes, less overtly humanoid and articulated and more akin to a bipedal robot, with cylinders for arms, ending in the gaping emitters for electron beamers. Their legs were unnaturally short, the knee joints covered with a jutting vambrace of armor sticking up from the lower leg, the base broad and octagonal.

Eight of them were flying out of the entrance to the base, jetting on shimmering columns of superheated air and firing as they came, their particle accelerators ripping up huge divots from the concrete pad in explosions of violently liberated water vapor. One of the beams came so close it blanked out my sensors for nearly a second and damage sensors flashed red, though I couldn't tell what was damaged and the suit kept running.

"Contact front!" I called instinctively. "A squad of High Guard!"

Slow is smooth, my gunnery instructor had said, *and smooth is fast.*

I targeted the closest of them and squeezed the control for the missile launch tube running up and down the right side of my suit's reactor shroud. Cold gas popped the missile from the tube, just far enough for the exhaust of the solid-rocket motor not to hit my own armor, and then it was streaking out across the hundreds of meters between us in the space of a second, nearly going hypersonic before it hit the enemy trooper.

I tried not to focus on the hit, knowing how little time I had and how much attention I'd just drawn to myself, but I caught a crimson flash on the targeting screen at the corner of my display, the indication of a thermal bloom that was supposed to mean complete destruction. I had my own missiles inbound and all sorts of ECM systems and a counter-battery rocket launcher on the left side of my back to protect me from them, but I was too close and I knew it.

My plasma gun was pointed right along the path of the incoming missiles and I had just enough time to pull the trigger. The packet of super-ionized gas held together and propelled by an electromagnetic field, shot out at thousands of meters per second and pushed a wall of superheated air ahead of it. The actual plasma blast hit one of the missiles, almost miraculously given how fast it was traveling, but the wall of heat did the real work, the turbulence kicking the other four incoming missiles aside just enough. They were guided and could have corrected, but we were way too close and by the time they curved back around, I'd be in the middle of the enemy.

Blasts rocked the concrete behind me, shaking me all the way up through the BiPhase Carbide of the suit, but I was too busy to worry about what the warheads had hit instead of me. I wasn't thinking, not at that speed. The interface made it easy to not think, to just act and react, like in a fight on the street. Back then, I'd been used to being outnumbered, and the key was always to get in close and keep them from ganging up on me, make sure they couldn't take a swing at me without hitting one of their own.

I hit the jets for just a half-second, a boot in the ass carrying me forward a bit faster than the suit's legs could have, and I was suddenly in the midst of the Tahni troopers, too close for missiles. Electron beams ripped apart the air itself only meters from me, their aim lagging just a fraction of a second behind my movements. They scattered at my approach, out of my line of fire, ignoring the other suits coming in behind me, and I hoped the rest of the squad would take advantage of it. I had my own problems.

Most of the Tahni had scattered, but one of them had decided to stick with me, swinging around his twin electron beamers, firing burst after burst as I circled just ahead of him. It was a him, that much I knew for sure; the Tahni didn't let their females fight, for some reason. I couldn't remember if it was biological or religious or whatever, but I suppose it was a relief. Momma had always told me never to hit a girl.

I hit the jets, twisting sideways to angle the exhaust away from the direction I'd been running and arcing over the top of the Tahni High Guard trooper. He tried to swing his weapons around to follow me, but the angle was wrong and his suit's shoulders didn't have the range of motion.

And he was dead already. I fired my plasma gun downward through the top of his helmet and then I was down again, not daring to stay on the air too long for fear of becoming too tempting of a target. The feet of my Vigilante thumped solidly into the concrete and I kicked it into a run for the opening of the base entrance. Behind me, the Tahni battlesuit stayed upright, immobile, reminding me of one of the statues at the entrance to the Marine base on Inferno, smoke pouring from the gaping, jagged rent in its helmet where the plasma had burned through the honeycomb boron-ceramic armor there.

I charged forward, knowing the second wave of High Guard was coming out before I actually saw them on the sensors. This first squad had been their ready force, the ones sitting in the hangar bay at the front, waiting for us, or whoever was coming. What came next would be everyone who was left, because there'd be no point to holding back. They couldn't fight with the suits much deeper inside, not effectively. Something three meters tall and two wide needed space to operate, and if they were going to throw their lives away on an Alamo, they might as well try to take as many of us with them as they could. At least that was what I would have done.

There were more this time, but they were strung out, coming in ones and twos and I wasn't going to give them the time to get organized. I launched one missile after another, emptying the magazine, locking each on a target in fire-and-forget mode. The fourth and last blasted out of the tube before the first had reached its target, and enemy missiles were streaking outward, but none of them were heading for me. I was a single suit and I had the intuition I was far ahead of the rest of the platoon.

Something whispered a doubt in the back of my mind, inserting the idea that the rest of them were gone, that they'd abandoned me and I was the only one left fighting by myself. It was insane, irrational. If nothing else, the Tahni High Guard were shooting at something behind me. But no one was giving me orders, and they *should* have been. Had Ackley frozen up? But Hayes would have been telling me what to do...

I didn't have time to think about it and I shoved it aside, concentrating on the enemy in front of me. Eight...nine...eleven... an even dozen, their sensor icons popping up all across the opening to the storage hangar. The green spikes of my missiles were already intersecting the red avatars of the enemy suits and blooming white on the thermal sensors, so I ignored those targets and fired my plasma gun at the closest of the rest.

The blast took him in the right hip and the High Guard suit stumbled between one step and another. And then the fuckers noticed me. Electron beams sought me out and I hit the jets for microbursts, taking giant steps in one direction and then another, trying to stay ahead of their aim. I was at the edge of the entrance now, past the main body, but more suits were coming out and I knew they had to have a full platoon stationed here.

It was too many, and the sheer inertia of being out front that had carried me this far was beginning to fade into the certainty of impending death. Retreating would leave me out in the open, far enough away for them to target me with missiles. I had to move forward, but I had to get out of the fucking way and get to some cover, and the only cover handy was the shuttles.

The helmet display combined infrared with optical and thermal, and combined it all into a computer-generated image as bright as broad daylight even on the cloudiest midnight, but somehow I could tell when the light changed from the coruscating lightning of the deflectors to the harsh overhead lamps and I knew I was inside without looking up. The jump-jets carried me centimeters over the scaly grey skin of the Tahni shuttles and I dropped down between two of the craft.

They looked a lot like ours, because physics trumped cultural differences if you wanted something to fly in an atmosphere, but the landing gear was more like furniture casters, solid spheres nearly as tall as my suit, and they were very effective cover. Electron beams lashed into the nose gear I had selected for cover and the fuselage shuddered at the expulsion of sublimated metal.

I needed to move, but fear nailed my feet to the ground, fear I hadn't let myself indulge in when I was standing out in the open and freezing up would have killed me. The shuttles were nice and big and protective, and I felt safe squeezed between them, unwilling to give up the shelter. I might have stayed there for the duration of the fight if one of the High Guard suits hadn't gotten a wild hair up his ass and followed me.

He almost got me. I was distracted by the beamer firing at the other side of the nose gear, my sensors blinded by the mass of the shuttle and the flare of heat coming off the disintegrating metal, and the only thing that saved me was my audio analyzers picking up the scream of the suit's jets. I rocked backwards, the only way the suit could look up, and saw a massive, backlit titan dropping down from over the fuselage of the shuttle, his twin particle accelerators swinging toward me.

There was nowhere to run. The other side of the shuttle was still under fire, going up would take me straight into the bore of his guns and I'd never be able to back up in time. The realization I was about to die took half a second, and before it had time to bounce from one side of my brain to the other, a missile moving at hypersonic speeds slammed into the Tahni battlesuit's torso and swallowed it in flames. The concussion was enough to knock me onto my back, leaving me rolling back and forth helplessly like an overturned turtle for several seconds.

I had just managed to get a leg beneath me when a Vigilante suit soared over the top of the shuttle and landed only meters from the fiercely burning wreckage of the Tahni trooper. The suit was faceless and silent and I realized for the first time what the insistent damage report blinking red at the corner of my display was telling me. My comm antenna had been damaged and I wasn't getting either radio or laser line-of-sight transmissions.

I tapped the side of my helmet with one of the articulated claws on my suit's left hand, the universal symbol for a dead radio and the other suit's helmet rose up on powered gimbals as the chest plastron cracked open a hair. Inside was Gunny Guerrero. I let out a breath

I hadn't realized I was holding and hit the control to crack open my own suit.

I'd been sweating since the drop started, but it all evaporated away with the blast of cold, dry air flooding in from the open hangar bay. Other things came in with the cold, the smell of burning plastic and sublimated metal and the sounds of pinging metal as it cooled and contracted.

"Are you all right, Alvarez?" he asked, his voice a low growl, the look on his face dark and utterly unlike the easygoing manner he'd shown before.

I nodded, then paused and took a sip of water from the nipple coming over my shoulder from a bladder stored behind my helmet.

"My radio's skragged, Gunny," I rasped. "And I'm Winchester on missiles, but I'm okay. Did we get them all?"

"We got them all," he confirmed. "You killed five of them all by yourself."

Damn. I didn't know how I should feel about that, but in the moment, I felt pretty good. I'd taken out nearly a squad of enemy suits.

"Second platoon is heading deeper in," he went on. "They're escorting Intelligence analysts and Fleet Security deeper into the base." He gestured upward. "The bombardment's stopped and we took out the air defense weapons, so our drop-ships are landing now. Go ahead and hook up with your squad. I'll let Hayes know your comms are down."

His tone, the set of his eyes, the tight clench of his jaw all told me something was wrong.

"What is it, Gunny?" I asked him. "Did we take casualties?"

"We did, Alvarez. Your team leader, Lance Corporal Kurita."

Oh, shit. No wonder I didn't see him behind me.

"Is he...?" I trailed off, not wanting to say it.

"He took two Tahni missiles pretty much the minute the enemy opened up on us." Gunny's mouth worked, as if the words were hard to get out. "He was killed instantly."

I hadn't known him that well. There just hadn't been time, not the way we'd trained during the flight from Inferno. He'd been quiet and competent, that was all I could remember. I felt like anything I said would sound stupid and insincere, so I said nothing. Guerrero seemed disappointed somehow.

"Get going," he told me, and his helmet began to descend, covering his troubled expression with the dead glare of the suit. "This fight's done."

And I'd lived through it. The thought struck me even harder than Kurita's death. I'd lived through it.

I wondered why it felt like a letdown.

14

HOT WATER WASHED AWAY SOAP AND SWEAT AND DIRT, BUT COULDN'T quite wash away the odd depression I'd been feeling since the end of the battle. I had the shower to myself, since my suit was with the techs being repaired and I wouldn't be able to perform PMCS on it until they were done. Everyone else had gone immediately to maintenance checks right after we'd made the jump to T-space and got gravity back. Well, everyone except the leadership, which had AARs to go over.

I wondered if they'd consider it a success. One KIA for the Marines. I'd heard Fleet Security had lost two, and a couple of Intel guys wounded from a squad of holdout dismounts in the base control room, deep underground, but that wasn't on us. We'd landed a company against a platoon and wiped them out, but that's what a company *should* do to a platoon, right?

I turned the water off and grabbed my towel, wanting to get dried off quick and dressed while I had the place to myself. I wasn't exactly shy, not anymore, but communal showers made me feel very vulnerable. Shorts, a T-shirt, and flip-flops went on quick, maybe even before I was completely dry and a sense of relief settled over me along with the shirt. I ran the towel over my hair one last time, blocking my ears. That's why I didn't hear the footsteps.

"Look who it is, boys. It's the fucking hero."

Not this asshole. Not now.

If anything, Lance Corporal Wade Cunningham was balder and uglier after two weeks in space than he had been back on Inferno, and the two other men with him weren't any better. They could have started a club for ugly, short white guys with buzzed haircuts and bad attitudes. I didn't know their names and didn't recognize their faces, but I assumed they were from his platoon.

"You got what you wanted now, hero?" Cunningham demanded, his voice echoing back from the shower stalls. "Got to kill some Tahni and show everyone what a big man you are?"

I didn't say anything, just kept my eyes on the three of them, edging toward the wall to keep them from flanking me. The asshole might just be talking now, but bullies always talked themselves *into* something. It was humid in the shower room, even with the fans running, and sweat trickled down my back, undoing all the good work the soap had just done.

"Tommy Kurita was a friend of mine, hero," Cunningham growled low in his throat, and the other two began to spread out.

Oh, this is just all kinds of not good.

"Kurita got hit by missiles from enemy armor." Maybe I should have kept my mouth shut, but it was possible he didn't know what had actually happened, and at the moment, I doubted anything I said could make things worse. "It could have happened to any of us."

"He was your battle buddy, though." Cunningham took a step toward me and I stepped back the same distance, eyes locked on his. "You were the one who was supposed to watch his back."

"I was riding point."

Useless. He wasn't going to listen to reason. I'd said it out of instinct, but I was already scanning his stance for weaknesses. He wasn't an experienced fighter; I could tell that much already. Most big loudmouths aren't. They're good at pounding someone smaller and weaker than them, but they never have to learn how to really fight. I hadn't had that luxury.

"You let Tommy get killed," he accused, sticking his finger in my face.

I wasn't sure about the other two. They were along for the ride, but they hadn't been prepared for a fight and the set of their feet told me they would try to push me around a little, maybe take a swing if the opportunity came open. I would have to bet they wouldn't jump in and gang-tackle me, which was a hell of a thing to bet on.

I edged toward the exit as I moved away from the finger, my towel still hanging from my hand, wet and limp. I just needed a step and I could make a break for the hatchway and have a good chance of making it. But credit to the asshole, he knew that, too. He lunged at me and I whipped the wet towel into his face and made a quick cut to my right, making for the exit.

One of the Ugly Bald Club twins blocked my way, arms in the act of extending to push me back. I'd anticipated that and rotated to my left, slapping my right palm against the outside of his left elbow, not hard enough to dislocate it, just enough to shock him, send him stumbling to the side. That was something I had learned the hard way. I could hurt people bad if I wanted to, but I didn't usually want to. Hurting people bad had a way of boomeranging on you, if the guy had friends or if he could find you again. It was important to just do enough damage to get away, maybe enough to make them hurt but not to hurt them.

He was out of the way and the hatchway was open behind him. I sprinted for it, but Cunningham had better reflexes than I'd hoped and he slammed into me from behind, driving me shoulder-first into the bulkhead beside the door. A whoosh of breath went out of me and pain jolted through my upper back.

Fuck it. He wants to get rough; I can get rough.

I swung my elbow back into something firm but yielding and Cunningham squealed like a rat in a trap, lurching backwards, hands covering his nose. Blood was streaming down his face onto his chest and the sight of it seemed to scare him…but it just made the other two angry. I knew it would happen, but the only other choice was to let Cunningham pound me a little, and he'd pissed me off too much for that.

The one I'd blocked aside gathered himself visibly, cursing at me loudly and incoherently before he rushed in. The third guy hadn't gotten involved yet and didn't seem in any itching hurry to make a move now. He just stood off to the side, anger in his expression but uncertainty in his eyes, mouth half-open as if he hadn't expected a real fight. I took a chance and focused on the one coming at me.

He wasn't any better at this kind of thing than Cunningham and I thought neither one of them had bothered to pay attention in unarmed combat training. Most people in my class hadn't. We were armor troopers, who cared about being able to wrestle with a Tahni? But I'd spent most of my life getting beat on by people bigger than me, and the Tahni were much bigger than these asshats.

I stepped back perpendicular to his rush and my foot came out of the flip-flops. I slipped backwards and still managed to keep my balance, but I'd lost a second, and a lost second was enough to give someone not quite as good as me but a couple centimeters taller and five kilos heavier just a bit of an edge. He swung wildly and his knuckles grazed my cheek hard enough for a dull ache to spring up behind my eye. I stepped into his guard and smacked my shin into the side of his thigh, bare beneath his shower shorts, the sound as loud as a gunshot.

"Fuck!" he declared and went down as if I'd chopped his leg off below his hip.

There was a big nerve there, the common peroneal. I'd learned about it long before Marine Corps unarmed combat class, way back when I'd been in the very last group home, the one I'd wound up running away from. Getting kicked right where the nerve ran up the side of the thigh was like having a hot knife stabbed into the muscle and twisted. I'd felt it before, more than once, and I was happy to be on the delivery end this time.

Bald Dude Number One was down and not likely to get up anytime soon, clutching at his leg and moaning, but Cunningham had gotten over his shock from the broken nose, at least enough to be angry about it. He tackled me low, around the hips. I didn't know if he did it on purpose or just lucked out, but it was just the right place for a takedown, and I'd been too distracted to try any sort of defense. My back smacked against the cold, wet tile of the shower compartment hard enough to make me see stars, and that was where Cunningham's luck ran out.

If he'd known what he was doing, that might have been it for me. He could have controlled my hips with his own, mounted me and started pummeling me with one punch after another and there wouldn't have been a damned thing I could do about it. But his face was red with blood and flushed with rage, and he just hauled back for a haymaker, not paying any attention to my legs. I hooked one of them up around his arm and tossed him backwards off me.

He didn't know how to fall, either. His head bounced off the ground when he hit and he came up cursing and groaning. I jumped up to my feet, ready to kick the shit out of him.

"What the hell?" Scotty Hayes' exclamation sliced through the fog over my thoughts and I stepped back, glancing over my shoulder at him but still keeping one eye on my opponents. "What the fuck is going on here?"

Hayes was dressed for duty, in utility fatigues, not for the showers, and I wondered if he'd just been passing by or if someone had heard us fighting and called him.

"Your boy here got my friend Tommy killed!" Cunningham's voice was comically distorted by the broken nose, and blood was flowing from it again after his fall. "I'm not going to let him get away with it!"

"Yeah, Wade," Hayes said, cocking an eye at the Lance Corporal's battered face, "you look like you're really teaching him a lesson. Want me to save some time and call a cas-evac unit to the showers for you, or can you make it to sick bay on your own?"

"If your fucking L-T had any balls, she'd have him up on charges!" Cunningham sputtered, blood from his nose flecking off his lip and mixing with his spittle.

"Shut up and go cool off, Wade," Hayes said, his normally relaxed expression going hard. "Or I'll finish what Alvarez started. And then I'll mention to Top that you've been swinging your dick around again and sit back and watch while she cuts it off." He looked at me and jerked a thumb toward the hatchway. "Come on, let's get out of here."

I grabbed my towel and my errant flip-flop and followed him out into the passageway. I thought he'd say something to me then, but he led me out of the crew quarters and past the ship's mess. I became suddenly self-conscious of the smacking of my flip-flops on the deck and the soaked-in water stains on my shirt. Finally, though, Hayes pushed open a hatch and poked his head through, checking carefully before waving me in behind him.

It was a storage closet for the mess, packed high with barrels of soy paste and powdered blue-green algae, the staples the military ran on, and there was a space barely wide enough to stand between the rows. Hayes pulled the hatch shut and rounded on me, a look on his face I couldn't quite read.

"Cam, I need you to tell me what happened out there."

"In the shower?" I asked, frowning. "Cunningham was angry and I was an easy target."

"No," Hayes clarified. "I mean down on Bluebonnet. What happened with Tommy Kurita?"

"I have no fucking idea," I admitted. "I was up front, first one off the bus, you know that. My comms were damaged by a beamer and I didn't even know Tommy was down until the battle was almost over. Gunny said he got hit by enemy missiles but I haven't even seen the footage."

"I have," Hayes said, his voice grim. There was something in his eyes I couldn't quite read in the dimly lit storage room, something I thought might have been envy tinged with bitterness. "I've never seen anything like it. You fired off your plasma gun just as the High Guard suits launched their missiles and you made them shoot wide." He snorted disbelief. "Somehow. And they missed you...but they hit Tommy."

"Shit." I squeezed my eyes shut. I suddenly felt drained and my hands were starting to shake, and I didn't know if it was the post-adrenaline-dump letdown that always happens after a fight. I leaned against one of the storage shelves for support. "I didn't know, man. I was just running on auto-pilot. I thought Tommy was supposed to watch my back, but I felt like I was out there alone."

"You weren't alone, though, Cam. None of us are. We have our battle buddy, and our fire team and our squad and our platoon, and we're supposed to watch out for each other."

I opened my eyes again, squinting at him, wondering if he was for real.

"I was up front," I said. I wasn't trying to sound sullen and resentful, but I could hear the tone in my voice, as if it was someone else was speaking through me. "I didn't have any comms and I didn't have time to look back."

Hayes looked as if he wanted to argue with me, to tell me off, and his jaw clenched visibly. There was a battle going on for self-control, playing across his features.

"You're probably right." I could tell that wasn't what he'd been about to say, but he had better self-control than I did. Maybe that's why he was a sergeant. "The fact is, none of us had seen real combat before and we all made some mistakes. That's probably what the Skipper and the platoon leaders are talking about right now. And I'm not telling you that you did anything different than any other PFC would have done. But Alvarez, you are *not* just any PFC. You have to know that."

"Yeah, I'm all sorts of weird," I acknowledged, laughing sharply.

"You are at home in that suit," Hayes told me, not letting it go. "You destroyed six enemy suits, Alvarez. *Six.* By yourself. How many people you think could have done that?"

"A lot?" I guessed. "The Tahni troopers don't seem that impressive."

"Don't you read the scansheet reports?" he wondered, spreading his hands like he was pleading with me. "Intelligence puts them out every week, the parts that aren't classified."

"I haven't had time." I really hadn't even heard of them but I didn't want to admit it to him. He looked skeptical, but he didn't call me on it.

"There have only been four skirmishes between Fleet Marine Drop Troops and Tahni High Guard since the Battle for Mars. Not really full-scale battles, just shit like this. Every single time, we've got our asses kicked." He shrugged. "Oh, you know, that's not how the reports read. The military likes to put smiley faces on everything. But if you read the numbers, we've taken four casualties for every High Guard battlesuit we've taken down."

My eyes widened and dull pain blossomed in my cheek where Cunningham had slugged me.

"Seriously?"

"And that's with veteran armored troops," he insisted, "Marines who've been training in Vigilantes for years. Most of us...." He waved a hand inclusively. "...have been in the Drop Troops for less than a year, except a few like Top and the Skipper. You've got a feel for the suit, something we can't really teach. We all saw it in the simulator, but lots of people are simulator heroes."

"I don't understand," I said. "You want me to kill Tahni, I'll do it all day for you." *Until they kill me.* "Put me at point every operation if you want, I don't care."

"Cunningham was right about one thing," Hayes said. "Something he said back on Inferno. You can kill Tahni all day and they'll keep coming. We don't just need people who can kill Tahni, we need leaders. And sometimes leaders have to leave themselves vulnerable to watch out for the other guy."

"I ain't a leader, Scotty. I don't want to be responsible for anyone but myself."

"You already are," he told me. "We all are, no matter what rank we wear. And now, I'm going to make it official."

"What do you mean?" I demanded, not liking the tone of his voice or the thin smile that passed across his face.

"Your fire team needs a team leader and you're it."

"I'm a fucking PFC!" I objected, straightening, pushing away from the storage shelf. "I can't be a team leader."

"Not anymore. I already talked to Gunny Guerrero and Lt. Ackley and she passed it up to Captain Covington. As of 1200 hours tomorrow, you are Lance Corporal Cameron Alvarez, leader of First squad, Alpha team." He winced just slightly. "You'll be getting a new recruit to fill out the team to replace Kurita."

My stomach was dropping out of Transition Space and back into zero gravity far behind us and my mouth was dry.

"You just got through saying how I wasn't watching out for the other Marines in my squad and now you're putting me in charge of a fire team?"

Hayes clapped me on the shoulder on the way to yank open the storage room hatch, as if the matter had been settled and there was nothing left to talk about.

"The best way to make someone learn how to do something," he told me, sounding awfully self-satisfied, "is to hold them accountable for it."

15

"Taylor, watch your interval," I snapped. "If you like Rodriguez that much, get her 'link address and call her after the war."

"Sorry," the quiet man said, his Vigilante backing off another ten meters in the Ranger-file line formation we were running through the city center.

I didn't really blame him for getting distracted. MOUT City was creepy, especially at night. Leave it to the military to find the most extravagant way to spend taxpayer money. Never mind that we had realistic virtual reality pods that could simulate any terrain, the Marines had built themselves a complete dummy city on Inferno a hundred kilometers outside the capital of Tartarus. I mean, right down to the business names on the marquee and the parking stickers on the windscreens of the cargo trucks parked at the curb. And furniture inside, for all I knew. Military Operations in Urban Terrain, an acronym older than the Commonwealth, or so I'd been told.

Someone had told me there were construction bots on call after every training run to rebuild any of the buildings that got damaged, which kind of made me want to smash into a couple of them just for shits and giggles, but I restrained myself. I was in a leadership position and, even if I wasn't too happy about it, I wasn't going to fuck it up on purpose.

I'd *thought* about it. Maybe, I'd figured, if I messed up bad enough, they might be forced to demote me back to PFC and put someone else in charge of the fire team. I still wasn't sure why I'd decided against it. It wasn't because I was afraid that they'd kick me out and I'd wind up in hibernation. I already knew they were too desperate to let any warm bodies get away and I'd also come to accept I was *very* good in a Vigilante, which they also wouldn't have wanted to lose.

But I couldn't do it to Scotty Hayes. He'd taken a chance on me and he really seemed to think I was worth it. I don't know why I felt like I owed him for that, particularly when I didn't want the job, but he was trying to be my friend, and it was more than anyone had done for me in the last ten years.

"First squad," Hayes said over the squad net, his voice calm and steady, "we got a frag-o based on a report from the drones. There's a company of Tahni infantry dug in at the constabulary. That's our target. We believe they're holding civilian hostages in the sub-basement cells, so we can't just bombard the building or call in an air strike. We have to draw them out and give Force Recon a chance to get inside and free the civilians."

I made sure my mic was turned off before I sighed in exasperation. The odds we'd ever get any useful intel from drones in real combat were somewhere between slim and none. If we could get drones past the Tahni ECM, we could have put missiles and guns on them and not have to send live humans in battlesuits and assault shuttles and fighters, but they had to have some excuse for a last-minute fragmentary order just to make everything more interesting for us.

"Alpha," Hayes went on, "at Phase Line Delta, you're going to break north and approach from the front, get their attention but don't get too decisively engaged. Bravo, I want you to hold back and pound any of the shock-troops we draw out. The rest of the platoon is heading around the rear of the building to the cargo entrance to bust through and take out the barricaded opposition and open things up for Force Recon. Be careful. We don't want to shoot through the building and frag our own guys. Everyone got that?"

"Roger, Scotty," I said.

After months of armor school pounding it into me to use proper communications procedure with callsigns and codewords and all that shit, it felt strange to just call everyone by their names, but it kind of made sense. We were using laser line-of-sight comms when we were close to each other and quantum frequency-hopping for the microwave signals, and if the Tahni could intercept that, we were pretty much screwed anyway. All the comms discipline was a holdover from wars between humans, when someone could check social media and intelligence reports full of stolen personnel records and put names together with units and use the data to strike at families and blackmail individuals. It was all pretty much a waste of time when we were fighting aliens. But the military ran on tradition, so we still used it when we were talking to anyone above company level.

"Betancourt," I said to the newbie, the guy who'd replaced me after I'd replaced Kurita, a recent AOT grad who was even greener than I was, "you're up at point." Might as well see whether the guy could cut it now, before we headed back out for another mission. Which I'd been told was coming up soon, and I could believe that as much as I wanted to.

"Go light on the jets," I cautioned the others. "We want to attract attention, but they might just waste an anti-aircraft missile on us if we give them the chance."

I was trying to sound authoritative, which meant I was just repeating what Lt. Ackley had told us when she'd read the Op order three hours ago. It sounded lame inside my head, but Hayes had assured me it was a good fallback when I didn't have any idea of what to say.

"It's what they'll expect," he'd told me. "Lt. Ackley is just repeating what Captain Covington said to her. It's how things work."

"Boost for a few seconds to stay out of their targeting screens if you have to," I continued, "but I don't want anyone over twenty meters up and keep a clock running in your head. Three seconds up, three down. Got it?"

"Yes, Corporal Alvarez," Betancourt said obediently, as if I wasn't the same age as him with a grand total of about two months' more experience.

The other two murmured agreement but I could tell they weren't too crazy about this arrangement. Everyone had liked Kurita and a lot of people still thought I'd let him get killed...including maybe Rodriguez and Taylor.

This is a horrible idea. Scotty, what the fuck were you thinking?

I didn't know MOUT City very well yet. They didn't use it for Armor school, so this was only my second pass through the place since we'd returned to Inferno after the raid on Bluebonnet. But I remembered from the briefing that Phase Line Delta was just past the pretend industrial district of the fake city, and even if my helmet display hadn't shown the divider as a red highlight across the map, it would have been obvious. The factories and warehouses and fabrication centers were big, squared-off, and stereotypical, while the government sector was decorated with buildfoam replicas of Greek columns and facades of red brick.

"Hook a left, Betancourt," I told him, just in case he'd lost track of which way north was.

I watched his movement with a critical eye, unimpressed. His Vigilante ambled with an awkward, broad-legged gait, like a toddler just learning to walk. They wouldn't have passed him through Armor school if he had that much trouble handling a suit, so I figured he was just nervous. I switched my comms to a private channel with him.

"Betancourt, relax a little. Stop overthinking it and just pretend you're walking to formation. The interface will do the work."

"Okay, sorry."

I wished the guy didn't sound so deferential. It was making me start to feel even more self-conscious. But his stride became more natural, which I guessed meant he was listening to me. The left turn on the imaginatively-labelled Third Street took us back behind a line of apartment buildings, the sort I would have associated with upwardly-mobile Surface Dwellers back in Trans-Angeles but were considered standard working-class housing in the colonies.

If I live through this war, they'll settle me on one of the colonies.

The thought scared the shit out of me and I didn't really know why. Maybe because it would be so totally different from the life I'd known. So was being in the Marines, of course, but that had a sort of temporary feel to it. Everyone talked like it would be temporary; wars didn't last forever, or at least they never had before. Then I'd be dumped on a world I'd never even visited, stuck with a bunch of strangers who'd never been to Earth. And doing what? Working on an algae farm or a construction company?

Cheer up. You'll never live through this, anyway.

The pavement vibrated like the skin of a drum under the feet of my suit and I wondered how anyone with ears couldn't know we were coming.

"Turn right in two hundred meters," I instructed Betancourt. "Up at that next street."

Hayes had told me some people actually got lost in the streets here, but I couldn't understand how. The place was laid out straight and square and open, and anyone who couldn't find their way around it would have curled up and died if they'd ever tried to get anywhere in the favelas of the Trans-Angeles Underground. I glanced at the map, noting the layout of the constabulary building. We'd be coming out on the far north end of the building, and although Hayes hadn't specified, I assumed he wanted us to pass from north to south on our sweep to draw fire.

"They're gonna open up on you right after the turn," I predicted, including the whole team on the transmission. "I want each of you to launch a missile at the enemy positions, airburst at ten meters up, and follow up with a plasma blast as each of you cuts south, to the right. Remember Bravo is going to be shooting across south to north, so stay out of their firing arcs."

"Yeah," Rodriguez said, her tone caustic, "I'll try real hard to remember not to get shot by our own guys."

I bit down on my response. Betancourt was at the turn and I didn't need to be arguing with her in the middle of a firefight. I was thirty meters behind Rodriguez and she was the same distance from Betancourt, so I was still looking at the side of an apartment building when the backblast from his missile flared, lighting up the shadows along the sidewalks. I called up the image from his helmet camera in a corner of my display and saw the front of the constabulary, squared off and fortified like a castle, with massive battlements hanging over the ground floor.

Anti-aircraft missile launchers squatted on wheeled carriages at the north end of the building behind concrete barricades, and the Tahni troops manned a pair of heavy KE-gun turrets in their shadow. Not actual Tahni and not even human Op-For with Tahni gear. This was a live-fire exercise, which meant remotely-controlled target drones. Bipedal and humanoid-shaped, they were molded to look as close to Tahni troops as possible. Real Tahni shock-troops wore powered exoskeletons to carry heavy armor and more of a weapons load, but the drones' armor was plastic, their servomotors cheap, recycled pot metal. And their weapons were just laser designators, thankfully. I wasn't sure if one of their heavy KE guns could penetrate a Vigilante's armor and I didn't want to find out the hard way.

Rodriguez's missile was in the air before Betancourt's struck and the two merged into a fireball a hundred meters across, and that was with warheads running on reduced charges. I turned the corner just as the fireball was rising into a miniature mushroom cloud, and I could already tell the plan had worked. Target drones were pouring out of the front entrance to the building, pushing heavy weapons turrets ahead of them, each with a splinter shield at the front of its three-wheeled dolly.

I put a missile into the middle of them and Taylor shot in the same place without being told, which made a nice change. I couldn't detect anything past the inferno of the explosions, but I fired my plasma gun into the general area of the front entrance anyway. The plasma gun was such a cool weapon and I didn't want to pass up a chance to live-fire it. The wall ten meters on either side of the constabulary entrance was crumbling, chunks of it vaporizing from the heat of multiple plasma burns, and the colonnaded portico covering the entrance had already collapsed, consumed by roiling flames.

But enough of the drone troops had emerged to start returning fire, and my tactical computer registered their targeting lasers as tantalum darts shot out at thousands of meters per second by their electromagnetic coils. A warning flashed yellow at the corner of my vision, telling me I'd been hit twice in the right thigh, hard enough to crack the BiPhase Carbide armor there. A scrawl cautioned me that the armor might no longer be airtight and I shouldn't take it into a vacuum. I uttered a silent but solemn vow to stay away from space until after the battle.

Betancourt hooked a right at the end of the street, where it ended in a T-intersection with the constabulary, and disappeared from view behind a parking garage. Part of my mind still boggled at the thought that there was any place where personal vehicles were so ubiquitous the city had to put up an entire building just to hold them.

"Third platoon!" Ackley's voice sounded urgent in my headphones. "We have an incoming High Guard squad, approaching airborne from the north at two kilometers! First squad, they're yours."

"Roger, L-T," Hayes acknowledged. "First, break off your attack and intercept. Alpha, take point."

I was at the corner of the parking garage, with Betancourt and Rodriguez already around the corner and Taylor behind me. I was the team leader, but I was closest...

Fuck it.

"Alpha, follow me."

I figured if Hayes had a problem with me running point, he'd say something. He didn't and I took his silence as tacit approval and thundered down the street, trying to catch the incoming squad on the suit's sensors. It would be more drones, but these were bigger and more elaborate, not truly armored and carrying no weapons, propelled by battery-powered turbofans, but they had actual missiles with dummy tagging warheads, and targeting lasers that my suit would register as electron beamers.

There they were, glowing bright on thermal, their signatures pumped up artificially by their onboard systems. There were always eight to a squad, same as us, though that was more a coincidence than anything else. Our Force Recon squads were larger, but everything in the Tahni society was organized around the number eight. Lt. Ackley had told us that in one of her little teaching sessions on the return flight from Bluebonnet. She'd said the Intelligence types figured the number eight had some religious significance, but she wasn't sure she bought it because that's what the analysts always said when they didn't know the reason for something.

They were only a kilometer out. I hit the jets and rose to meet them, knowing the others would follow my example. Urgency burned inside my chest brighter than the fires consuming the front of the constabulary, not a bit dimmer in intensity than what I'd felt on Bluebonnet, and I wondered if that meant I got too keyed up during training or not keyed up enough in real combat. The pressure coming from below with the boost of the jets was countered for a half-second by the ejection of a missile from my launch tube, then a second, each locking onto a different enemy thermal signature.

"Incoming!" Hayes warned, but I'd seen it already.

The spread of missiles was unnaturally uniform, more even and precisely timed than a Tahni squad could have managed in combat, synchronized by the drone controllers, each of the weapons launched aimed at a different target. My countermeasures activated automatically, their computer systems faster than my human reaction times, and three small, unguided rockets loaded with warheads full of electrostatically-charged chaff launched from the left side of my reactor shroud within a half a second.

I paid no mind to their missiles. Either they would hit or they wouldn't, and there wasn't anything I could do to stop them. I was more concerned with the fate of the ones I'd launched, and I cursed as their indicators winked out on the targeting screen, showing me that they'd been neutralized by the enemy's ECM. Whether they would have been in a real fight, I wasn't sure, but they didn't make things too easy in training.

One of our missiles hit. I wasn't sure whose, but it knocked a High Guard simulator drone out of the air in an expanding globe of white gas and smoke. One down.

I was thirty meters up and moving forward at top speed, plenty close enough for guns, and the targeting reticle was glowing green in my helmet display, inviting me to take the shot. But something distracted me, a flashing on one of the IFF transponders, enough to draw my eyes to the name. Betancourt had taken a hit from one of the enemy missiles and...

"I'm going down!" he squawked, his suit jets automatically setting him down safely.

In a real fight, he'd have been dead, or so badly injured they'd have to haul him up to orbit and throw him into a nanite vat for a month. But the training program wasn't nearly so accommodating, making sure to list him as wounded, his armor as simply disabled, which meant we'd have to take care of him.

"Taylor," I snapped, annoyed with the newbie and with the need to deal with his ineptitude, "break off and watch out for Betancourt. Rodriguez, stay with me."

The delay had taken seconds, but it was seconds too many. The drones opened up on us with their targeting lasers and an alarm screeched shrill warnings of damage to my left leg, of penetration and radiation burns and emergency medical systems activating. I twisted and danced in mid-air to try to avoid the incoming simulated electron beamer fire and my Vigilante behaved sluggishly, limited by the computer's stubborn assertion that I was being medicated and my reflexes would have been slowed down had this been for real.

I was barely fifty meters from the nearest of the drones now and curving around behind their formation, near enough to notice how fake the drone battlesuits looked close-up. And to remember how *light* they were. Light enough that I wouldn't actually have to *hit* them to make them go down. I was spinning and twisting still, trying to avoid their questing targeting lasers, way too unstable to get a fix on them with my plasma gun. But I fired anyway, simply pointing it in the general direction of the cluster of drone suits.

The coherent packet of ionized gas tore apart the night, lightning and thunder and terrible heat accompanying its discharge. The wave of hot air was even more effective in the thick atmosphere of Inferno than it had been on Bluebonnet, and two of the drone suits tumbled out of control, their turbofans completely inadequate to the task of correcting from the bloom of thermal energy and the turbulence it had created.

We were only thirty meters off the ground and that wasn't nearly enough time for them to pull out of the stall. The impact of the lightweight plastic and ceramic drones was disappointing, a clatter against the pavement and a shower of broken pieces pinwheeling down the street.

I was about to yell at Rodriguez to do something, but she was smarter than I'd thought. She blasted a shot of her own between two of the drones descending only two meters apart and both of them went out of control, smacking into each other before slamming into the ground. The last four were nearly a kilometer farther out, the second wedge in the enemy formation, and there was no way we were going to be able to take them down in time. They had the distance to launch missiles and the only reason they hadn't yet was that Rodriguez and I had been mixed in with their own forces.

"Down!" I said to Rodriguez, cutting my jets and descending just ahead of two targeting lasers.

A flight of missiles came from over our right shoulders, so fast I didn't even register seeing them on the sensor display, just acting on the instinctive knowledge they were there. The weapons weren't aimed at us, though. The remaining four drone suits disappeared in a wave of pressure and a wash of white light, a storm passing overhead as Rodriguez and I touched down.

"Index, index, index."

The deep, gravelly voice wasn't Lt. Ackley's, it was unmistakably Captain Covington's. I hadn't even known he was monitoring the training, though I probably should have. And he didn't sound happy. Which probably meant none of the rest of us would be, either.

"Did I screw up, Corporal?" Betancourt asked me. His Vigilante was standing by itself, somehow managing to look forlorn despite its featureless face.

"Not any more than the rest of us," I assured him, waiting for the call. And right on cue, there it was.

"Alvarez," Hayes said. "Report to the Range Control Center. Gunny wants to talk to you."

"Of course he does," I murmured, off-mic. Then I went ahead and keyed it, just for Hayes. "I told you this was a bad idea."

"Yeah," he sighed. "And maybe you were right."

16

"GODDAMMIT, ALVAREZ, WHAT THE HELL AM I GONNA DO WITH YOU?"

"I don't know, Gunnery Sergeant," I clipped off, still standing at ease in front of the man. "Bust me back to PFC and make me a grunt again?"

Gunny Guerrero eyed me balefully from under hooded lids, leaning back in the chair. The Range Control Center was spartanly decorated, the thick, concrete walls bare and cracked by age and baking heat. The monitors and displays were ancient, decades old and dating back to the last war, and the office furniture could have been just as old, judging by the cracked plastic and squeaking casters of the chairs. Every flaw of the room was magnified in the stark glare of lights bright enough for a medical operating theater.

"Don't think we haven't considered it," he answered darkly. He sighed and sat up straighter, the chair groaning in protest. "But Scotty was right before and he's still right now, though you'd better not let him know I said that." He rubbed at his temples as if he had a fierce headache. "At least tell me you know what you did wrong."

"I probably shouldn't have taken point with the enemy suits," I admitted.

"There ain't no fucking 'probably' about it!" the platoon sergeant bellowed and I shut my mouth. "You're a team leader. And yeah, sometimes you gotta lead from the front, but that's in a combat situation when there ain't no choice! Not in training when the fucking Skipper is watching!"

He blew out a breath as if he was trying hard to rein in his temper. I seemed to have that effect on people.

"Did the Skipper say anything about it?" I knew I shouldn't ask, but I kind of wanted to know. He was someone who I genuinely believed was a badass.

Guerrero glared at me, working his jaw like he wanted to spit.

"He laughed. When you knocked the drones down like the paper airplanes they are, he fucking laughed, he called the exercise and he left without saying another fucking word."

I opened my mouth, closed it again, thinking better of what I'd been about to say, given the Gunny's mood.

"Okay, okay," he said, raising his hands in a quelling motion, as if he was trying to calm me down instead of himself. "Besides running point, besides managing to get your newbie PFC killed, you also totally fucked with the integrity of the live-fire exercise. *Everyone* knows the drone suits are a joke, but you can't treat them like one or they won't let us do live-fires anymore and we'll be stuck in the damn simulators all the time!"

My face fell. I hadn't thought of that.

"Still," Guerrero admitted, scowling as if the words had to be yanked from his mouth like an infected tooth, "it usually takes someone five or six runs through the range before they realize the weakness the drones have. So, I guess there's that. Look, kid, here's the bottom line. We all know what you can do. You ain't the best I've ever seen in a Vigilante, but you're up there with 'em. So, stop showing off what you can do and start thinking about how to get your team to act like a team."

I grimaced.

"Does this mean you're not busting me back down?"

"No, dammit!" he yelled, hopping to his feet and getting in my face. "You don't get off that easy! Now get back to your team and get your shit ready to head back to the base. Tomorrow is an off day, so the quicker you finish PMCS, the faster you can all get out of my fucking hair!"

"Yes, Gunny."

I about-faced and got out of there the back way, not wanting to parade past Lt. Ackley who I'd seen talking to Captain Covington out front. Hayes was waiting for me by the back door, arms crossed, occasionally swatting at a mosquito drawn in by the light.

"So?" he asked, shaking his head.

"I didn't get fired," I told him, not trying to conceal my disappointment. "But I think Taylor and Rodriguez hate me."

"Well, I'm giving you the chance to get 'em to like you. Tomorrow at 1900, we're all meeting up at Myths and Legends."

"At where?" I shook my head.

"It's a semi-respectable enlisted type bar in downtown Tartarus. We're all going, the whole squad, and maybe people from other squads and other platoons, but I guaran-damn-tee you one person is going to be there, and it's you." He tapped a finger into my chest. "That's a fucking order, and I don't give that many of 'em, so you'd better obey this one."

"I'm not old enough to drink," I protested, weakly. That was one of the many laws I'd been breaking since I was twelve.

Hayes laughed, turning away.

"If you're old enough to be here, Alvarez," he threw over his shoulder, "then you're old enough to drink."

———

The rest of the squad left for the bar at 1800 hours and I should have gone with them, but I was still feeling resentful enough to want to sulk a bit longer, so I caught a later bus and got lost. It shouldn't have been possible, not with 'links and GPS mapping satellites, but this place wasn't on the maps and the name wasn't in the planetary database. After a half-hour wandering around downtown, sweating through my only set of civilian clothes, I was ninety-nine percent convinced Hayes had been fucking with me.

Finally, I broke down and messaged him.

you should have come with us, he replied. myths and legends is a nickname.

A coordinate pin popped up on the screen with the heading "War Heroes" and an address. On the bright side, I was only three blocks away from it. And it was starting to rain.

I was only slightly soaked by the time I made it to the place, and without the coordinate pin, I never would have found it. It was a hole in the wall wedged between a fabricator repair shop and a virtual reality gaming center, without as much as a sign or a window, and only a crack of light coming from beneath a door labelled "WH" told me I was in the right place.

A wave of noise hit me when I pulled the door open, and I had to look twice to confirm the bar wasn't bigger on the inside than it was on the outside. It was, upon closer examination, a creative use of mirrors. The mirrors also made it tougher to find the squad. The place was packed and seemed doubly so with the reflections behind the bar and along the walls.

The furniture, the bar, the flooring all looked like real wood, which I had never seen before outside of gossip reports on Corporate Council execs and rich celebrities. It was darkly-tinted and polished to a high gloss, reflecting the light from a dozen wall lamps, more than enough to keep the place glowing brightly with the strategic use of the mirrored surfaces. There was an actual human behind the bar rather than a drink dispenser with a chip reader, and he was as dark and lined with age as the polished oak of the tables. He smiled and laughed as he poured liquor out of what must have been actual glass bottles for the patrons.

And the patrons, unless I totally misread the haircuts, were all military. Not exactly hard to guess here on Inferno, but they all had that rough-around-the-edges look of enlisted and junior NCOs, laughing a bit too loud and drinking a bit too hard to be officers or senior gunnies. They were, I judged, all Marines, but not all of them were Drop Troopers. For some reason, that bothered me.

There were the techs, of course, the ones who worked on our armor, the shuttles, and the vehicles, and we all appreciated the work they did and some of them were great to hang with, but it seemed to be the universal feeling among Drop Troopers that the techs weren't exactly "real" Marines. The officers and the little pop-up ads from the Defense Department could lecture us to the contrary until the stars burned out, but they weren't going to change anyone's mind.

You could spot the techs and maintenance crews and the armorers. They didn't have 'face jacks and they generally let their hair grow longer than we did. Most of the Drop Troopers, men and women both, kept the sides of their head shaved to keep the jacks clear. Some of us wore the rest in a sort of barely-regulation mohawk, but I just kept it all buzzed short because anything else just seemed too pretentious to me. There were other differences, though. Armored Drop-Troopers had a certain walk, something I didn't notice in myself but I saw in others. It was kind of a hesitant sway to their gait, something Drop-Troopers picked up from so much time in the suits. I imagined I'd wind up with it eventually, if I lived long enough.

The wrench-and-bucket types being here was okay, I supposed, but they even let Force Recon into this bar, and no one liked Force Recon. They all had their noses in the air, like they were the elite or something, the best of the best. They wore their hair long, right at the edge of regulation, like they were rubbing it in our faces that they didn't have jacks, didn't *need* jacks.

Okay, if I was being honest, I hadn't ever actually *talked* to a Force Recon puke, but we all just *knew* that was how they felt about us.

"Cam!" Hayes' voice carried across buzz of conversation and music that had been ten years out of date back home and not in a genre I liked, something twangy and full of banjos. "Over here!"

I edged my way through the crowd, nearly colliding with a waitress carrying a transparent cooler full of some sort of dark ale and brushing up against a barrel-chested, shaven-headed guy who scowled at me from a face that must have been scarred long before he'd enlisted in the Marines or else the military docs would have fixed it. I tried not to stare as I moved past him to the high-top table where our squad was sitting.

"What the hell took you so long?" Hayes wondered, winking at me. "Maybe next time instead of being all sulky and bitchy, you'll ride with the rest of us."

"Yeah, yeah," I acknowledged, raising a hand as I settled down onto a stool. "I didn't know the place had its own nickname. Sorry, but most of us haven't had as much time to sham as you."

"That's what being an E-5 is all about, Corporal Alvarez," he said, offering me a glass of beer. "Optimizing your opportunities to sham."

I took the beer and downed half of it in one chug, trying not to make a face. I didn't particularly care for the stuff, but I'd learned to fake it. An underage street criminal living in the tunnels drank whatever they could get their hands on.

"You always got to go it alone, don't you, Alvarez?" Rodriguez asked, staring down at her drink, not seeming too happy to have me here.

Taylor said nothing, taking a sip of his drink, his eyes boring into me. Betancourt glanced back and forth between Rodriguez and me, wide-eyed and looking shocked at the hostility of her question.

"What?" I asked, trying to play it off as a joke. "Did you miss me that much? It's only been a couple hours."

"I wouldn't say I missed you." She smirked. "But maybe Betancourt did."

"I'm your team leader, not your momma, Rodriguez," I said, giving in to the annoyance gnawing at my last nerve. "You want me to hold your hand out there?"

"I want you to have my back," she snapped back at me, finally meeting my eyes. "That's your job, right?"

"And I'll do my job." I downed the last of the beer in my glass, then thumped it onto the table. Glass on wood made a very satisfying sound, one I'd never heard before. "Part of doing my job is finding out how good each of you is. It's training, right?"

I was talking out of my ass, but it was something I'd learned to sound confident doing.

"It was my fault," Betancourt lamented. He was such a puppy dog, his big, dark eyes constantly seeming on the verge of tears. "The damn drones hit me with a missile."

"They could have hit any one of us," Taylor told the younger man, shrugging.

"Not me!" The voice took me by surprise. I'd heard it before, but I hadn't expected to see Vicky Sandoval out tonight. She was sitting at the next table over with the rest of her squad, but leaning over into our conversation. "Those paper airplanes have never taken me down once. There's a trick to it."

"Oh, really, Corporal Sandoval?" Hayes asked, leaning forward on his elbows. He hadn't intervened when Rodriguez was going off on me, but now that Sandoval was involved, he was suddenly a conversationalist. "Please share this secret with your fellow Marines."

"Hell, no!" Sandoval said, looking at him askance. "If I tell you, everyone would know and they'd fix the glitch! Then how would I keep my record spotless?"

"Oh, fuck me," Taylor muttered, staring at something across the room. "I didn't realize Fourth would be here tonight."

I followed his eyes toward the sound of a half-drunk laugh and the shaven, egg-shaped head that had produced it. I'm not sure how he managed it, but Wade Cunningham looked even more self-important and obnoxious in civvies than he did in uniform. One of the dumbasses he'd had with him in the shower room during our fight was with him again tonight, pretending to laugh at whatever lame joke Cunningham had made while they waited at the bar for their drinks.

"Cunningham is enough to make me give up on men," Sandoval muttered.

"I thought you did that years ago, Vicky," Rodriguez said, with more salt than I'd have expected. Sandoval grinned a challenge at her.

"You trying to convert me, Nancy?"

I watched, fascinated, almost forgetting Cunningham…until his voice cut across the bar in a foghorn bellow.

"Watch where you're going, you fucking ground-pounding prick!"

Cunningham was squared off with a broad-chested, square-headed dwarf of a man with the haircut of a Force Recon Marine. The guy might have been from a heavier gravity world and looked as if he could bend lead pipes with his hand, and I wouldn't have fucked with him on a bet, but Cunningham wasn't that smart.

"You made me spill my drink!" Cunningham insisted, holding up a shot glass as if it was evidence in a murder trial. "You're gonna fucking buy me another one!"

"Fuck off, jack-head," the broad, short man rumbled, not backing off a centimeter from the man. "Buy your own damn drink and get out of my face."

I didn't hear what was said next because Cunningham's ugly, bald friend was yelling and three other Force Recon types jumped up and started shouting back. The words lost coherence in a wall of sound.

Hayes and Rodriguez pushed off their stools, wary expressions on their face, their drinks forgotten, and so did Sandoval and a few others from her squad.

"Is there gonna be a fight?" I asked, having to yell it in Hayes' ear to be heard.

"It's Cunningham," he answered. "What do *you* think?"

Shit.

The first punch was lost behind a wave of bobbing heads as Recon and Drop-Troopers began to move in on the confrontation, but the next flurry came from Cunningham and I was impressed he'd lasted past one shot from the big guy. His friend had grabbed the troll from the back and was trying to put him in a sleeper hold but other Recon guys started wading in, as if two on one was unfair when the one probably outweighed the two of them.

And that was it, it was on. Hayes was rushing in, followed by the rest of the squad and I was somewhere in the middle, caught up in the tide of people and adrenaline and sound. Instincts acquired over years trying to avoid other people's fights sought out the nearest exit and safe routes through the crowd and I had to force myself to go against my better judgment and do something stupid, which was the opposite of the way things usually went.

I was lost almost immediately, swept into a press of bodies and drowned in the competing odors of body spray and alcohol, and I couldn't tell who was who except by haircuts and the occasional flash of a face I recognized. Fists were swinging and I put my arms up to guard my head and threw my shoulder into anyone who came too close. I wasn't trying to hurt anybody, mostly because I wasn't sure who they were, but I did my best to push people away from each other and avoid getting hit myself.

That worked for about thirty seconds. A skinny, long-armed Recon Marine zeroed in on me with eyes glazed over in an alcohol haze and shot a pair of surprisingly controlled jabs at my head. One of them clipped my left ear in a flare of pain and a sudden, tinny ringing and I decided I'd showed enough restraint. I ducked inside his guard and buried a fist in his gut. The breath gushed out of him in a waft of stale beer and I managed to smack a forearm across the side of his neck and knock him aside before he puked all over me.

His fall knocked three other people backwards and opened up a space right in front of me. The thought hit me of using the bit of open floor to get the hell out of the bar, but someone beat me to it. Wade fucking Cunningham was blasting past the fight he'd started and right out the front door before the hole closed up behind him and two Recon Marines lunged for Nancy Rodriguez right in front of me.

Random blows were raining down around me, but I kept my hands up and stepped into a kick to the side of a leg and one of the Marines trying to grab Rodriguez squawked and tumbled into the other. I thought I saw her glance at me in recognition before the fight drifted in and forced us apart like a flood. Something hit me hard behind the right ear and I went down, stars filling my vision, and I caught a boot or three to the legs and ribs that I barely felt through the pain in my head.

I was in a bad spot and I had the stray, nearly coherent thought of how ridiculous it would be to go off to war only to get my head caved in during a stupid-ass bar fight. When I heard the siren, I wasn't sure if it was real or just part of the symptoms of a major concussion, but the feet pounding around me began to part and the shouts of the combatants faded under the amplified assault of loud and very authoritative voices.

"Everyone against the fucking wall unless you want to be fucking stunned!"

It was the MPs. I was going to live. I closed my eyes and blacked out.

17

"You awake?" Someone yelled in my ear, shoving at my shoulder.

Light speared into my eyes and I threw an arm over my face. The floor was cold beneath me, smooth and hard like tile and I rolled off my back, pushing myself up to my knees. I put a hand to my head, thinking it should hurt, but finding to my surprise, that it didn't.

I opened my eyes and looked up into the not-unpleasant face of Vicky Sandoval. She looked very different dressed in civvies, and since I didn't feel as if I was nursing a serious concussion anymore, I took a moment to appreciate the view.

"I think I am," I answered her question. "Though I've had dreams that started this way."

She rolled her eyes and walked away from me, accompanied by a guffawing laugh from behind us.

"If you have dreams about sex in a jail cell," she said, "then maybe the crack on the head did you some good."

Jail cell?

My eyes focused past her face on the bare, concrete walls, the white, tile floor, and a wall of transparent plastic a couple centimeters thick, peppered with tiny holes to let in sound and fresh air. Beyond the polymer barrier was a corridor marked with warnings in big, glowing letters.

military police holding facility: no weapons permitted.

do not attempt to communicate with detainees unless accompanied by authorized personnel.

24-hour video and audio monitoring. anything you say or do can and will be used against you in a military court.

"Oh, yeah," I said, remembering the last thing I'd heard before I passed out. "The MP's. I was hoping I'd hallucinated that part."

"You were pretty out of it when they hauled you off the floor," Rodriguez agreed. She was huddled on the floor, arms wrapped around her calves, head resting on her knees. She had a bruise on her right cheek. "They must have let the medics take care of your head. They only dropped you in the cell a couple minutes ago."

"How long was I out?" I asked, coming to my feet, suddenly spooked at the thought of missing morning formation. "How long have we been in here?"

"Just a couple hours," Taylor said. He and Betancourt were leaning against the opposite wall. The newbie looked pale and panicking, as if he was convinced this was the end of his military career. "They just dumped us in here, haven't even offered us a pee break yet."

"And I got to go," Rodriguez complained.

I looked around, noting who wasn't there.

"Did they get Scotty?" I looked over to Sandoval. "What about your squad? Did anyone get out before the cops came?"

"God only knows," the Lance Corporal from Fourth squad replied, hands turned upward. "I was too busy trying not to get hit with a sonic stunner to see."

"Scotty got out," Rodriguez said, sounding confident, or at least sounding like she was trying to be confident. "I'm pretty sure I saw him head out the back door."

"What happens now?" Betancourt wondered. "Are we going to be court-martialed?"

Sandoval barked a laugh.

"If they court-martialed every Marine who got into a bar fight, the courts would run sessions 24-7-365. Plus, most of the damned platoon got picked up. They can't afford to lose that many Marines."

"Article 15, max," Taylor added. "Non-judicial punishment. Maybe your next promotion gets delayed a cycle, if you were up for one. No big deal."

I sagged against the wall, feeling both relief and exhaustion. Whatever the medics had done to my head had taken care of the concussion, but left me drained. Since my next promotion would require NCO school and another six months in grade, and I never wanted to be a squad leader, I didn't care how many article-15's I racked up. As long as I didn't get stuck in a cell for too long.

"Hey Sandoval," I said, the sudden looseness combining with the effects of the concussion or maybe whatever they'd used to treat it to make the words tumble out of my mouth unguarded, "do you like to be called Vicky?"

She regarded me with a cautious glare, the way I might have stared down a dog in the street if I wasn't sure if it would bite.

"My friends call me Vicky," she said, a bit cool and detached in her tone. "My *close* friends."

I shrugged.

"So, when do I find out if I'm close enough?"

I was not a particularly smooth talker. Where I came from, flashing a wad of paper trade-notes or, better yet, a few tabs of Kick worked better than words. I had the sense things weren't like that here. I kept eye contact, though, because I'd been advised it was the thing to do to let a girl know you were interested. Her eyes were hazel but they might as well have been ice blue.

"Alvarez," she said with deliberate care, "I don't know you let anyone close enough to call them by their first name."

Motion caught the corner of my vision and I turned just in time to see two MP guards stomping toward the cell. They both wore bulky, padded armor designed more to protect against physical strikes and blades than guns or energy weapons, and holstered in a mount on the shoulder of each of them was a sonic stunner, the size of a giant handgun but with a bell-shaped nozzle at the end. Their helmets were of the same material and design, with visors they could pull down to protect their faces at need. The visors were up now, and the cop in the lead had one of those eternally-old faces I'd seen on veteran cops back in the Underground, the kind where you couldn't tell if they were bored, angry, or tired.

The woman behind him seemed younger and less jaded and cynical, and I could sense the disapproval in her glare, as if we had all let her down personally with our actions. And behind her was Scotty Hayes, a smirk on his face.

"I am so disappointed in you guys," he said, hands on his hips as the MPs unlocked the cell door. "I can't believe you'd get involved in a bar fight! It's so damned irresponsible!"

"Tell me you're here to get us out, Scotty," Sandoval begged, "and not just to gloat."

"Yeah, you're sprung," he confirmed, motioning toward the door. "Hurry up before the MP Watch Commander changes her mind."

I stumbled and had to catch myself on the door frame and the female MP gave me a dirty look.

"Don't let me catch any of you at that bar again," she warned, stepping close enough to shove me back a centimeter with the shoulder plastron of her armor.

"You won't catch me again," I promised. She seemed satisfied at first, then frowned as the comment sank in, but I was already past her and heading for the exit.

It had stopped raining, anyway, though it was still as humid as the inside of a shower stall when we stepped outside. I looked both ways down the street and realized I had never been to this section of Tartarus before.

"Where the hell are we?" I asked, slowing from the urgent stride I'd been using to exit the police station as quickly as possible.

There were no other military headquarters offices around the MP garrison as far as I could see. It was out among beat-up and worn-down warehouses and covered storage lots filled with cargo trucks and a few armored personnel carriers that probably hadn't seen use in decades.

"Utility and storage district," Hayes informed me, "or, as we like to call it, Bartertown. About as far from the brass as possible, because none of the admirals and generals want to see how the sausage is made."

"Which bus do we catch to get out of here?"

Hayes laughed and Sandoval's low chuckle was a counterpoint.

"The busses don't run out here."

"Then how did you get here?" I asked him.

"The same way we're getting back. Shank's Mare. The Shoeleather Express."

I frowned at him, uncomprehending, and at least this time, I wasn't the only one.

"Did you get hit in the head too, Scotty?" Taylor wondered.

Hayes laughed again, gesturing down the road.

"We walk," he elaborated. "And before any of you miserable pukes complains, kindly remember that I had to walk both ways and then get on my knees to beg Gunny Schmidt to release you all into my custody."

"I'm sure she enjoyed that," Sandoval said, rolling her eyes before following him down the street.

"I'd like to know where the hell Cunningham is," I said, rubbing at the side of my head, not feeling any pain from the blow I'd taken but still feeling the resentment. "He's the one who started all this. He should have stayed and got busted like the rest of us."

"Like the rest of us except Scotty," Sandoval amended, still digging at the squad leader.

"There's very little justice in life," Hayes lamented, though whether he was speaking of Cunningham's escape or his own, I wasn't sure. "If there were, I wouldn't have to spend one of my rare nights off bailing your asses out of jail instead of getting drunk and getting laid."

"At least you can be relatively sure you'd have got drunk," Rodriguez said, joining in on the fun.

"We aren't going to get in any trouble, then?" Betancourt piped up, apparently still unable to grasp the situation.

"Not *officially*," Hayes corrected him. "I'm not going to say anything, but that was most of the platoon in there, and *someone* is going to blab. And if I know Top, she'll have her own way of making sure her own version of justice gets done. You can fucking count on it."

———

Why the hell did Hayes always have to be right?

"All right, motherfuckers," First Sergeant Campbell barked at our platoon, lined up outside the company area in the rain, all by ourselves on what was supposed to be an off day. "Since you seem to think having time off is an excuse to go bust up a bar and get yourselves picked up by the MPs, I guess *this* platoon won't be getting any more liberty!"

I didn't dare look to the side, not while we were at attention, not in the mood Top was in this very early morning. But I wanted to. I wanted to glare back at Fourth squad and give Wade Cunningham the death stare for getting us all into this.

"Now, normally," Top went on, "I would have you painting fucking rocks and sweeping dirt for the rest of the day, but there's a complication." She snarled and rain ran down from her cover into her face. "And I don't mean the fucking weather. You would have heard this at the same time as the rest of the company, but *they* didn't act like a bunch of idjits, so they'll hear it when they get back from liberty. But you're getting the news first. We're shipping out again in three days."

I forgot about Cunningham, my mouth falling open just a bit. I tasted rain and shut it again.

"That's right. So, I'm going to do you sorry sad-sacks a favor and let you have some *extra* training in the virtual reality pods. All damn day long until dinner. You can eat packaged meals for lunch, so Gunny Guerrero, you'd better go grab some now!"

It wasn't as bad as it could have been. I'd frankly been expecting the whole painting rocks in the rain thing, so a day jacked into the pods was a step up. Gunny Guerrero wasn't happy because we'd made him look bad, but on the good side, Lt. Ackley was otherwise occupied with the Skipper and the other platoon leaders, so at least we wouldn't have to watch her be embarrassed for us.

It was a typical setup, a night drop onto a colony world occupied by the enemy. There were a lot of those, lately, but this one was fairly barren, a single city surrounded by smaller settlements, each of them surrounded by smaller farms. The Tahni had taken the city and fortified it, putting their base at the outskirts next to the fusion reactor and re-channeling its power into their deflector screens and the ground defense laser, then surrounding it with air defense missile turrets.

The Op order came in over the pod's helmet simulator display, simple and direct: drop twenty klicks away from the city, work inward on foot by platoons and infiltrate by squads to the deflector dishes and take them down with a missile strike to the power feed lines while the Fleet pounded from orbit with proton cannons. Just one shot would be enough. Under stress from the orbital bombardment, the feedback from a single lost circuit would collapse the whole thing catastrophically.

"First squad," Gunny Guerrero ordered, still sounding disgruntled at having to run all this himself when he hadn't even had the chance to go out and get drunk, "since you're so talented at deflecting charges for disorderly conduct, you're going to hit the deflectors. Since fourth has so many people who prefer to sit back and watch other Marines do their fighting for them, they'll take up an overwatch position and cover your approach. Second and third, you'll hit the anti-aircraft batteries to open things up for Fleet air support."

Ouch. I couldn't see Cunningham, but I knew that had to hurt, even for a blockhead like him.

"Alpha team," Hayes said, almost stepping on the echo of Guerrero's words, "you're up front. Alvarez, that means your *team* is up front, not you personally. Got it?"

"Roger that," I said, muting my mic for the sigh that followed. It seemed like such a waste. I knew what I could do, knew I could count on myself.

"We drop in thirty seconds," Guerrero announced.

The pod shook slightly, simulating the motion of the aerospacecraft we were notionally flying in. Having flown in a drop-ship, I could finally testify that this was one of the things the simulators didn't do a great job at. Actually riding a drop-ship into combat was much more of a gut-wrenching, head-spinning roller-coaster ride than anything I'd experienced in the simulator pod, but I guess there was a limit to how much physical motion they could work into a line of virtual reality booths only two meters tall and a meter wide. The feed from the exterior cameras helped with the illusion, though.

The horizon was flat and distant and I couldn't see any sign of the city itself, but the bombardment was a coruscating arrow of lightning running down into the half-sphere of a deflector shield, an arrow on a giant map telling us which way to go. It was visible from hundreds of kilometers away, interrupted only by the curvature of the planet, but we'd inserted from orbit just a few dozen kilometers away. Or that was the idea, anyway. The truth was, they didn't want to waste a lot of time on simulated suborbital flight when it wasn't pertinent to our training.

I snorted. It might have been the first time I'd ever experienced the government worried about wasting something.

"Drop!"

Again, something the simulation couldn't quite duplicate, the reason we still had to do live drops and live-fire drills. Here in the pod, it was a gentle shaking, a roar of jets, with none of the visceral, hind-brain panic of free-fall or the almost-pain when the jets first kicked in from the spinal compression.

Rodriguez was on point, with Taylor to her right rear and me and then Betancourt on her left and I was tracking them in the IFF and trying to look through their sensor signals to the world beyond. There was no sign of enemy forces yet and I was sure there wouldn't be, because the simulators seemed to think the Tahni would just "hunker in the bunker" under orbital fire. It had happened once or twice and it was automatically the way it would be. I wasn't so sure of that, but it made beating the simulators easier when I didn't have to worry about armored patrols during a drop.

We came down in seconds, pushing the edge of survivable braking thrust, both because it was necessary to avoid detection and, admittedly, because it was a simulation and our bodies wouldn't have to pay the price for the hard hit.

"Nineteen klicks to Objective Delta Sierra One, First squad," Hayes told us.

He was nestled in-between Alpha and Bravo teams, and Fourth squad was just now deploying from the drop-ship behind us. I'd read the op order and if we stuck by it, Gunny would come out after Fourth, at the center of the formation. Watching him wasn't part of my responsibilities though, thank God. I shuddered at the thought of being Lt. Ackley, just a few months out of the Academy, only a few years older than me and responsible for the whole platoon and all our equipment. Too damned many lives and too much money. All the responsibility and none of the authority. I'd almost rather have been in Captain Covington's spot. Yeah, he had the whole company on his shoulders, but he also had real power to go with it.

I snorted again. I didn't even feel ready to lead a fucking fire team and I was day-dreaming about being a company commander.

No way in hell.

The run in seemed short and I wondered if the simulator was fucking with the clocks. Hayes had told me it did that sometimes, when we were going to be crossing long distances with no opposition scheduled. The suit had a clock counting up from the drop, or sometimes a countdown to a deadline, and the simulator program would speed up the clock and the passage of landscape beneath you while recording the same speed you were traveling at, just to get you to where the action was.

I'd asked Hayes if he thought it was a feature or a bug, but he'd just shrugged it off as one of the eccentricities of the Drop Troopers. Me, I was starting to think, with the benefit of one whole combat drop under my belt, that anything taking away from realistic training was probably a mistake.

No one asked my opinion in whatever objective time it took us to get into position near the Tahni base. We were walking up a draw through a seasonal riverbed, the water only centimeters deep under our feet. It was nighttime and I wondered why we bothered attacking at night. We had thermal, sonic, and infrared, and the computers to mesh them all together in a coherent simulation of day, and so did the Tahni. Their sensors wouldn't be any more compromised by the proton bombardment at night than in the day, the ECM would be no less effective, and I had to think the reason was psychological. Maybe in the sense that their physiology would be more sluggish at night or maybe in the sense that we felt more hidden by the darkness.

There was no darkness at the base. It was lit up like the Central Square at Christmas time by the incoming proton blasts, one artificial lightning bolt after another slamming into the deflector shield so close together it could have been a continuous beam. Return fire would spear upwards when the capacitors recharged, a crackling tunnel of static electricity and ionized air that was the visible signature of a huge defense laser buried in the ground, firing up through thick focusing crystals. I'd never seen a laser that large fire in real life, and I wondered if it was actually this impressive or if they were exaggerating it for effect in the simulation.

I fought against its distraction, fought against the glare and the digital noise in my sensor display and tried to find the target. The deflector dishes were easy to find, I just had to look directly beneath the big glowing hemispheres of roiling energy, but the power feeds were short and heavily shielded, with as little of the connection above ground as possible. The helmet display highlighted them in red and I knew where they were but still couldn't see them, even on thermal.

"Hold where you are, First," Gunny Guerrero called just as we were about to emerge from the draw into the valley where the city and the Tahni base were located, about three kilometers away. "Fourth, get into cover position."

Rodriguez skidded to a halt, water spraying around her suit's legs. We'd fallen into a tight wedge in the draw and I was at the edge of the riverbank, the soft dirt giving way under my right foot with each step as I pounded to a halt. The security halt seemed to drag on longer than the terrain march to the objective and I wondered if the rest of Fourth squad was as thick-headed as Cunningham and his friends. Sgt. Saleh was the squad-leader and he seemed like a competent NCO, but as the saying goes, you can't make chicken salad out of chicken shit.

"All right, First," Guerrero finally said on our squad net. "You're up."

"Move 'em out, Alvarez," Hayes told me. "Take it slow and quiet and we'll be on 'em before they figure out we're here." He sounded confident and I wished I was.

Static electricity was thick in the air, crackling off our suits, curling up the ends of the tall grass in little tails of smoke, and I wondered how long an unarmored soldier could survive in these kinds of conditions. There had to be some serious residual radiation from the deflectors, not to mention the heat, and maybe a man could live through it but I wouldn't have wanted to be the one to try. I'd leave that shit to Force Recon.

This is going to work. We're going to pull this off.

The thought came with a sense of wonder. No simulation was ever this clean. Something *had* to go wrong or they wouldn't bother. I was looking for it, so I wasn't surprised when it popped up about a kilometer into the sprint across the open field. We hadn't seen them because of the interference from the field, but there were three armored bunkers spaced out across the front of the installation, dug halfway into the ground, their heavy KE gun turrets sticking out the front.

"We got defensive gun turrets," Rodriguez said before I could get the words out. "I don't think they've seen us yet."

That was the advantage of the bombardment. It made it hard for us to see them, but it would fuck with their sensors, too, and we weren't huge thermal targets just running across the field nearly two kilometers away. We were still moving, quick and steady.

"We can do it, Scotty," I told Hayes. "If we can get within a klick of them, we can hit the jets and be over the top of them before they adjust.

"Go," Hayes decided, not hesitating. "Keep moving, keep cold as long as you can."

We were low to the ground, hunched over, our profile small and cold as long as we didn't push it over a certain speed.

We can do it.

One klick to go…

The ball of glowing plasma flashed by in slow motion, a bolide meteor streaking across the sky. It burned itself out in the armor plating at the front of one of the bunkers, charring the metal black and searing the dirt covering the lower half into polished glass. It didn't penetrate through, but it did a great job of letting the Tahni know we were there.

"The fuck!" I blurted, disbelief freezing my decision process for a half a second…which was a half a second too long.

The heavy KE gun was a rapid-fire electromagnetic weapon, shooting tantalum darts the size of my little finger at thousands of meters per second, at a cyclic rate of a dozen a second. That weapons-stat data card from Armor School flashed through my head along with the knowledge the three or four centimeters of BiPhase Carbide armor I was carrying wouldn't be enough to stop it.

"Jump!" I ordered, but the word came out too late.

I didn't feel the impact, of course. There was a flash of a red warning light and then my helmet display went dark and I was back inside the simulator pod, the controls as dead as I notionally was.

Cursing in three different languages and a couple of obscure dialects I'd picked up in the favelas, I yanked the leads out of my 'face jacks and smashed the flat of my hand against the pod release and pushed the hatch open, squinting at the light flooding in from the simulator room. A technician glanced over at me, smirking just slightly, obviously amused at my outrage.

"Hey, is there any way I could see a replay of the last thirty seconds of the simulation?" I asked him, biting down on my initial response to his unsympathetic expression.

He was a Technician Second Class, what the Fleet calls a Tech 2, which is the equivalent to a Marine PFC, so I technically outranked him even though I wasn't even in the same service, much less the same chain of command. He shrugged and waved me over to a small monitor set in the wall.

"Let me guess," he said, still smirking, "you want to see the part just before you got killed, right?"

I responded with a silent glare and he cowed just a bit, running his finger across the touch-screen to scroll back in the video. It was a 360-degree view, since the whole thing was simulated, and all I had to do to get a look at the forces behind us was brush a fingertip against the screen. The plasma shot had come from off to the right. I'd figured that when it first happened. It wasn't from our squad, it was from Fourth, from the overwatch position. And I had a gut-feeling I knew who it had come from before I even checked the IFF.

"That son of a bitch."

The words slipped out and with them slipped away any trace of coherent thought. I knew where Cunningham's simulator was in the even rows of oval, man-high pods and I stalked over to it without a moment's hesitation and ripped the hatch open.

Cunningham blinked at the sudden glare of the lights and, before his eyes could refocus from the simulation to my face, I pulled the plugs out of his head, hit the quick release on his restraints and hauled him out of the pod.

"Alvarez?" he squawked, too shocked to even pretend to be outraged. "Hey, wait a minute…"

I slammed him up against the wall, jaw aching from how hard my teeth were grinding together.

"Is that what you're gonna do in real combat, Cunningham?" I'd meant the words to be a low, threatening growl, but they came out as bull-bellow. "You gonna buddy-fuck me and let the Tahni do what you didn't have the balls to do yourself? Is that the plan?"

"I was just messing around, man!" he raised his hands in surrender. The fucker was scared, and he should have been. I was watching myself from over my shoulder, not under control, not even trying. "It was a joke! I'd never do it for real!"

My right hand hurt, and it took me a second to understand it was because I was clenching my fist so tightly, my arm cocked backward, ready to slam into his face.

"You were messing around?"

I almost thought I'd said the words, so disconnected was I with my own actions, but then a hand so much stronger than I'd imagined yanked backwards on my shoulder and I was pulled back a step from Cunningham. Gunny Guerrero was easygoing for a platoon sergeant, but his face was a mask of rage, and if I looked half as angry as he did, I didn't blame Cunningham for being scared.

"You were fucking *messing around*?" Guerrero repeated, finger poking into Cunningham's chest. "Do you think this is a fucking *game*? Do you think we're here *playing*? This shit is to teach you, to keep your sorry ass alive! This is a fucking *war*! Tell me something, you stupid fucking moron, what do you think Top would do if she was here? What do you think the fucking Skipper would do? Do you think he would slap you on the back and buy you a beer and tell you how funny your fucking joke was?"

"No, Gunny," Cunningham said, his voice squeaking.

"You're Goddamned right he wouldn't. He'd have you in the fucking brig! He'd have your ass up on charges! Do you want me to bring Top down here? Do you want her to involve the Skipper in this?"

"No, Gunny!" He was more enthusiastic about the answer this time, standing up straight, eyes going wide.

"Then I fucking suggest you apologize profusely to Lance Corporal Alvarez and then get your ass back into that pod and do your fucking job!" He snarled, his lip curling back over yellow teeth. "And we'll take care of your punishment later, on a platoon level."

Cunningham nodded, turning to me, his mouth working as if he didn't know what to say.

"I'm sorry," he said, finally, what might have been honest shame alongside the fear in his eyes, the knowledge he'd gone too far. "I don't like you, but I wouldn't do that to another Marine if it was real, you gotta believe me."

I was about to say something about how he'd run out on the bar fight and left us to rot, but the Gunny interrupted.

"Now, Alvarez," he said, grinding his teeth as he forced a smile on his face, "why don't you tell Cunningham you accept his apology and we can fucking get back to training?"

I didn't want to. I wanted to tell him exactly what I thought of him and then smash him in the face until my knuckles bled. But to do it now, I'd have to fight Guerrero, too. I saw Scotty Hayes walking up behind him, a concerned frown dragging down his normal, cheerful expression.

"Yeah, fine," I muttered. "Let's get back to it."

Guerrero hitched a thumb back at Fourth squad's pods and Cunningham scurried away like a rat spared the trap. I started to turn away myself but Guerrero stopped me with a hand thumping against my chest.

"Dumbass!" he snapped, and I frowned at him in confusion. "If you could have kept your shit together, I'd have had a perfect excuse to get that fucking moron out of our platoon," Guerrero growled low enough that only I could hear him. "Now, if I take this shit to Top, *your* ass will be swinging right next to his. Do you know you get a for-sure Article 15 for fucking with another trooper's simulator pod without authorization? And that shit would go on your record and *never* come off." He tapped a finger against one of my 'face jacks and I flinched away instinctively. "This shit is wired into your fucking *brain*, dumbass! That operation is not cheap! You fuck with it wrong, they have to go back in there and fix it, you think the one who cost all that money isn't going to spend some time in the brig?"

"Oh." The anger had expanded far enough out of me to fill the whole room, but now it shrank back inside and back into the little box at my center where I kept it locked away. "Shit."

"Yeah, shit is right!" Guerrero spat, throwing up his hands. "Now I gotta call in every favor I got stored up with the Warrant in charge of the simulator and get the whole thing erased from the tapes and all I can do to fucknuts over there...." He motioned over at Cunningham. "...is make him clean the barracks floor. And we're gonna be back on the *Iwo* in three fucking days! Jesus help me..." He shook his head. "If you can't keep your fucking cool, Alvarez, I don't care how good you are, I am busting you back to PFC."

He turned back to the rest of the platoon, all of them out of their pods and staring, and began shouting orders, but I was too numb to hear.

Hayes blew a breath out the side of his mouth and stuffed his hands in his pockets like he didn't know what else to do with them.

"Cunningham is a prick," he told me. "But you're from the city, Cam. You had to have run into a lot of pricks there. How'd you deal with them?"

"I usually ran away," I admitted, "and hid someplace small and dark."

"Well, we got the small and dark covered," Hayes said, motioning at the pods and the battlesuits they represented. "But there ain't no running away. When we hit the drop, we're all each other has. Learn to deal."

Fourteen Years Old:

"Cameron," Mr. Portillo sighed the name, sitting back in his chair, hands clasped across his knee like the useless poser he was, "you have to learn to deal."

I sat on the edge of the uncomfortable folding plastic piece of shit he'd pulled out of the closet for me, my feet flat on the floor. I'd rather have stood, but Portillo had insisted. He'd wanted to talk to me "man to man." I wondered who he was going to bring in to carry off his half of the arrangement.

"Deal," I repeated, my tone flat and unyielding. "You want me to deal with Tony and Valdemar pimping out twelve-year-old kids to the gangs?"

I said it like I was so immeasurably older and more mature than the twelve-year-old kids, which maybe I wasn't, but at least I could defend myself against the two ringleaders of the group.

"You want me to deal with them beating up anyone small enough to not fight back, stealing anything they have, or making them their slaves? You think that's something I should deal with instead of you?"

Portillo sighed heavily, dramatically. He always did that, and I wanted to wrap my hands around his pencil neck and strangle him every time I heard it.

"Cameron, I've told you and the rest of the staff here have told you, you can't just go around making these sorts of accusations. It's disruptive to the good order of the facility."

I felt my eyes go wide at his sheer balls.

"And letting a couple small-time gangbangers run this place is just fine for the good order?"

"If you have any evidence of any illegal behavior against Tony or Valdemar, you should present it to me and Ms. Neymeir or anyone else on staff and we will see to it that they are investigated by the proper authorities." He was smug and self-satisfied, as usual.

"How do you think I'm going to get evidence against them?" I was wasting my breath; I'd known that before I'd come in the room. But I had the conviction of a teenager that if I just presented the facts in a passionate and clear enough way, I'd win the argument. "You guys have the security monitors. You're telling me you've never seen any of this?"

"I am a duly empowered officer of the City of Trans-Angeles, Mr. Alvarez," Portillo told me. His lip twisted into a half-smile and in that moment, I was sure. "If I ever saw any illegal activity, I would be required by law to report it to the Juvenile Crimes Authority."

"Yeah," I murmured, leaning back against the cheap plastic, hearing the creak as it threatened to give way beneath me. "I suppose you would."

"And since you have no evidence, the only choice you have here is to learn to deal with your fellow occupants in this facility, until such time as someone adopts you or you become a legal adult and are allowed to move out on your own." He pursed his lips, trying to seem authoritative and *intimidating but only succeeding in making himself look like more of a tool. "I trust we understand each other."*

"Oh, yeah," I confirmed, not looking away from his dark eyes. "I understand completely."

"Then I suppose we have nothing left to discuss."

I didn't slam his door behind me, but it was an effort. The hallway outside Portillo's office was dimly lit and cloaked in shadows, but I saw Valdemar waiting for me at the top of the stairs, saw his perfect white smirk. He was good-looking and he knew it, which made him even more of a douchebag.

"You tried to narc on us, Alvarez," he said, arms crossed over his chest. "What do you think's going to happen to you now?"

He wasn't expecting the shoulder to his chest, definitely wasn't expecting to cannonball down the winding stairwell. I heard the crunch of breaking bones, but I didn't look back to see how badly he was hurt. I ran, not stopping for the cries and shouts and commands behind me, not stopping to grab anything from my room. There was nothing here I needed or wanted.

I ran and didn't look back.

18

"THIS IS THE BIG ONE, BOYS AND GIRLS."

Captain Covington's face was unreadable, exuding the same cool reserve whether he was angry, excited or depressed. I'd hate to have played poker with the man. But I thought I detected just a hint of enthusiasm behind his words, as if the novelty of the coming operation had lit a fire in his jaded soul.

He paced back and forth across the *Iwo Jima's* docking bay, a caged lion, watching the rest of us with hungry eyes. We weren't at attention, weren't even in any real formation. This was as informal as it got for the Skipper, and I could see from the scowl on Top's face that she wasn't crazy about it. If she'd been running the briefing, we'd all be at parade rest. Or maybe in the push-up position, depending on her mood.

There wasn't as much room in a troop carrier's hangar bay as I'd thought before the first time I'd been in one. The drop-ships and assault shuttles were nestled into hollow recesses folded into the ship's hull, stored in the vacuum, only their airlocks accessible through the hangar bay docking umbilicals. But the main passageways were broad and usually kept clear to allow cargo to be loaded onto the drop-ships, which meant there was barely enough room for all of Delta Company to gather, and hope to God we'd all showered.

Rodriguez had, but I wasn't sure about Betancourt.

"This isn't some staging base," Covington went on, "or an isolated ammo dump with a platoon guarding it. We are going to be making the first attempt at retaking a human colony world from Tahni occupation."

Nods all around, as if everyone had been waiting for this, eager for it. Me, I was thinking we'd have lost a trooper hitting one of those isolated ammo dumps with just a platoon of enemy.

"It's not a mainline Commonwealth world, just a small, squatter colony out on the Periphery, a place called Brigantia."

Top had tasked a couple of "volunteers" to haul a portable holoprojector from the ship's conference room to the hangar bay and it snapped to life at Covington's tap on his 'link, bringing up a star map showing the established Commonwealth. The former Neutral Zone with the Tahni was highlighted in a deep purple, which seemed to be a lot of trouble given how useless and irrelevant it was now.

The Skipper ran his thumb across the screen of his 'link and the image zoomed in to a star at the edge of the Neutral Zone, marked with the letters and numbers of an astrographic notation but no colloquial name, a sign of how unimportant the place was even to the mapmakers. Closer in and five planets manifested out of the darkness, an ice ball at the farthest edge, a pair of medium-sized gas giants, a burnt husk of rock in the nearest orbit to the G-class star... and the only habitable in the system, Brigantia.

"It's close to Earth-normal, nine-tenths of the gravity, about three-fourths the density, so it's a bigger planet. Dryer than Earth, at least on the surface, a lot of water trapped underground. The capital city...." He snorted as if at a joke, though no smile crossed his graven-image of a face. "...Hell, the *only* real city is a place maybe five kilometers by either, mostly industrial fabrication and trade centers. Called Gennich, after one of the founders of the colony. Big enough it has its own fusion reactor and a defense laser the Fleet was kind enough to build for them at taxpayer expense."

There were a few chuckles at that, but not from me. I had never paid taxes and didn't expect to.

"The Tahni grabbed the colony right about the time they bombed the squatters in the Neutral Zone. They didn't nuke these guys, maybe on the theory that they didn't commit the cardinal sin of violating the Truce, just took their colony and have been using it as a communications relay station."

He scanned the company, searching for comprehension in our eyes.

"How many of you know about the wormhole gates?"

The officers and the platoon sergeants all raised their hands, along with a couple of junior NCOs and maybe three or four other enlisted. I didn't raise mine, though I'd read something about them. I knew he'd explain whether I raised it or not and I just wanted him to get to the mission brief.

"All right, here's the short version. We're in Transition Space right now, I hope you all know that much." He cocked an eyebrow, as if daring anyone to claim they hadn't realized we were traveling through another dimension. "Transition Space runs along the gravito-inertial Transition Lines between connected star systems, but the only way we found out about it was when we discovered the wormholes. Each system that's connected with a Transition Line has a microscopic wormhole, too small to fit a person through it, much less a ship, but big enough to transmit a signal through if you know where it is. That's how we can communicate with the colonies faster than just sending ships back and forth carrying messages, using communications arrays positioned close to the wormhole, what we call the Instell ComSats."

How anyone could be in the damned Marines and not know about the Instell ComSats was beyond me, but then, Cunningham was in our platoon.

"The Tahni use the same system, of course, but they have a choke point. The only way for them to get messages back to their homeworld from the Periphery is through the wormhole in this system." He jabbed a finger toward Brigantia. "But they can't use a ComSat hanging out in space, because they know we'd destroy it just as quick as they put a new one up. They use a high-power transmitter on the surface of the planet, powered by the same fusion reactor the Commonwealth built for them." He shrugged. "Sure, they can only transmit when that side of the planet is in the right place, but there's not a damned thing we can do to shut it down, unless we want to nuke the city…or take it back."

He'd mentioned nuking the world so casually, as if it was something the Fleet had actually considered. I wondered if they had.

"Our job, first, last and no questions asked, is to take out that communications array. If everything else goes the way it's supposed to, the Fleet's cruisers are going to be bombarding the deflectors with their proton cannons from orbit at the same time. The feedback from the array going down should run right back into the deflectors and bring them down, which means no more deflectors and no more Tahni barracks. Now, of course, they're not going to sit still while we do that. We don't know if they have any High Guard in the garrison here, but they definitely have a shitload of Shock-troops and crew-served weapons."

To my surprise, Sandoval raised her hand.

"Yes, Lance Corporal?"

"Sir, they got to have a shitload of air defense around there, probably outside the deflectors and camouflaged." She shook her head. "How're we gonna get through that in the drop-ships?"

"You're exactly right, Sandoval," Covington said, a very thin, barely-noticeable smile creasing his face. "You may have noticed we're carrying a company of Force Recon on this ship."

Oh, boy, had we ever. Top had pounded it into us with the decibel level of a sonic stunner that if any of us got into it with the Force Recon troops, she would cut our guts out with a rusty knife. And it was so damned hard to keep my mouth shut when the pricks called themselves "operators," as if they were some sort of Fleet Intelligence spooks instead of just straight-leg foot-soldiers.

"Yes, sir," Sandoval said, her cheek quivering slightly, as if she was clenching her teeth not to say anything else. "I noticed."

"They're going to HALO in with glider chutes and take out the air defenses to let us insert low enough to drop."

Shit. I didn't say it, but I was thinking it, and I heard a couple people actually curse softly at the news.

"At ease!" Top growled and the murmuring ceased.

"You'll get a detailed op order from your platoon leaders," Covington continued, ignoring the exchange, "but this is the basic plan." Another tap on his 'link and a diagram popped up in mid-air above the projector. The town, the fusion reactor complex outside its boundaries and the shielded emitter of the defense laser were all actual stock images from just after their construction, but the deflector dishes and the transmitter array beneath them were all computer simulations.

"We're dropping in as close as we can, less than five kilometers away unless we're facing untenable ground fire. They're sure to have dug-in bunkers and weapons turrets guarding the approaches to the reactor complex, so we're going to have to distract them, get their attention. Fourth and First platoons are going to provide the distraction. You're going to circle around and come in from the south, from the city side of the complex, draw fire that direction, while Third and Second approach from the northeast and northwest. Second will suppress the enemy bunkers while Third takes out the communications array."

He motioned expansively.

"Once the deflectors come down, we need to un-ass the area, because the proton cannons aren't going to cease fire, they're going to take out the barracks, the laser, and anything else that happens to be in the area. Are we clear?"

A chorus of voices responded in the affirmative. He cocked his head to the side.

"I said," he repeated, "are we clear?"

"Aye-aye, sir!"

That, apparently, was better, and he nodded satisfaction, touching his 'link one last time. The map was replaced by a file photo I'd seen in Basic, and again in AOT. It was a full-body shot of a Tahni male dressed in what passed for a utility uniform for their military. He was broad-shouldered and deep-chested, with arms that seemed long for his torso and fingers almost like a human's but with extra joints.

The face was what always got me. Like the hands, so *close* to human, too close for it to be an accident, or at least I thought so, and I wasn't the only one. Close enough that if I saw one on a dark night or from far enough away, I might mistake it for a man. The jaw was too big, though, like a steam-shovel, and the brows were heavily-ridged, the doll-black eyes barely visible beneath them. The ears were broad, and flat against the side of the skull and the skin was a dark tan, though that varied between individuals, or so I'd been told. The hair was cut into a mohawk that ran all the way down the back of his thick neck and then trailed into a long queue wrapped around his throat. Someone had told me only their blooded warriors wore it that way.

"This," Covington said, "is the enemy." A low murmur went up and a few wisecracks quickly shushed by the platoon sergeants. "Most of you haven't been told much about the Tahni other than where they've invaded and what sort of weapons they use, and I think that's a mistake, so I'm going to tell you right now what we know about them."

Now, I was interested. I'd been trying to look up information about the enemy but it seemed like everything was classified.

"The Tahni Imperium has been around in one form or another for about four thousand years." He eyed us all significantly. "Four *thousand* years. It conquered the entire planet a thousand years ago, hundreds of years before the Tahni even achieved spaceflight. For the last thousand years, they've shared the same government, the same religion, the unshakable belief that their Emperor is the living embodiment of their god.

"They also believe they are the living extensions of their god, His hands in the universe. That's why they don't use AI-controlled weapons or autonomous drones. Hell, they don't even like to use remotely-fired weapons if they can avoid it. To them, the closer they can come to killing the enemy with their bare hands, the closer they are to their god.

"To us, their society, their religion, their biology would be considered insane. They go into rut when their females are in season and lose all reason. The only way they've been able to maintain an orderly society is to keep their females totally separate from their males and only come together for prearranged marriages purely for procreation."

"No wonder the fuckers are always trying to fight someone." I didn't know who said it, but it caused a general chuckle through the company and Covington didn't clamp down on it, though he didn't laugh.

"Among other reasons," he agreed. "And that fucked-up religion of theirs tells them that all the habitable planets in the galaxy belong to them, and anyone else is trespassing. That anyone else being us. Do not make the mistake of thinking the Tahni will ever give up on this war. It's part of who they are, part of who they believe their god is, and the only way we'll ever force them to come to Jesus is to beat them so bad we rub their noses in their own shit like a bad dog." He tapped his 'link to shut down the projection. "That starts now. Ooo-rah?"

"Ooo-rah!" The reply was deafening, echoing off the bulkheads, and I was as loud as anyone. I knew it was a psychological prop, but sometimes we need psychological props.

"Platoon leaders, see to your platoons. We drop in sixty hours, so I want everyone familiar with the op order and rehearsed till you can do your part of the mission and your leader's part, too, in your sleep. Dismissed."

"Hang out here a bit, Third," Ackley told us as the others began to filter off to wherever their platoon leaders were going to take them for their individual briefings. "Take a knee."

I bit down on a sigh and kneeled down with the rest of the platoon. Taking a knee was a military tradition I'd never understand. It's no more comfortable than standing up and everyone looks like a complete idiot. But I suppose officers got taught in the Academy that it was more intimate and personal than standing around, so we all went down on a knee in the middle of the damned hangar bay.

Lt. Ackley waited until they were all out of earshot before turning back to us, kneeling down herself.

"We're up front again," she said, and I wasn't sure if she was bragging, exulting or lamenting the fact. "The Skipper is putting his trust in us and I don't mean to let him down." She turned to Scotty Hayes. "First, you're on point."

"Jesus, ma'am," Hayes said, laughing softly. "I can't tell if you're rewarding me or just trying to get me killed."

Ackley smiled, a genuine smile and not the put-on, bravado-heavy grin some officers tried to use to make themselves look all tough and nervy.

"You know what the reward is for work well done, Sgt. Hayes," she told him. "More work."

"I've heard that, ma'am," he admitted. "I just never thought I'd experience it."

"The op order will be available on your 'links and I expect you all to be familiar with it before we launch, but it's pretty straightforward stuff. We'll drop and then cover as much distance as we can in the air without overheating, try to stay out of the firing arc of their ground bunkers until the cover platoons can begin laying down suppressive fire on their positions. We're going in platoon column."

I nodded. That made sense. Platoon column had the individual squads in wedges, one right behind the other rather than spread out. Spreading the squads out would just give the weapons turrets in the bunkers a bigger target to shoot at.

"Stick with your squad, but there's no finesse about our role in this operation. First squad puts missile fire into the communications array until the damned thing blows up, and the rest of us make sure no one shoots them in the back until they're finished. We back each other up in Third Platoon, am I clear?"

Her eyes flickered toward Cunningham and I pressed my lips together to force back the twisted grin trying to break through.

"Aye-aye, ma'am!"

"Good," she said, nodding. "Because, boys and girls, when it comes down to it, we can't count on anyone but each other. Whether you love your buddy or hate him, he's still your buddy. You still have to look out for him and hope to hell he looks out for you. I know we've seen combat now, and some of you may think it wasn't that hard, that it'll be easy, that the enemy's a pushover. Well, I don't have any more combat experience than the rest of you and I can tell you that's horse shit, and it'll get you killed. The only easy day was yesterday, and the only good time was last time. Brigantia will be harder than Bluebonnet and what comes after Brigantia will be even harder than this, until we invade the Goddamned Tahni homeworld."

She smiled wanly. "And I know that's not an ooo-rah thing to say, but it's something you need to hear. We're here to win the war, but if you want to live to see the end, you need to keep your eyes open and look out for each other. Ooo-rah?"

"Ooo-rah, ma'am." The reply was subdued, but sounded more heartfelt.

"We have sixty hours," she said. "Let's get in the simulators and work the mission." She snorted. "And hope the damn straight-leg Recon pukes do their job."

19

THE ARMOR WRAPPED ME IN THE COLD EMBRACE OF THE DEAD.

It took the space of two or three breaths before the systems booted up and the Heads-Up Display alleviated the total blackness inside my helmet. Some people had a tendency towards panic in that moment of darkness. The ones who lasted through Armor school learned to endure it. I'd learned to appreciate it. It was peaceful, a womb, a fort made from chairs and bedsheets by a child, a shelter from the harsh emptiness without.

The insistent, annoying nasal tone of the drop-ship flight crew ruined the mood.

"Separation in five, four, three, two, one…launching!"

The jolt slammed my head into the helmet's interior padding as the docking mandibles cut loose and the dropship's maneuvering thrusters pushed us away from the monolithic mass of the Fleet Marine Transport *Iwo Jima*. Muted cursing crackled on the squad net and I saw on the IFF display it was from Betancourt.

"Take your finger off the transmit key, newbie," I snapped at him, hoping he wouldn't make me look even worse by saying he was sorry.

The last sixty hours had been absolute hell, one drill after another, one ass-chewing after another because Betancourt kept fucking up. The guy was scared, and while I didn't blame him, I also had no idea what to say to him. I'd tried to talk to him anyway, and so had Scotty Hayes, but there hadn't been the time for any psychological counseling, so I'd just had to hope he'd get his shit together.

And hope Cunningham didn't stab me in the back, and hope the Force Recon boys got the job done and…

I didn't like it. I didn't want to hope. Hope was counting on shit I couldn't control, and that had never gone very well for me.

"Ignition in five seconds," the same relentlessly cheerful crew chief announced from the cockpit. "Prepare for acceleration."

I rested my head against the padding at the rear of the helmet and sucked in a deep breath just in time for the crushing press of six gravities of boost. I wasn't linked into the lander's exterior cameras this time, mostly because I'd decided I didn't want to see death coming if I couldn't do anything to stop it, but I knew there would be a sun-bright flare from the boat's drive bell, taking us down to the southern continent of Brigantia just as fast as they could.

Even six g's couldn't outrun a missile, but there were ECM and chaff and automated CWS for that. The heavy boost and the frequent jinking and deking were to keep the ground-based lasers from swatting us out of the sky. Theoretically.

The fist squeezing my chest let up and I realized we were leveling off. I figured we were maybe five minutes out from the drop zone only seconds before the warning light flashed in my HUD and let me know I was right. I pulled up the mapping software, getting interested in where we were if not what was coming up to meet us. Lt. Ackley was gabbling about something, but I shut it out for the moment. Not that she wasn't competent, but I'd noticed she was talking to hear herself talk just before the drop and if there was anything really important, she'd cast the frag-o onto my HUD. I was trying to get my head right before I had to start worrying about everyone else.

Our target glowed with a red halo a few kilometers outside the city of Gennich, but nothing on the map told me whether the Marines had done their job and taken out the anti-aircraft batteries. They only needed to miss one…

We were low now; I knew it without looking at the instrument readings. There was a thickness to the air, a shudder in the wings, a deeper register of the engines. Not low enough for the drop yet, still another few hundred meters to go, but I started running system checks on my jump-jets. I snuck a peek out the exterior cameras and still saw nothing. It was night on this side of the planet.

Night, again. It was always night.

"We drop in thirty seconds," Gunny Guerrero announced over the platoon net. "Keep your intervals, hundred meters between you, and no one stops moving until we're at the target. First squad…"

Whatever he'd been about to say vanished in a flash of light and the agonized shriek of metal ripping, and the very fist of God shaking the dropship's fuselage mercilessly. I didn't have the time to deliberate, didn't have the luxury to speculate, I only had instincts borne of endless repetition.

I dropped. I didn't remember hitting the control, but the external deployment hatch had popped. I'd cut loose the magnetic locks holding my Vigilante in the drop carriage and I was falling free with the dropship close, too damned close above me when it exploded. The moment seemed frozen, as if I suddenly had all the time in the world to think now that the decisions had been made and my fate sealed.

The bird had taken a hit from a coil gun; it was the only thing that fit. A missile would have killed us all instantly, a laser would have given us a moment's warning before it was able to burn through the hull. It had taken us in a wing and the ship had torn itself apart in less than a second, and when the engines had cut loose from the fuselage, it had exploded. One other suit was silhouetted against the blast...no, two others, blown free of the ship.

Then the moment was over and time was moving on and the glowing ball of gas and debris that had been our dropship was tumbling forward with its leftover momentum, and I was falling, way too high and way too fast. We were over a thousand meters up and still traveling at 700 kilometers an hour, and the jump-jets in my suit didn't have nearly enough power to slow down 600 kilograms of armor, weapons, isotope reactor and very fragile human flesh to a survivable landing in that distance.

But seeing as how I don't have any other choice...

The flare of the jets was a faint glow in the night sky, but it made me feel obscenely exposed, a thermal "shoot me" sign hung around my neck for the Tahni gunners to see, and it was all for nothing because I would still plow into the ground at...

No, not the ground. The lake. My HUD map showed it. Water would be as hard as concrete from this height, but if I could minimize my surface area when I hit...

I had ten seconds and the black, featureless surface of the lake was screaming up at me; it was now or never. I gave the jets a long, continuous burst and stood the armor vertically, its arms tucked in, joints locked in place, then bit down on the mouthpiece built into the helmet. I'd been too busy to be afraid till now, but in those last few seconds I had the time…and still felt no fear. It surprised me.

So did the impact. The interior of the suit was lined with foam cushioning for just such an occasion, but the designers apparently hadn't planned on the armor going quite this fast when it hit. There was a dull, concussive pain, the sort of feeling I remembered having the morning after a beatdown, and when I opened my eyes, I was fairly confident I'd passed out; everything was black, my helmet systems were down, and though not a drop of water made it through the seals, I had the unmistakable feeling that I was sinking fast.

The emergency ejection switch was inside my right gauntlet and it ran from its own, integral battery. I whispered a prayer that it hadn't been damaged, sucked in as much air as my lungs could hold, and squeezed the control. Explosive bolts blew with a chest-deep thump, there was a tug against my temples as the interface jacks yanked out of the implant sockets, and the armor fell away around me. I was swallowed up in a cold so bitter and sudden that I very nearly gave in to the compulsion to gasp the carefully-hoarded breath out of my lungs.

Up. Have to go up.

I couldn't see a damned thing; the water was just as black as the inside of my dead helmet had been. But I had a sense, something gut-deep, of the way the suit had gone when it had disappeared beneath me and I kicked desperately in the opposite direction. Pressure squeezed at my chest and the cold leeched the power from my arms and legs and I felt a soul-deep conviction that I wasn't going to make it to the surface before my air ran out, yet still panic eluded me. I longed for it, wanted an excuse to give in to the cold and exhaustion dragging at me, to let the carbon dioxide burning inside my lungs escape and accept the frigid water in its place.

It wouldn't come and I was forced to keep swimming, keep fighting. Lights flashed in my vision, not beacons guiding me to safety but a flash of warning that my air was gone and I was about to lose consciousness and still I kept swimming.

Air, suddenly, without warning, somehow so much colder than the frigid water, so cold it made my lungs hurt when I sucked it down. Water went down my windpipe with the air and a violent cough racked my chest. Desperate, I threw myself onto my back and let myself float. The night was clear and Brigantia's solitary moon was out; enough illumination for me to see just how far away the lake shore was.

And more...I could see the fiery deaths of dropships lighting up the sky, one after another, a platoon of Marines and four flight crew per bird. Missiles streaked out from the escort fighters, beams scored the atmosphere as orbital ships offered fire support, but they were answered with the eye-searing blast of a fusion-fed laser slicing the black apart. Assault shuttles disappeared in clouds of superheated gas thousands of meters above me, the stars of their passing reflected in the flat, mirrored surface of the water, and the lasers continued up through the atmosphere to target the ships in orbit.

It's gone to shit. It was a revelation, slapping me in the face with a wash colder than the lake water. *They're going to have to pull back.*

It felt like a lump inside my gut. Everyone could be dead. I'd only seen two suits pop free of the drop-ship. Was it Scotty Hayes? Rodriguez? Sandoval? Was Lt. Ackley dead? Gunny Guerrero? Was I the only one?

But beyond that, down at the base of my deepest thoughts was one thing, one concern. There wouldn't be any Search and Rescue lander coming for me. I was alone. I cursed softly, turned over and started swimming.

"Wake up," Poppa urged, shaking at my shoulder. "You have to wake up."

No, that was wrong. Not Poppa...I'd never see my father again. I opened my eyes and found myself shivering fitfully and staring up into the yawning muzzle of a rifle.

"Shit!" I scrambled backwards against the rough bark of the century-old oak, seeded by the original colonists along with various other genetically altered Earth life.

The cold of the incipient dawn was forgotten in a rush of adrenalin and it took another second before I could look past the gun and see the old man holding it. Well, even out here in the Periphery, no one actually got *old*, but a life spent outdoors in the sun and weather had cracked and lined the lean, sharp-edged face, darkening it into the color of the desert rock outside Trans-Angeles.

"Take it easy, boy," the old man drawled, swinging the barrel of the gun upward and raising a calming hand. "If I saw you burn in here last night, the Tahni surely did."

He waved the hand in a "follow-me" motion and headed off into the woods, not turning back to see if I would follow. I considered it for a long moment, trying to shake off the disorientation. I didn't remember falling asleep last night, but I'd obviously passed out immediately after crawling up on the shore. The skinsuit was insulated, which was probably the only reason I hadn't died of hypothermia on a night where the temperatures had dipped down close to freezing and even with it, the morning chill permeated through my core. The cold made my decision for me; I needed to move.

"Who the hell are you?" I asked the old man, struggling to keep up in soft boots not meant for outdoor use.

The local seemed to know the surest way through the trees and I did my best to follow in his steps without turning an ankle.

"Dak Shepherd."

I waited for elaboration, but none seemed to be forthcoming and we were almost through the trees. I stepped out into the open, grassy plains and froze, as if all the fear I'd anticipated last night had been stored up and unleashed on me at once.

Seven Years Old:

I didn't want to come out from beneath the blanket, didn't want to leave the vehicle, but it was too hot to stay inside; I felt as if I couldn't breathe. The sun was naked and harsh, the sky yellow with dust and sand, and all around me was nothing, emptiness. The old road stretched out from one horizon to the next, cracked and broken by time, buried under sand in places but stubbornly persisting for the long decades since it had fallen out of use. Buttes jutted red and lonely in the distance, but nothing else interrupted the desolation.

I cried out for my Poppa, for Anton, but no one answered. I was alone.

"Are you comin', boy? Or would you rather wait for the Tahni to come haul you off to an internment camp?"

I blinked and the haze of years past cohered into the lined mask of Dak Shepherd's face again. He was frowning and the expression seemed redundant. Beyond him, the open grasslands carpeted the river valley, spread out under an endless, bleak sky and my gut twisted in unreasoning panic.

"Agoraphobic?" The word wasn't spoken with the scorn I expected. I nodded, trying to force my eyes to focus on Shepherd's face.

"Slightly," I gasped the word out. I closed my eyes and tried to slow down my breathing. "Usually not this bad."

"See that a lot from Earthers. Keep your eyes on me, don't look around, but move fast."

That helped. I studied every detail of the man, trying to focus on the rough, hand-made work clothes the old man was wearing, patched and stitched in a dozen places, trying to identify the odd lines of the rifle he carried. It wasn't a military issue weapon; it looked as old as he was and had probably been custom made on a fabricator from a black-market pattern. All I knew was that the hole at the end of the barrel was big.

I kept my eyes down, watching the damp grass, imported and gone wild, slapping insistently at my thighs. Mosquitos swarmed in our wake, diving with singular purpose at my shaven head, mocking the futility of my flailing hands.

"Why the hell did they bring mosquitos here?" I wondered, not expecting an answer.

"Same reason they brought cockroaches and rats," Shepherd responded with an amused snort. "By accident. Watch your step, we need to start running."

"Why?" It came out more plaintively than I'd intended.

"Listen." He nodded off to their right, back toward the lake.

I started to turn, then reconsidered and closed my eyes first. I heard it then, the distant rumbling...not thunder, there wasn't enough cloud cover for that. It was a turbofan engine, not close yet, but coming our way.

"Maybe it's Fleet Search and Rescue." I tried to sound more hopeful than I was.

The only reply was a humorless snort. Shepherd broke into a long, loping run and I sprinted to keep up with his lanky, long-legged stride. I wanted to look up, wanted to see where we were running, but something deep in my chest clenched icy fingers at the idea and I kept my head down and my legs churning.

I wasn't out of shape; they didn't *let* Marines get out of shape, whether we operated a battlesuit or a desk. But I was huffing and puffing trying to match Shepherd's pace and I wasn't even weighed down by a rifle. The old man was like a length of coiled spring, thin and wiry and mechanically efficient. I was just beginning to wonder if I'd have to suffer the humiliation of asking Shepherd to slow down when the older man abruptly dropped out of sight. My arms pinwheeled and my heels dug into the ground at the sudden realization that I was about to fall into a creek bed, then the soft ground at its banks crumbled and I was sliding down on my back, trying not to yell out.

My butt slammed into the flat side of a rock worn smooth by water, arresting the slide after only two meters and sending me sprawling head-first into the fast-running water. The creek was only chest-deep but the current was strong, I was off-balance and the water was shockingly cold, even through the skinsuit. I tumbled, desperately trying to stand but unable to get my feet beneath me; the current began to carry me away...

I could feel Anton's arms through the blanket, could feel my brother lifting me into the car, even though I couldn't see it. I knew the car; I'd watched it pulling up outside. It looked impossibly old and battered and I wondered if it was an original gas-burner someone had squirreled away in a garage out in the boonies or if it had been fabricated off an old pattern by someone too poor to spring for a newer model.

"Be quiet, Cam," Anton whispered to him as he laid me down on the floor in the back seat. "Be quiet and stay here and everything will be okay."

Liar.

A hand wrapped around my right forearm with the grip of a power loader and yanked me upright, then pulled me to the shore just a few meters away.

I nodded thanks to Shepherd and expected the local to make some scathing remark about my clumsiness, but the man put a finger to his lips in warning, dark eyes traveling upward. The scream of the jets was close now, over the lake, and from the change in the pitch, I was fairly sure the aircraft was hovering. Shepherd waved for me to follow and headed upstream, away from the lake, splashing through the shallows.

"How long do we have to stay down here?" I asked, after the third time I'd nearly slipped on the unstable, rounded rocks of the creek bed.

"Until they go away." Shepherd indicated who "they" were with a jerk of his thumb back toward the lake. "Or we're over the horizon. Or they find us and kill us."

He fixed me with a glare.

"Shut up and move."

20

I STUMBLED BLINDLY IN THE DEEP SHADOWS OF THE CANYON, TOO exhausted to pick up my feet and too stubborn to ask Shepherd for another break. The system's primary was close to setting somewhere behind those red canyon walls, and we'd been walking or running since dawn with only a handful of five or ten-minute breaks, carefully-rationed water and very little food. And I'd spent most of the trip with my eyes glued to Shepherd's back, not daring to look up for fear of another panic attack.

"Heads up," Shepherd said, his voice as even and free of strain as if he'd just taken a stroll in the park. "This is it."

I forced my eyes upward, expecting another break and hopeful that the walls of the narrow canyon would keep me from freezing up. It was so dark I almost missed the trailer, and that was probably the idea. It was backed into a crevice where the side of the sandstone canyon had collapsed, shielded from overhead view by camouflage netting, with dirt piled over its sides to break up its outline. I jumped back when the door in the exposed side of the mobile work shed squeaked open and a woman stepped out.

She was a younger, smoother version of Shepherd and from the resemblance, I guessed she was the man's daughter. The work clothes were similar, though she'd opted for a pistol holstered at her waist instead of the massive rifle he carried, and skin and hair were half a shade lighter.

"So, this is our guest?" Her voice was a strong contralto, her eyebrow arched in skeptical assessment.

"I'm Corporal Alvarez, 187th Marine Expeditionary Force," I blurted, barely stopping myself from following up with my ID number.

"Cam," I amended, trying to salvage my composure.

"Maria," she offered, and I had the sense that she was about as chatty as her father.

"He's what's left," Shepherd declared sourly. "Let's get inside before their drones make a pass through here."

It felt incalculably comforting to be inside the shadowed confines of the trailer, despite the accumulated sand on the floor, the dingy, peeling paint on the walls and the battered and ripped upholstery on furniture that could have come from the pre-spaceflight era. I was so relieved to be indoors again that it took me a second to realize there were other people in the trailer, two of them sprawled out over a sofa that might once have been some shade of green and a third huddled over a folding table, leaning against it despite its questionable stability.

They were all dressed in similar fashion to Shepherd and Maria, all with the weathered look of locals, and all armed, both with obvious weapons and skeptical expressions. I was staring at them uncertainly when the door slammed shut behind me and Shepherd's hand on my shoulder guided me toward a chair.

"Hope they didn't track you," one of the two men lounging on the sofa rumbled, picking at his teeth with a sliver of wood as he regarded me from beneath shaggy, sand-colored brows.

"We have bigger problems," Maria assured him. She looked around at the others, her face going grim. "Fleet Intelligence just sent a coded message…"

"You're in the Resistance?" I asked her, eyes going wide. I knew the cells existed on all enemy-occupied worlds, organized by the spooks to get intelligence on the Tahni and sometimes sabotage their on-planet facilities, but to meet one…

Maria didn't answer, but her baleful glare told me what she thought of the question.

"They're not going to try another conventional attack," she went on, instead.

"They're abandoning Brigantia?" the woman seated at the table asked, her eyebrows going up in surprise. She looked older than Maria, more stolid and stable, though not the desiccated fossil that Dak Shepherd was.

I shook my head, knowing the answer before Maria gave it, and liking it about as much as she seemed to.

"They're gonna' nuke the Tahni base," I said. Maria glanced at me, looking surprised at the insight. I shrugged. "We got our asses kicked and we don't have enough troops for a repeat, not without getting beat up just as bad."

"But a strike that close to Gennich…" One of the men on the couch pushed himself to his feet, stepping closer to me as if I were the one launching the missiles. "It'll take out the whole city!"

"They've given us sixty hours to evacuate as many people as we can," Maria said. "They said they're going to try to keep the Tahni pinned down with orbital bombardment while we do it."

There were spluttered protests and hands slapping furniture in frustration, but I ignored them, my thoughts churning, my mind kicking back into gear now that it no longer had to fight back the panic constantly.

"The shields will be at maximum output," I mused, and didn't think anyone had heard until the others fell silent, staring at me as if I'd grown a second head.

I shrank a bit under the scrutiny.

"During the bombardment, I mean," I explained, trying to remember the important parts of the briefing past the Skipper's morale boosting. "It's got a fusion reactor powering it, but it's still going to be close to the edge deflecting all that shit. It would only take a nudge in the right place to blow it out."

"Yeah?" Shepherd was at my right shoulder, so close I could feel the man's breath. "What's this right place?"

"You guys must have taken some photos of the base, right?" I spread my hands hopefully.

Maria pulled a datalink off her belt and set it down on the table, touching a control on the side. The hologram the device projected wasn't just a photo or a video, it was a detailed schematic not too dissimilar to the one they'd showed my platoon during the target brief, and I didn't bother to ask how she'd got it.

"Here," I said, pointing at a section of the squared-off, blocky construction of the base. The transmitter was a universal dish shape, its form a slave to its function. "That was our target…shit, was it just yesterday?" I shook myself, trying to get my head working right.

Maria shoved a canteen into my hand and I swallowed half of it down before handing it back, nodding gratitude.

"The antenna is the only external structure connected to the power supply," I went on. "It's got overhead cover by the shield, but the ground approach is open."

"What good is blowing up an antenna gonna' do?" Toothpick Man demanded, gesturing with the wood sliver. "I don't give a damn if the Tahni can call their mommas back home."

"Jesus, Charlie." Maria rolled her eyes. "It's connected to the power system. If we blow it up while they're drawing maximum from the reactor…"

"They told us the power surge would overload their systems," I agreed. "It'll shut down their shielding, at least until they can reset."

"The Fleet will be bombarding the shield," Shepherd mused quietly.

"Do you have any explosives?" I asked. It wasn't my specialty, but every Marine got classes on handling explosives in Basic and I was sure I could remember enough to work with it.

"We have something better than that." It was the man sitting beside Charlie. He was short and skinny and unimposing and he hadn't said two words until now.

"You got it?" Shepherd seemed surprised, and the expression didn't fit on his hard-edged face.

"Out in the truck. Drove it in last night."

"Damn."

There was a reflexive relief in my exclamation, and on its heels a tide of guilt.

"It was the only one that survived the crash," the little man was saying, leaning into the powered lift bed of the all-terrain cargo truck, shaded and shielded by the camouflage netting pulled over the truck like a carport. I winced when the man slapped a hand appreciatively against the leg of the prone battlesuit. "Took me all night to dig it out of the wreckage and get it on the truck."

The suit was battered and scorched, and I could already see that the jumpjets were so much scrap metal, but the joints didn't seem damaged and the weapons were intact. I hesitated, his hand near the latch to release the chest plastron.

"Is there still...?" I trailed off. The whole thing seemed disrespectful.

Maria put a hand on my shoulder, obvious sympathy in her eyes.

"Oh," the little man realized what I was asking. "No. The lock that attaches the helmet to the chest came loose in the dropship crash. I left the body there...didn't have time to bury him."

I pulled myself up into the bed of the truck and examined the armor with a critical eye. There was blood inside the helmet, nearly dried now. I swallowed hard and grabbed the leads of the interface cables, plugging each into the jacks implanted at my temples. There was a silence inside my head, a complete darkness that meant lack of input and I began to despair...until a blinking yellow indicator let me know the suit's system was rebooting.

Nearly a minute for that, then another few seconds while it checked my identity. I wasn't the Gunny who'd worn it originally and warning lights flashed red as it told me in no uncertain terms where I could go and what I could do with myself for trying an unauthorized connection, and I could feel the impatience radiating off the others. I ignored them and tried to remember what Mutt had told me, the tricks to perform a field-expedient ID reauthorization for a Vigilante operating system.

The process dragged on from one prompt to another and I hunted through menus and hoped I was remembering the key sequence right or else I'd have to do the whole damned thing over. Finally, it granted me the blessing of authorization and all the lights in the identification display went green. Then I switched to suit status and yellows and reds began to replace the green with depressing uniformity.

"It's operational," I said, my voice distracted, most of my consciousness still buried beneath the interface. "Barely. The booster jets are trashed, the chest plastron latch is busted but I can fix that if you have some tools." I clucked with exasperation. "Targeting system is damaged. I'll only be able to guide them manually, and short-range at that, almost point-blank. The isotope reactor is intact, but the leg actuators are damaged. They'll last short-term, but I wouldn't be counting on them to get very far."

"But you can blow that dish, right?" Shepherd asked. For the first time since I'd met the man, I thought he seemed worried.

"I'll have to be close." I yanked the interface jacks out of my sockets. "And I won't be walking there in this suit."

"If we're going to do this," Maria said to her father, "we have to do it now."

"I don't know about this." That was the older woman, Delta they'd called her. "We're staking a lot on this jack-head and one beat-up suit. We should evac the city."

"As my grandfather liked to say," Shepherd replied, "why not get both?" He pointed to Delta. "You and Charlie get the word into the city, get the people ready to go." He smiled thinly. "If the Tahni hear about it, that should make them even more ready to believe we're giving up."

"How are we gonna' get the suit to the base?" I asked him. "This banged up, I wouldn't want to try running it more than a few kilometers."

"At night," Maria told him, eyeing her father with what might have been doubt. "And with a distraction. Are you sure about this, Dad?"

"We got next to no time, no other weapons that'll do the job, and no one else who can make this thing work," Shepherd said flatly. "You got a better idea, you tell me now."

She grunted and regarded me dubiously.

"You have an itch to get yourself killed?"

I just want back in a suit. But she wouldn't understand that answer. I just agreed with her, instead.

"I must. I volunteered for this shit."

"What do you need, son?" Dak asked me. He was projecting a confidence I wish I shared.

I'm a Lance Corporal. I thought it but didn't say it. They needed me to sound like I deserved their confidence.

"Can you get me some live drone shots of their defenses?"

"Probably," he allowed. "Nothing high-resolution or three-dimensional, but I think we got some stuff that's small enough to go undetected that can get you a regular two-D view."

"If you have any way to transmit to the Fleet, you should tell them what we're going to try. They might not call off the nukes, but at least they'll know to support us if we can pull this off."

"We do have a transmission antenna," Maria said. "But it's hidden in an old grain storage building, and we can only use it once before the Tahni detect it and send a missile down on top of the building."

"If you're saving it for a special occasion," I told her, cocking an eyebrow, "I think this might be it."

"Right," Dak said, finality in his voice as if he was ending the argument right there. "Anything else?"

"Yeah," I said, looking down at the busted chest plastron. "I need a wrench."

21

"You don't like it out here, do you?"

I looked up from the open maintenance panel in the chest of the battlesuit, taking the moment to wipe sweat from my forehead. Maria stood by the tailgate, holding a bottle of water and a military ration pack. I didn't know where she'd gotten the rats; they certainly hadn't come out of the battlesuit. Maybe Fleet Intelligence had dropped supplies for them.

"Why do you say that?" I wondered, setting down the tools they'd loaned me and taking the food eagerly. I felt like I hadn't eaten anything for days, and enough raw hunger could even make military rats palatable.

"When you go from the trailer to the truck, you keep your head down and walk just as fast as you can." She leaned against the bed of the truck, watching me rip open the packaging and begin spooning down a self-heating packet of stew.

I hadn't thought about it before, but she was sort of pretty. Not the kind of flawless beauty you got when the doctors worked your genes to perfection before you were even conceived, like the rich people back on Earth, but something more natural and appealing. I shrugged it off. She was probably older than me, likely not interested and certainly way too preoccupied.

I finished off the mouthful of stew I'd been using as a delaying action and started to form a likely-sounding lie, but hesitated. *What the hell difference does it make?*

"I don't like it outside; haven't since I was a kid." I scooped up another bite before I continued, trying to loosen up the tight controls I usually wrapped around the truth. "Have you ever been to Earth?"

"I was born here." She tilted her head in a philosophical shrug. "I'll probably die here. But I've done ViR tours of a few of the megacities."

"Over half the population lives in them, and everyone that doesn't, wants to. Except for the people rich enough to have a house, but I never met one of those."

"Only rich people have houses?" She seemed shocked; maybe her ViR tour program hadn't included that tidbit.

"There are hellacious taxes on anyone who doesn't live in the cities. Only rich people can afford to pay them. Everyone who doesn't live in Trans-Angeles or Capital City or one of the other mega-cities is stuck in the old towns, the pre-war towns." I looked down at the remains of the heated food packet; it didn't seem as appetizing as it had a few minutes ago. "My family lived in Tijuana...what's left of it. It's a hell-hole, a place everyone forgets about because they'd rather pretend it doesn't exist or it's someone else's problem."

My mouth felt dry; I grabbed the water bottle and sucked down a gulp.

"When I was seven, my dad stole an old junker of a car from one of the local gangsters and tried to make it across the desert to Trans-Angeles. Mom...she'd been killed in the gang fighting, and Dad was desperate. He'd heard if you just showed up, they'd take care of you, get you an apartment, that no one cared if you were registered or not. It was just me and him and my big brother, Anton. He was twelve."

I could see Anton's face, long, narrow and serious, always so serious, like the weight of the world was on him. He already had a scar across his chin where he'd caught a fragment from a car bomb. More than mom's face or dad's voice, I remembered Anton's sad, haunted eyes.

I realized I hadn't spoken in a while, and that Maria was staring at me.

"We didn't make it. The bandits caught up with us in the desert south of the city. They took everything we had. Anton should have stayed in the car with me, should have tried to hide, but he had to try to..." Pain squeezed my chest worse than any g-forces ever had. "Afterward, after the bandits had left, I walked through the desert for two days before I collapsed. I woke up in the Trans Angeles East Hospital; a maintenance worker checking the solar power satellite rectennae outside the city had found me."

"Jesus Christ." I thought at first Maria was just cursing, but I looked up and noticed her crossing herself. Something else you didn't see much in Trans-Angeles. It reminded me of Momma.

"I bounced back and forth between the government youth centers and one foster family after another, until I ran away and did the best I could on my own." I laughed softly. "That usually meant petty scams, ripping off the gangs, whatever, just to make a quick score. I got caught and would have wound up in an Ice Cube—a punitive hibernation center. But the war meant I had a choice, and enlisted in the Marines."

I picked up a wrench and made a show of going back to work on the chest latch, trying to shove the emotion back down where it belonged.

"I'm no psych councilor," Maria said softly, "but I'm guessing you don't tell many people that story."

I shook my head, still pretending to concentrate on the armor.

"Everybody's got their own problems."

She put a hand over mine, stopping the clanking of the wrench and bringing my eyes back up.

"I'm not out here because I'm some kind of patriot," she said. "I'm out here, my dad is out here, because the Tahni killed my mother, my husband, my daughter. They killed everyone I ever loved."

I would have expected the words to be tinged with anguish or fury, but instead I thought I heard something softer, something that might have been empathy, if I even knew what that sounded like. I couldn't recall the last time I'd heard it.

"I'm sorry." It sounded totally inadequate, but it was all I could think of. "How…how old was your daughter?"

She squeezed her eyes shut for just a half-second, the only indication she might be on the verge of tears.

"She was thirteen. Her name was Jackie and she loved horseback riding and soccer. And not a day goes by that I don't think about her, and how old she'd be."

She wiped at her nose.

"Everyone has a reason to be out here," she went on, letting her hand slip off of mine. She smiled, and I thought it might have been the saddest expression I'd ever seen. "Listening to yours doesn't make mine less important, it just means I know why you wear the armor."

"Some days," I admitted, "I wonder if the armor wears *me*. I'm not sure if there's anything of me inside it. Every new group home I went to, every new scam I pulled, every rip-off, I stripped away another little piece of that seven-year-old boy from Tijuana, and I'm not sure what's left."

"Dad says we're all like coral reefs."

The non-sequitur stopped my thoughts in their tracks and I stared at her, uncomprehending.

"Oh, you're from the city," she realized. "Have you ever heard of a coral reef?"

"They're in the ocean or something, right?" I guessed, fishing blindly back into my memory for something I might have read as a kid.

"Coral," she explained with the patience of a teacher, "are little sea animals that live together in colonies. They find something like a rock formation or an old shipwreck or whatever, something solid, and they stick to it and secrete these little shells. Millions of the shells grow up around whatever piece of rock or metal was down on the ocean floor, and they just keep building up over time until there's this huge, colorful mass of life built on dead memories. It makes a home for fish and other sea creatures, a sort of oasis in an underwater desert."

She waved a hand as if she were wiping the image off a screen.

"I've never seen them live and in person, just videos from Earth. But Dad says our lives are like that, built on hard, cold rock, or the wreckage of someone else's junk, but we keep making new memories on top of those, building up in layers, something new always on top of something older, life on top of death. And you aren't that rock at the center, or that old piece of discarded junk, you're what you built on top of it, one layer at a time."

"So, I should go jump in a lake and shit all over myself till it hardens?" I was trying for funny, but managed only bitter sarcasm and I shrank in on myself, knowing I was doing the same thing I always did, and I'd get the same result.

I expected Maria to realize what a worthless shit I was and leave me stewing in the sun. I was ready for it, preparing a rationalization in my head; how she was just some backwoods local girl and we had nothing in common and I should learn to keep my mouth shut.

Then she kissed me.

An electric shock ran down my spine and back up again, the lightness in my head and the warmth in my face reminding me I hadn't as much as touched a woman in nearly a year, since Pris ran off with a bag full of Kick and left me to the cops.

Had that been a year? Shit, I wasn't that kid anymore.

"Make better memories," she told me, drawing away, her hand still burning white-hot against the skin of my cheek, "and you'll make a better Cam Alvarez."

"We, uh…," I stuttered as she rose to her feet and pulled me with her. "We don't have a lot of time. I still have to fix the suit."

I wasn't sure where we were headed, just someplace back behind the cluster of buildings, towards the lean-to's shaded from the afternoon sun.

"You have plenty of time to fix the suit," she assured me. "Let's work on the man inside for a little while."

"That's gonna be a stone-cold bitch," I declared with morose certainty, staring at the frozen frame of black-and-white video from the drone feed.

"Well, it's all gonna be a gigantic…." Dak hesitated, squinting over at me in the dim light of the trailer. "What'd you call it again, Cam?"

"Clusterfuck," I supplied.

"Yeah, that. But what specific bitch are we talking about?"

"Those." I touched the screen to freeze the video, then swept my finger back and forth across what looked like a line of dirt mounds stretching across the front of the Tahni installation. "They're fortified bunkers. Each of them has a heavy KE gun turret and at least two or three Shock Troops inside."

"Shock Troops?" asked Charlie, the one I'd mentally designated as Toothpick when I first met him. He still had the toothpick, or another just like it, walking back and forth across his lips.

"It's what the military types call their line infantry," Maria reminded him. "The ones in the powered exoskeletons."

I tried not to stare at her, but I knew that was nearly as obvious as staring would have been. Her hair was tied back into a ponytail hanging down her neck, but I'd preferred it loose and wild and spilling across my chest. She'd smelled of dust and sand and the faint fragrance of whatever body wash she'd last used, and her skin was preternaturally smooth, and I could have stayed with her on the ragged old mattress inside the tin storage shed for the rest of my life.

Shit. I was staring, and not talking. Maria rolled her eyes. I shook my head and tried to ignore Dak Shepherd's sly smile.

"Anyway," I went on, trying to wrestle my thoughts back to the subject at hand, "you've got over two kilometers of cleared, flat ground all around the base, and those emplacements will rip your trucks apart before you can get anywhere near them."

"Well, how the hell do we get past them, then?" Delta asked, spitting a stream of tobacco juice into a plastic cup. I shuddered. I'd never seen anyone chew tobacco back on Earth, not even in Tijuana. "You're the fucking Marine. How would you do it?"

"I'd do it with air strikes and missiles, but we got no air support and only two missiles." I rubbed the heels of my hands against my temples, trying to concentrate. "I never thought I'd say it, but I wish we had some Force Recon pukes along. They could sneak in ahead of time with sniper teams and take these things out from two kilometers, easy."

"Snipers, huh?" Dak murmured, peering closely at the image. "How?"

"The Tahni religion is weird," I told him. "They believe they're all sort of the living embodiment of the will of their god, so they like to stay as close as possible when they kill someone. They don't have remote firing turrets, they have a crew on every one of those guns, which means they have to be able to fire from cover…"

"Which means a gap in their armor," Dak surmised. He was a man who was quick on the uptake. I appreciated that.

"Two kilometers, Dad," Maria mused. "That's a hell of a long way, especially at night."

"Better at night," he corrected her, shaking his head in a curt, decisive motion. "Less heat mirage, less chance of updrafts at the end of the trajectory."

"You think you can make that long a shot with your rifle?" I asked him, a little skeptical. "I mean, it's not a Gauss rifle or a laser, right? It's just a hunting rifle, right?"

"It's an 8mm electric-ignition, electromagnetically stabilized Tannhauser," he rattled off as if it would mean anything to me. "It fires variable-velocity, tungsten-jacketed ammo at up to 2,000 meters per second with less than a meter of drop at two thousand meters."

"I know all those words you said must be related, somehow," I told him, shaking my head, "but when you put them together like that, they just seem like one giant wall of static to me."

They all chuckled as if that was the funniest damned thing in the world, even Maria.

"I've taken elk at two thousand meters up in the mountains more than once," he elaborated. "I reckon I can hit one of those big Tahni fucks, or at least make them keep their heads down long enough for you all to make it through their lines."

"I hope you aren't the only one," I said, looking doubtfully at the others. Maria, I trusted, though maybe it was a mistake to judge her marksmanship by the fact she and I had knocked boots a few hours ago, and Dak seemed utterly competent, but Charlie, Delta and the others? I wasn't so sure.

"I might could make the shot," Delta ventured, chewing on her lip. "I mean, I've shot that far in practice, never had to take any game from that distance." She smirked at Dak. "*Some* of us can actually stalk up on an elk or an oryx without having to try popping them from outside sniffin' range."

"I think Johnny could do it," Maria said. "He's got the rifle for it, and he always brings home an elk when they're in season."

I resisted an urge to ask who Johnny was, not wanting to sound jealous or possessive.

"Get him," Dak ordered. "And someone go find Carmelita, too. She's not as good as Johnny, but we need at least one sniper team for each bunker."

"They'll spot you after the first or second shot," I warned him. "They have thermal imaging, sonic detectors, ballistic calculators to run reverse vectors on your shots…. You're going to have to be ready to move."

"Don't worry about us, son. Whether we live or die, the only thing that matters is you getting that suit to the target. That city is the heart of this world. If the Fleet destroys it, this colony is dead, no matter how many of us survive. I'm too old to outlast my home." His eyes were bleak. "I've outlasted too much already."

22

"I still don't like you coming along on this haul," Dak insisted, having to yell into my ear to be heard over the rumble of the alcohol-fueled truck engine and the thump of the tires on the rutted dirt road.

Clouds of dust billowed around the ancient vehicle, obscuring the primary star—I had to remind myself not to call it the Sun. It felt weird being out in the day, but everyone had assured me we would have stood out even more at night, when the ground cooled and our hot engines lit up the enemy's thermal sensors. They'd also assured me the Tahni didn't care about the dirt farmers going about their business, since they were seizing about three quarters of their output to feed the hostages in the city.

"If anything happens to you, the whole thing is…" Dak squinted at me. "What was that term you used, again?"

"FUBAR," I supplied, bouncing off his shoulder in the back seat of the cab. It was like ramming into an oak tree. "Fucked Up Beyond All Recognition."

Another Marine term I'd only learned in the last few months, but it had come in handy. Along with goat-rope, SNAFU and candy-ass, among others. The military had no end of terms to describe how badly the military sucked.

"Yeah, that," Dak agreed. "You're the only one who can operate that damned suit. You should be back at the trailers with Maria." He sneered. "Making believe the Goddamned storage sheds are soundproof."

I tried hard to swallow the frog in my throat and it did its best to choke me on the way down. Dak stared hard enough to burn through BiPhase Carbide, and I thought I might not have to worry about the Tahni killing me, but he couldn't keep the expression up and it cracked into a grin.

"Don't worry about it, kid," he assured me. "Maria is a grown woman. Normally, I'd be worried about you being too young for her, but I get the sense you've seen too much in this life to be too young for anything." He shrugged. "But you should still be back where it's safe."

"There's nowhere on this planet that's safe," I said earnestly. If I was being honest with myself, I was glad Maria had been too busy planning for the assault to come along. "But you're going to need me for the transmission. They're not going to just take your word for it that you have a functional Vigilante and someone qualified to operate it. I'll need to include my biometric data in the transmission. Otherwise, they'll just go right ahead and launch those nukes and everything we do down here won't mean a damned thing."

"And you know so much about how the Fleet brass makes its decisions from your vast experience as a corporal?"

"I don't remember anyone saying you shouldn't be listening to a corporal when you were all asking me what to do about the Fleet nuking you," I reminded him.

"Point," he acknowledged. "But if you get yourself killed, I'm going to make sure there's a memorial to how damned stupid you were."

"If you two are ready to stop arguing like an old married couple," Charlie said, leaning back over the front seat to yell to us, "we're coming up on the Mendelssohn place."

I tried to catch a look through the windshield at the road ahead but couldn't see much more than dust and a few green patches among the red and brown.

"Are these Mendelssohns going to mind us being out here?" I wondered.

"They're dead," Dak declared, his voice flat. "Ian and his son made the mistake of thinking they could take on the Tahni landing force with hunting rifles and a few machine guns."

"Isn't that what we're doing?" Charlie asked, not turning around this time. I was glad of it. Having a human driver was nerve-wracking, and every time he looked away from the road, I expected the truck to hit a ditch and flip over.

"Just drive, Charlie," Dak echoed my unspoken sentiment.

The wreckage of the house was old, dating back to the invasion, the charred and blackened remains fading now, washed by rain and baked under the system primary until it almost seemed a natural formation.

"Lot of those around outside the city," Dak commented, but didn't elaborate. I wondered if the house he'd shared with Maria's family had been one of them.

The truck rumbled past the ruins and on by the silent memorials of storage sheds, still standing but long neglected, down nearly another kilometer before we reached the silo. It was tall and cylindrical and I had never seen its like before.

"What the hell is that for?"

"Grain storage," Dak said, giving me a curious glance, as if anyone should know that.

"Grains? You mean like corn?" Momma had grown corn in her garden, though not much of it. Mostly, we'd traded with neighbors for it.

"Corn, wheat, oats, barley," he listed off. "What, you don't have those on Earth anymore?"

"Except for corn, I don't even know what the rest are," I admitted. "And I only had corn as a little boy. We just had soy and spirulina in Trans-Angeles." I shrugged. "And the occasional rat. At least in the Underground. I imagine the Corporate Council execs up in the towers got to eat whatever they wanted."

"Damn. That's no way to live." The old man shuddered slightly, as if the thought horrified him.

"That's the way ninety percent of the people on Earth live. Probably six billion people, between all the megacities."

"Like fucking bees in a hive," Charlie commented, pulling the truck up beside the silo, braking hard enough to throw me against my harness.

"Worse," Dak argued, seemingly unaffected by the rough stop. "At least the bees get to go out in the fresh air before they die."

"I'll probably never see it again," I mused, stepping out of the truck. "Whether I live through this war or not."

"Don't tell me you miss it!" Dak said, and I snorted a laugh at the instinctive distaste in his words.

"I don't know. It's the only home I've had for most of my life." Which was short, compared to his, but it was all I had to go on.

The silo seemed as dilapidated and neglected as any of the other buildings on the property, except for the thick, solid-looking padlock securing the broad, sheet-metal doors. Charlie touched a keycard to it and it popped open with the snap of an electromagnet de-powering. The hinges shrieked in protest at the man's attempt to pull the doors open, finally yielding after an honorable struggle, allowing light into the cavernous interior of the grain storage building.

It might have once held corn or one of those other things Dak had been ticking off, but right now, the only thing it contained was a skeletal contraption about two meters tall, folded in on itself and affixed to a wheeled base. If I hadn't already known it was a transmission antenna, I would have had no clue.

"Where did you guys get this thing?" I wondered. "You made it sound like Fleet Intelligence only sent down a drop pod barely big enough to hold your communications gear."

"They did. But they had the key components for this thing in there, and they gave us the instructions on how to fabricate the rest from raw materials we had laying around." Dak went down to a knee in front of the machine and unfolded a keypad, exposing a small, 2D screen beneath it. "Tell me what we need to say, since you're so damned indispensable, boy."

Luckily, I'd been thinking about it. He hit the record button and nodded to me.

"Message to Commander, Commonwealth Expeditionary Force," I said, hoping I sounded official and not just overly dramatic. "Aware of your plan to deploy fusion missiles against the Tahni base. We have a Marine drop-trooper with a functioning Vigilante battlesuit available and plan to utilize him in conjunction with local militia forces to take out the Tahni InStell transmission antenna while you bombard their deflectors with proton cannon fire. His biometric signature will be attached to this transmission."

I sucked in a breath. This was the hard part.

"We are asking you to hold off on missile launch until 2330 local time to give us the chance to take down the deflectors. If we fail in our mission, we understand you will have to follow up with the nuclear strike. We are attempting to evacuate as many colonists as possible from the city, but clearing them out entirely won't be possible given the Tahni presence. This is a chance to preserve as many innocent lives as possible."

Dak hit pause, and I thought I saw respect in his eyes.

"Not bad, kid." He motioned me over. "Now show the screen your face and handprint and we'll haul this outside and set up for the transmission."

"How long of a timer can we put it on?" I wondered, remembering what Maria had said about the Tahni homing in on the thing when it began transmitting.

"We could do an indefinite timer," he said with a shrug. "But the Fleet ship is only going to be in position to receive the signal for another hour, so help me get this thing unfolded and arranged outside so we can get the hell out of here."

"Dak!" Charlie slammed through the door, breathless, his face pale. "There's a vehicle coming up the old access road from town! It's still a good klick away, but I think it's a Tahni patrol!"

"Shit." Dak's eyes clouded over in concentration and I almost thought I could make out the gears turning in his head. He unslung his rifle and shoved it at me, followed it up with the belt of magazine pouches he'd worn buckled at his waist.

"What the hell am I gonna do with this?" I demanded, holding the rifle awkwardly. It wasn't the first time I'd handled a gun, but this thing was a qualitative difference from the military Gauss rifle I'd qualified on in Basic.

"You two stay in here. I'm gonna close the door and lock it, and I want you both to be quiet and not move an inch until I come back."

"How the hell are you going to face down a Tahni patrol?" Charlie demanded. "You think you can talk your way out of this?"

"I think I have a better chance doing that than we have of standing them off with an Alamo in a fucking grain silo."

He backed out the door, not waiting for any more arguments, and the doors swung shut with a grim finality, meeting at the center with the solid thump of a coffin lid. Metal scraped metal and I knew he was putting the lock in place. The interior of the silo was plunged into darkness and shadow and I became instantly aware of every rustle of dried grain beneath the soles of my boots.

"Fuck this," I murmured.

I buckled the ammo belt around me, slung the rifle and scanned around for the source of the stray beams of light leaking in from somewhere above us. Gaps in the sheet metal glowed in the afternoon glare, just narrow fissures here and there…except for the unmistakable square of a door positioned at the front, along a service catwalk. I followed the scaffolding around to a rickety-looking wood and metal ladder and I tried not to make too much noise as I climbed up it.

"What the hell are you doing?" Charlie asked. He had his handgun out but didn't seem to know where to point it or what to do with it.

"He's going to need cover if this doesn't work," I hissed an explanation. "Shut up and get up here with me."

"This is a bad fucking idea," he insisted, absurdly tip-toeing across the grit-strewn floor, stifling a yell into a barely-audible squeak as something I couldn't identify ran across his foot.

Rat, probably. Another accidental tourist, like me.

The scaffolding creaked under my weight and I winced, hoping it couldn't be heard from outside. I held my breath for a second and listened. The hum of the Tahni engines was eerie in its unfamiliarity. Someone had told me they used hydrogen-burning vehicles. We had them some places, or at least I'd been told we did, but the military didn't use them. Why bother when we had isotope reactors that would run for years without servicing?

Polymer tires scuffled and thumped over the dirt road, scritching and scratching their way to a stop. I edged closer to the small doorway, idly wondering what it was for. Maybe to let cargo trucks dump grain into the silo from the top? I looked for a latch and finally found something crude and metal and nearly rusted shut. A gap of about a centimeter marked the boundary of the hatch and I squinted through it, barely making out the enemy vehicle.

It was wedge-shaped, utilitarian and ugly like nearly everything Tahni I'd seen, open-topped with a crew-served KE gun swinging back and forth at the guiding touch of an armored Shock Trooper.

Dak approached slowly, hands held out by his sides, fingers spread. I kept my eyes on him as I worked at the door latch, firm but patient, trying to break it loose without slamming it against its stop and giving us away.

There were four of the Tahni, half of one of their squads, and they clambered out of the vehicle's open sides, their weapons scanning in every direction, searching for threats. Metal crunched under their boots and the servos at the joints of their powered exoskeletons hummed and whirred quietly, supporting their extra armor and heavier weapons. They didn't have battlesuits, and I wondered if there were any High Guard on the world at all.

"Hello!" Dak said loudly. "What can I do for you gentlemen?"

I used his voice as cover and put a little more force into the latch. It broke loose with a gentle rasp and I managed to keep it from slamming into the metal, letting my knuckles take the brunt instead, barely restraining myself from crying out from the impact. I held up my hand and sucked at the blood welling up from my knuckles.

"What are you doing here, Earther?"

The voice was harsh and yet also somehow soulful and rhythmic, like a chant, coming out of the speakers on the exterior of the Tahni's helmet. It was eerie hearing the alien try to speak English, a haunting unfamiliarity, beyond another human trying to speak a different language and more like a chimpanzee trying to speak.

"Still got to feed the family," he said. His voice was plaintive, attempting to sound a bit indignant at being questioned, though I wasn't sure the Tahni would be able to detect the emotions in his tone. "I need to repair the feed funnel for the silo."

"Where is your authorization?" The sing-song chant was the same cadence as before, rote terms learned to deal with us without any real understanding.

I pushed the hatch open a few more centimeters, just enough for me to squeeze the barrel of the hunting rifle through. The scope was simple and intuitive, nothing more complicated than the manual sights of the Gauss rifles we'd trained with, just a matter of putting my eye to it then settling it on the helmet of one of the Tahni. It focused automatically, following the movements of my retina, and the six-centimeter wide visor swam into stark clarity. Something flickered behind the polarized polymer, maybe the alien's eyes glancing around. My thumb found the clearly labelled safety and flicked it off.

"I wasn't given any special authorization," Dak said. "I thought you guys needed the output from our farms to feed the population of the city."

"You are not allowed away from your residence without authorization." The Tahni Shock-trooper raised his KE gun to cover the older man. "You will be taken into custody."

The same tone, the same inflection, but to my ears, it was the handing down of a sentence by a judge, condemning us all to death.

Shit. Shit, shit, shit, shit.

"Search me," Dak invited. "Search my truck. I'm only here to repair a grain silo so we can all eat. You want us all to be able to eat, don't you?"

The Tahni was having none of it. He took long, loping steps towards Dak, one hand maintaining cover with his KE gun, the other reaching out to grab at the human's shoulder. I made a decision. I'm not sure when the flip had switched, and I knew I'd probably be getting us all killed, but I couldn't let them haul Dak away. Not only would he most likely wind up dead, but I was fairly certain the whole attack plan would fall apart without him.

I was no sniper, nor was I Force Recon, but the range was only fifteen or twenty meters. There was no way I could miss.

Famous last words.

"Dak, get down!"

I pulled the trigger.

23

THE RIFLE PUMMELED MY SHOULDER, THE STOCK THUMPING AGAINST my cheek like a short jab from an opponent I'd let in under my guard and I cursed in surprise and dull pain. But the bullet was gone and my inexperience hadn't been enough to throw off its trajectory. Time slowed with the decision to pull the trigger, tachypsychia gripping my thoughts in its adrenaline-soaked claws, and I thought maybe I would get to see a Tahni face live and close up, but when the slug punched through the thick, polymer faceplate, everything behind it splashed back in a spray of red and the legendary too-human face was erased, splintered and torn, before I even caught a glimpse.

The shot had been a crack of summer thunder and it echoed off the sheet metal silo and rolled across the rolling fields of untended grain. Before its echo had quite reached the closest rows of wheat, time slipped back into regular motion, and the Tahni moved with it. I had seconds. Their armor would tell them where the shot had come from by analyzing the sonic waves and projecting the trajectory on their equivalent of an HUD, the same way ours did in the Vigilantes. Their reaction would be slower because the Shock-troop exoskeletons weren't hooked up via an interface link to their brains, so I had seconds. Just long enough for one more shot.

Picking the next target was instinctive, deducible only in hindsight, long after my subconscious had made the decision. There were three Tahni remaining, one standing to the left of the vehicle, blocked off from Dak by the bulk of the ground-car and the corpse of the team leader, still propped upright by the locked joints of his exoskeleton. The second was behind the car, probably not even understanding what had happened yet, while the third was still behind the controls of the gun mount. He was the biggest threat, in a position to take me and Dak out, and firing the biggest gun.

The scope seemed to take forever to focus on his helmet visor, the targeting reticle swimming into view with glacial slowness, but

I forced myself to hold my finger off the trigger until the red ring solidified across the tinted polymer. I heard the report this time, a pressure wave hitting me in the sinuses and the chest and blasting through my ears with a painful whistle.

The Tahni behind the KE turret must have been off-balance, because the powered joints of the exoskeleton didn't keep him standing. He pitched backwards off the rear of the vehicle, somersaulting head over heels into the dirt, and then I moved.

What would have made sense would have been jumping back into the silo, sheltered from view if not from the tantalum darts of their KE rifles, but that would have left Dak alone and unarmed, exposed to enemy fire. I pushed Charlie down off the ladder back inside and leapt forward out of the hatch, my stomach staying up on the platform while the rest of me dropped the three meters to the dirt.

I hit hard, striking on the balls of my feet and falling to the side, calf, thigh, hip and shoulder, and the breath went out of me with a star-filled burst of pain in my upper back, but I kept my hold on the rifle. The Tahni Shock-trooper on the left side of the car had opened fire on the hatch where I'd stood just a moment before, the shockwave of the stream of tantalum darts a chain of miniature sonic booms. Sheet metal shrieked in death agony as the barrage tore it to pieces, yet I ignored the shots, ignored that enemy soldier and concentrated on the one coming around the back of the car.

I wished I could afford to look back, to figure out which direction Dak was moving, but the Shock-trooper approaching from the rear of the ground-car was going to have a clear shot at me in about two seconds. I could have tried to crawl to my left, to keep the body of the vehicle between me and the enemy, but I was lying on my back and time wasn't my friend.

I rolled onto my belly, hugging the rifle to my chest like a security blanket, centimeters ahead of a burst of tantalum darts. The sound of the incoming fire was nothing I'd ever heard before, an unending chain of painful, supersonic snaps reverberating inside my head, their incessant beat taking my heart rhythm with it into a tachycardic drum solo. I fired and missed. The stock banged into the top of my shoulder like the backhand slap of a disappointed marksmanship instructor at Basic.

I could hear him screaming in my ear as if he were a specter of a former life.

Damn it, Boot! You will *achieve a proper cheek weld before you touch that trigger! You take another shot without proper cheek weld and sight picture and I will shove that weapon up your ass sideways!*

"Yes, Drill Sergeant," I murmured.

I shut out the sound, the fear and the prospect of immediate death and put the aiming reticle over the trooper's lone vulnerable spot. Something tugged at the borrowed work shirt where the fabric billowed up around my right shoulder, a scoring line of heat from the passage of the round only half a centimeter from my flesh, and I touched the trigger. The recoil was satisfying, comforting in its precision and I knew I'd hit what I was aiming at without bothering to look at the results.

Because now I really had to move. I had no direct shot at the Tahni on the other side of the car and by now, he'd know exactly where I was and what I was doing.

Forward. I needed to move forward, take the chance he'd head toward the silo and I could keep their ground car between us. It wasn't a brilliant plan, but it was as close as I was going to come up with while crawling on the ground on my belly. I couched the rifle in my arms and scuttled like a cockroach fleeing the light, cursing softly at the rocks and gravel digging into my knees and elbows. Something itched in the middle of my back, maybe sweat, maybe an insect inside my shirt, but I imagined it was the phantom touch of the enemy laser sight tickling against my skin. I was about to die. I put my head down and kept moving.

The KE gun thundered again and there was something different about the sound, the direction of the echo, and I knew instinctively that it was firing from this side of the vehicle, that I was too late. I waited for the kill shot, for the end, and discovered, to my shock, that the idea scared me. I'd never wanted to die, but I'd also never had any particular fear of it. I was going to die scared, and somehow that bothered me.

The gunfire stopped.

That didn't seem right. I raised my head and saw nothing but the side of the assault vehicle, heard no hum of servomotors or clanking of armor.

"Get up, junior."

Dak stepped out from behind the frozen statue that was the first Tahni casualty, the enemy soldier's KE gun cradled in his arms, the power cable still connecting it to the battery pack hanging from the dead alien's shoulders. The muzzle was glowing and I looked from him to the other side of the car. The final enemy soldier had toppled onto his side, his chest armor ripped apart by a long burst of tantalum darts from his dead comrade's gun.

"You'd better not have messed up my rifle," Dak said, letting the Tahni weapon fall. It came up short on the power cable, the muzzle scraping across the ground, sweeping dirt back and forth.

He grabbed the hunting weapon from me, checking the safety and grunting in satisfaction before he slung it over his shoulder.

"Where the hell's Charlie?"

"Oh, shit," I realized, running back over to the door.

Dak hadn't fastened the padlock, just threaded it through the hasps, and I yanked it out and tossed it to the ground, pulling the door open. Charlie was on the ground, cursing and holding his ankle, the afternoon glare shining down on him through the shredded metal a few meters up.

"I think I broke my fucking ankle!" he said, glaring at me. "Why the hell did you push me off the ladder?"

"So you wouldn't get shot," I said, hauling him up off the ground. He leaned into me, cursing some more when he tried to walk on his right foot.

"Get in the truck," Dak ordered, leaning into the carriage of the transmission antenna and pushing it out through the open doors. It looked pretty weighty, so I assumed the wheels were motorized and it was assisting his movement.

I half-supported Charlie as he limped out toward the cargo truck, past the Tahni dead. Two of them still stood, as if they'd been turned to pillars of salt like Lot's wife in that Bible story my Momma had told me.

"They'll be coming to check this out, Dak," Charlie warned him, grabbing the handle on the truck's passenger side door to support himself, "once that patrol doesn't come back."

"We'll be long gone," Dak said, not sounding bothered by the prospect.

He was unfolding the sections of the transmission dish, a flower unfolding to accept the attention of the sun.

"You know how to drive this thing, kid?" Charlie asked me, pulling himself into the cab.

"Not even a little," I assured him, climbing up behind the wheel.

The fact it even *had* a steering wheel was troublesome. There were no personal vehicles in Trans-Angeles, but I'd seen a few down in Tijuana. The military had trucks and ground-cars on Inferno, of course, but even those had computer-assisted controls. This thing was completely manual and the prospect of trying to keep it on the road was terrifying.

"Well, there's a first time for everything. Hit that start button on the console and get us ready to take off."

The machine rumbled plaintively, some great beast wanting to be fed, and the vibration of the internal-combustion engine shook the hard plastic of the driver's seat like a warning. I tried to pay attention to Charlie's explanation of how to operate the thing, but my eyes were glued to Dak's systematic assembly of the antenna and the conviction it was taking too long.

"Did you get that, kid?" Charlie asked and I stared back, wondering if I should admit I hadn't caught a word of it. He sighed and rolled his eyes. "I said," he repeated, "you just push the 'forward' button on the panel beside the wheel to shift it into gear, then press the accelerator, the pedal next to your right foot, to make it go. The one on the left makes it stop."

"Oh, right, sure." I glanced down at the panel and tried to find the button. It didn't actually say "forward," but there was an F lit up across it, which I supposed was close enough.

When I looked back up, Dak was climbing into the rear passenger's side, frowning at me, eyes narrowed.

"What the hell, Charlie? Can't you drive with one foot?"

"I could if it was my left foot," the man in the seat beside me replied, then motioned at me before Dak's door was even closed. "Go, damn it! You waiting for an engraved invitation?"

I hit the button and jammed my foot down on the accelerator. The truck's polymer tires sprayed dirt and gravel and the big vehicle fishtailed wildly, nearly hitting the Tahni armored car. I clenched my teeth, gripped the wheel tightly and let off the gas just slightly, steering us around the circle and away from the silo. The transmission antenna watched silently, a man with his arms raised in prayer, oblivious to my struggles.

"Jesus!" Charlie was fastening his safety restraint with desperate haste. "Slow the hell down!"

"No," Dak said sharply. "Floor it. We need to be far away from here before that transmission gets sent or their drones will trace the truck back to this place."

"Whatever you say." I pushed the pedal down and tried like hell to keep the truck between the ditches.

The truck shuddered and rattled its protest and each rut in the road tossed me from side to side but I didn't let up. My fingers clenched the wheel so tightly my knuckles were going white, and I let them, because otherwise, my hands would have been shaking. My heart was hammering against the inside of my chest, and sweat was pouring down my neck, plastering my shirt to my back, and it wasn't the driving, or the open spaces, or even the throbbing pain in my shoulder from where I'd landed. The adrenaline was leaching out of my system and taking with it the cool detachment I'd felt during the brief gunfight.

"Hey," Dak said. Something about the tone of the word caused me to risk taking my eyes away from the road long enough to glance back at him. There was understanding in his expression. "You did good back there. You made the right call."

"I guess there's a first time for everything." My voice broke a bit and something quivered in my chest. I felt like I could have sobbed and only an iron grip on my emotions pushed them down.

It was ridiculous. It wasn't like it was the first time I'd almost got killed.

Dak was silent for a moment, and I thought maybe he was disappointed in my reply, but then I heard him whispering a countdown.

"...zero." He twisted around in his seat, looking behind us. "It's transmitting. Any time now."

The terrain had changed; the flat plains of the abandoned farm disappeared behind us, giving way to rolling hills. I hadn't remembered to check the distance, but I thought it had to be at least six or seven kilometers. My eyes flickered down to the display showing the rear-view camera just in time to spot the missile.

I don't know what I'd expected, maybe an assault shuttle, or a squad of High Guard, or even an orbital kinetic kill strike. I suppose I should have known better. The missile was efficient and versatile and the rising globe of fire coming over the hillside was plenty impressive, certainly enough to wipe the transmitter, the silo and the dead Tahni patrol out of existence.

The sound rolled over the hills like distant thunder about the same time the dome of white expanded into a mushroom cloud rising hundreds of meters into the sky. Not a nuke, of course, but enough Hi-Pex, chemical hyper-explosives, to make a good try of it.

"And maybe we're next," Charlie murmured, staring at the screen, face drawn.

"No, we're good," Dax insisted. "They'd have gotten us by now."

I didn't know if he was trying to convince Charlie or himself, and I wasn't at all sure he'd convinced me.

But I kept driving.

"Why the hell were you driving?" Maria asked, hanging off the side of the door as I clambered down from the truck.

I winced when I saw how close I'd come to scraping the bumper of one of the open-topped rovers crammed into the narrow draw. It looked like a huge, mutated beetle with curved armor plating welded across the engine compartment and covering the passenger cab, and a decades-old assault gun peeked out above the shielding on a pintle welded into the floorboards.

"Charlie sprained his ankle."

"It's fucking broken!" Charlie insisted from the other side of the vehicle.

Shadows were invading the depths of the canyon and I could barely make out his pained grimace as he limped around the front of the truck, waving aside a few younger hands and their offers of help.

"I guess that means we'll be pulling off the attack without you," Maria said, raising an eyebrow as she regarded his pitiful limp.

"Oh, fuck that!" Charlie blurted, looking askance at the woman. "Just get somebody to wrap my damn ankle and I'll stand on one foot and shoot!"

"If you want it wrapped," Delta scolded the man, grabbing at his arm, "then stop pushing away everyone who tries to help you and let's go wrap it!"

Charlie looked as if he were about to argue with her, but he reconsidered and let her slip an arm around him and help him walk back toward the trailer.

"Wait a second," I said, turning back to Maria. "You're talking like the attack is a sure thing. Did we hear back from the Fleet?"

Dak was at my right shoulder, appearing there like a wraith, remarkably silent for a man his size, and I could see the same question in his eyes. Maria nodded, seeming sober more than jubilant.

"We did. They've given us until the original deadline to hit the Tahni. They'll start the bombardment just as they planned and if the shields aren't down by the time they already planned for the launch, they'll hit it with nukes." She looked between Dak and me. "We have to attack tonight."

"It's what we figured," Dak allowed. He fixed me with the sort of glare I would have expected from Top or Gunny Guerrero. "Is the suit ready to go?"

"It's as ready as it's going to be," I told him. If I didn't sound confident, it was because I had learned all too well from Mutt just how many things could go wrong with a Vigilante even when it hadn't fallen out of the sky at a thousand meters per second. "The missile launchers work and that's about all I can swear to."

"Then that's going to have to be enough." He slipped an arm around his daughter. "I guess I won't bother to ask if I can talk you into sitting this one out."

Her only answer was to lean into the man and return his hug. He shook his head and headed off, yelling orders at a gaggle of younger men and women who were clustered around one of the up-armored trucks, ooh-ing and ahh-ing over the ancient assault gun as if it were the coolest thing in the world instead of a weapon gone obsolete before their grandparents were born.

"Are you all right?" Maria asked. I supposed I must still look shaken up, though I was actually beginning to level off from the adrenaline dump and the subsequent fall.

"Nothing a few years of psychological counseling wouldn't cure," I assured her, seeking out her hand with my own.

Her hand was warm and the sheer human contact seemed to breathe life back into me. She tightened her grip and leaned her shoulder against mine. I wanted to ask her what we were, what this meant, and I didn't know why. I'd never asked Pris, never asked any of the other girls over the last four years. It wasn't something you talked about out on the street, and even if it had been, I wouldn't have cared. They were just someone to have fun with, someone to warm my bed…on those rare occasions when I had one.

"Do we have any time before we need to get ready?" I wondered, and I hoped I didn't sound desperate.

"Not enough," she told me, and it sounded like a lament. Then the corner of her mouth turned up and she tugged at my hand, leading me away from the crowd. "But we'll make time."

24

THE VIGILANTE HAD BELONGED TO A GUNNERY SERGEANT FROM Second Platoon, and I felt oddly nervous wearing it, as if the man's ghost might start yelling at me from beyond the grave for dishonoring his armor. More practically, it felt like putting on someone else's underwear and it made me profoundly uncomfortable. I pulled the chest plastron down, hoping the feeling would fade in the darkness; instead, it intensified. For the first time in my memory, I was scared of the dark.

The HUD crackled to life and began searching for satellite signals it wasn't going to find, and the return of the light brought with it the breath I'd been holding. The passive sensors couldn't make out much stuck in the covered bed of the cargo truck, and I didn't want to chance active lidar or radar driving through the wasteland trying not to get noticed.

"You read me up there?" I wouldn't have risked radio either, but this close I could get a line-of-sight hookup with Maria's datalink up in the cab. For once, I didn't want to be alone.

"You got that shit working?" Maria demanded, all hard edges and bluff now, her own armor back in place, maybe for my benefit or maybe for the gunner in the seat beside her. He'd looked way too young and way too scared to be doing this. "That bombardment's going to kick off pretty soon and it's not like we can call the Fleet and ask for a time-out."

"As well as it's going to." I winced. I hadn't meant to sound that harsh. "I'll make it work," I assured her. "How much farther?"

"Just a few minutes till we hit the end of the draw."

I tried to remember the map she'd shown me earlier; the suit's mapping software was useless without a satellite lock. If I recalled right, we should be no more than six kilometers from the base, heading up a draw that would dump us out onto the flat plain outside Gennich. Three kilometers of open killing ground, and if the Tahni didn't believe in automated weapons turrets for religious reasons, they made up for it with the sheer number of manned positions they dug into their perimeter.

And I knew exactly how they planned to get me through that killing ground. I wanted to ask her to drop me off at the end of the draw then turn around and go back, wanted to make her promise not to charge across the open field in the truck to draw fire away from me, but I knew how little good that would do.

A flare sparked out in the darkness, like far-off lightning just outside my field of view, then a peal of thunder rolled across the hills above the draw. Another, louder, and the flashes grew brighter, reflecting off the clouds. It was no storm.

"Show's starting," Maria announced. "Be ready to jump."

The sides of the draw were getting closer, and I steadied myself with the broad palms of the armor's hands as the truck swerved sharply around trees and rocks. The thunder was getting closer too, adding a new timbre to the vibration of the truck bed beyond the uneven dirt and gravel of the path. It blended together, a single, bass note reverberating off the narrowing walls around us, just as the sporadic lightning became a constant glow, a fire blazing across the sky and turning night to day.

I rose to a crouch, feeling the suspension of the truck bed shift beneath the weight of the suit, the gyros keeping it balanced despite the wild swerving like one of the surfers I'd seen on livestreams back in Trans-Angeles. The wave of terrain we were riding arched upward sharply and the armor's footpads scraped against the metal of the truck bed. I grabbed instinctively at one of the struts of the cargo frame, the metal bending under the claw-like fingers of the armor's glove. The whole strut began to pull loose from the frame, ripping free of the canvas with a tearing sound I could hear over the engine, the tires, and the thunder of laser weapons burning down through the atmosphere.

Then we were over the top, out of the draw and onto the flats, and I let go of the strut and slid backwards off the truck bed, with Maria's redundant yell of "go!" ringing in my ears. The truck was going fifty kilometers per hour when my armor finally went out the back, and I hit the ground running at nearly the same speed. Tufts of grass and clods of dirt flew up around the Vigilante as the foot pads ripped into the soil; the hip actuators screamed in protest and yellow warning lights flashed in the periphery of the HUD, but I kept the suit on its feet, slowing down gradually until it reached a speed I thought the suit could handle without ripping apart.

The truck pulled away, its rear end jostling and bouncing over the ruts in the dirt and gravel road, and suddenly everything was laid out in front of me, a surreal tableau of the end of the world. The Tahni base stretched out before us, still over two kilometers away but large and looming for all that. It was a utilitarian square a kilometer on a side, glowing with the crackling, sparking static of the deflector shields rising from dish-shaped projectors at the perimeter of the featureless outer walls, trying to absorb gigajoules of energy from the proton cannons spearing down through the atmosphere, pounding at its defenses. Air heated to plasma around the microsecond pulses and the plasma forked in bolts of lightning, visually impressive but harmless compared to the raw, actinic energy of the particle beams, and the super-ionized air formed a dome over the boxy lines of the enemy base, outlining it in fire.

God Himself pounded down on the Tahni redoubt with a judgement from Heaven that couldn't be contested, only endured. Until the answer came, blasting from a concealed emplacement at the edge of the shield coverage, a laser fed directly from the fusion reactor buried a hundred meters beneath it, rending reality itself with the raw energy it embodied, tearing the night apart with a flare brighter than the naked sun.

Protective filters in my helmet were all that saved me from immediate and perhaps permanent blindness, and I hoped the goggles I'd noticed Maria wearing would be enough to preserve her vision. She kept the truck more or less straight, and I ran in the perceived concealment of the dust cloud billowing out from its tires, the Vigilante's footpads striking the ground like hammer-blows.

The turrets could be shooting at us by now, if they'd seen us. I thought maybe that was a sign the sniper teams were working, at least distracting the Tahni if not actually hitting them. I had no way to tell. The Tahni KE guns had little thermal signature and I wouldn't be able to see the snipers firing unless I was looking right at them.

Whether they were doing the job or not, the only direction worth going was forward.

The interface wrapped my mind in a protective skin of raw data, highlighting possible targets, selecting weapons systems, calculating distances. I buried myself in the information, trying to ignore the certainty of death gnawing at my hindbrain, the expectation of the enemy slug, missile, or beam that would seek me out and end me...or end her. The sensor readings were a fireworks show, energy flooding them in every spectrum, and I knew the others were out there, charging across the open plain in all-terrain rovers, four-wheelers, dirt-bikes or trucks, but I couldn't make them out through the heat and the lightning and the smoke rising from the charred ground at the edges of the deflector shields.

I couldn't make out the Tahni defensive positions either, couldn't detect any incoming fire, and I dared to hope for just the space of a few seconds that even if the snipers hadn't gotten them, maybe the enemy troops had retreated underground to ride out this battle of the gods. We were less than a kilometer away from the windowless, grey ramparts, close enough now that I could see our target, a dish antenna just to the two o'clock from our angle of approach, huddled in a niche in the wall...that was when the Tahni saw us and the KE turrets opened fire.

Tantalum darts launched by an electromagnetic coil gun at 3,000 meters per second tore into the dirt to my left, then sliced across the front of the truck; it slewed to the right, the tires digging in, then it was yawing leftward, time stretching out as it slowly went over under a hail of gunfire. It tumbled in a barrel-roll, bits of the chassis flying away like rats abandoning a sinking ship, and I was only two steps from crashing right into it and being swatted away.

I jumped. If the Vigilante's jets had been operational, it would have been a two hundred-meter arc landing me all the way at the InStell antenna, but with just the byomer muscle fibers and a pair of wonky hip actuators, I cleared the rolling cargo bed of the truck by only centimeters. And landed nearly on top of the Tahni weapons emplacement.

There were three Tahni Shock Troops inside the clamshell cover of the half-buried bunker, all in powered armor a head shorter than my battlesuit and a quarter of the weight. The opening in the front of the bunker was just large enough to operate the crew-served KE gun; I grabbed the emitter of the weapon and yanked it out, ripping it off its pintle mount and tossing it behind me. The gunner nearly went with it, letting loose at the very last second, while the loader and the security trooper tried to bring up their laser carbines.

I stuck half of his suit's right arm into the opening where the KE gun had been and fired a pair of grenades out of the launcher affixed to the armor, then jumped again. I didn't need to see what came next; the flare of thermal energy on my rear cameras told the story. I wondered if they screamed. I'd never heard one scream, never seen the faces inside those mirrored helmets except in the pictures they showed in mission briefings.

I came down with just a hundred meters to go, and one more line of defenses to get through to do it. They were already firing at me from the last bunker off to my right and fifty meters away. I bounded back and forth like a skater on the ice, feeling the tantalum darts zipping by me more than seeing them. The armor moved with grace and power, connected directly to my thoughts via the interface, and I reveled in the feeling of being truly whole again for the first time in days.

I swept my right arm around, aiming not with my eyes but with the instinctive feel of pointing a finger, and fired the plasma gun with the whisper of a thought. The packet of super-ionized gas speared through the weapons port just millimeters above the crew-served KE weapon and exploded when it contacted the gunner. White glare filled the darkness of the bunker for just a fraction of a second, then the weapon fell silent and there was no movement.

I tilted back the suit's upper torso and looked up. The deflector shield was a star, stretched and flattened, and hovering only a few hundred meters above me, holding back the fury of the primary laser batteries of two Fleet cruisers firing from orbit, but only just. It was a domino waiting to be tipped.

The antenna was just over a hundred meters away, the dish at a slight angle, aimed for one or another of the system's Transition Hubs, the only way to send messages faster than light other than sending them on a starship. It would have been more efficient to use a satellite, but Fleet could shoot those down as fast as the Tahni put them up. I could see the armored cables running from the base of the transmitter through conduits under the walls, leading all the way down to the reactor…almost point-blank distance.

The missile launchers swiveled into place, rotating forward from a vertical position on either side of the nonfunctioning jump-jets to lock horizontally over both of my shoulders with a solid, metallic clunk, a coffin lid closing. Warnings flashed in the HUD, repeating the list of targeting malfunctions I'd already seen, and I ignored them, scrolling down to manual guidance and activating the laser designator built into the helmet.

When I fired, if things worked out the way I hoped they would, the shields would collapse in seconds, and anyone out in the open within a kilometer or so of the base would likely be dead. Including the resistance fighters keeping the Tahni defenses occupied.

And they all knew it when they volunteered. Just like I did.

I wished I could look away, but I had to guide the laser designators; I stared down my fate with eyes wide open. The battlesuit rocked back on its heels as both missiles shot from their launchers at once, covering the hundred meters in less than a second, and everything was light and sound, pressure and confusion. I was on one knee, my other leg stretched out behind me, the suit's torso low to the ground as the shockwave from the blast of the warheads passed above me, and I had no idea how I'd gotten into the position.

The suit must have done it, I thought dully, watching the fireball climb into the sky, spreading out across the deflector shield as it rose…

Got to move.

I pushed himself to my feet and turned away, wanting to witness but knowing it would be the last thing I ever saw. There wasn't time to get to a safe distance, but I ran anyway, as fast as the suit would go, ignoring the warnings of failing actuators, trying to ignore the scene above me even as it teased at my eyes in a projection on the upper right corner of the HUD. The deflector shield was flickering, and I had only seconds…

She was there, at the truck, staggering, blood streaming down her face and soaking the side of her jacket. Two thoughts collided in my brain like the clash of cymbals.

Maria.

And,

The bunker.

Only a couple hundred meters away from the walls of the Tahni base, it was still far too close, but it was half underground and *hell, there's no better idea.*

I grabbed her with my left arm across her waist and swept her in front of me, too rough for her condition but there was nothing else to be done. And there was the bunker, the entrance seeming way too small, but I pushed her ahead of me and squeezed through with the scrape of metal on metal that set my teeth on edge, and there was just no time…

The world ended in fire.

25

"GUNNERY SERGEANT MCINTIRE?"

My eyes fluttered, then squeezed tightly shut at the harsh light.

"It's all right, Gunny, you're going to be okay."

"Ain't no Gunny," I murmured, my voice sounding harsh and raspy, my throat sandpaper. "I'm a fucking Lance-Corporal."

I forced my eyes open just a slit, saw the habitually concerned face of a med-tech hovering over me, backlit by glowing ceiling panels. Inside. I was inside, somewhere. A hospital? A plastic cup was brought up against my lips. I tried to move my hand to grab it, but I didn't seem to have any strength in my arms. The water was heaven, washing away the cotton in my mouth and soothing my dry throat.

"Your armor's ID said you were Gunnery Sgt. Alan McIntire," the soft-edged face said, slowly withdrawing the cup. The guy was young, maybe as young as I was, with hair cut to a fuzz that barely showed up against his pasty skin and the unmistakable white duty uniform of a Fleet medical technician.

"Cameron Alvarez, Lance Corporal, 187th Marine Expeditionary Force," I recited. "My armor was a write-off and Gunny McIntire…" I let my head loll back against the pillow. "He didn't need his anymore." I tried to look down at myself, but couldn't seem to sit up enough to manage it. "Where the hell am I? Why can't I move?"

"You're at a Fleet aid station in Gennich," the med-tech told me absently, absorbed with entering my newly-discovered name in his work tablet. He looked back up and smiled. "We took over the local hospital once we chased the Tahni out of it."

The smile thinned out. "And you can't move because we had a neural block on you for the last three days to keep you under and motionless while the regen packs did their job. I'm afraid you were quite badly burned, but you're fine now." He held up a hand to forestall the panic he'd anticipated. I didn't feel panic; I felt nothing. "It should wear off in a few minutes."

"Three days," I repeated. I wanted to move, wanted to sit up and look around. *Where was she?* "There was someone else with me when..."

"Let me check," the man offered, cutting me short with the air of someone who'd been asked the same sort of question too many times. "I can pull up the record of when they found you."

He scrolled through screens on his tablet, and I could tell when he found the report by the way his eyes flickered back and forth, skimming the text. I could also tell by the way the corners of his mouth tightened against a scowl that what he found wasn't good news.

"I'm sorry, but the woman they found you with in that Tahni bunker didn't survive. Only the armor saved you...and it almost didn't."

I wasn't listening anymore. I'd known, of course. On an intellectual level, I'd known she couldn't have lived through it. But I'd held out the barest scrap of hope in the irrational recesses of a child's brain that still believes in Santa Claus.

I pretended to sleep, hoping the man would go away.

"Alvarez."

I sighed. Couldn't the guy take a hint?

When I opened my eyes, the med-tech was long gone and Dak Shepherd stared down at me.

I fell asleep. This is a nightmare...

But the smart bandage wrapped around the old man's left arm, the bald spots where hair had been burned away from the side of his head and the charred fringes of his shirt told another story. This was too depressingly real to be a nightmare.

"Mr. Shepherd, I'm sorry..." I began. I tried to push myself up in the bed and this time I could; I actually *had* slept and for long enough that the neural block had worn off. I realized I was wearing disposable hospital clothes, neutral grey. My skinsuit had probably been burned off along with a few layers of the skin beneath it, but what I could see beneath the sleeves looked fine, pink and baby smooth.

"Don't." The man's face was still carved from hardwood on the side of a totem pole, but there was something else behind the dark eyes now, a pain I hadn't seen there before. Shepherd sat on the edge of my bed, not a familiar gesture but more a near-collapse.

For the first time, I noticed the room around him. Cheery yellow painted on local wood, a single window with the shades pulled against the mid-day sun. It was built for three, but I was alone. Not many wounded then; probably a great many dead.

"We tried," he said, his voice infinitely tired. "I hit one of the gunners. I could see it in the scope. The gap in the turret was just ten centimeters or so, but I hit him right in the helmet. But the damned armor was too thick. I got his attention, but I couldn't take him out. They barely wasted a half a dozen rounds on me, and it was just about enough." He motioned with his injured arm. "None of the other shooters made it. Delta, Johnny…none of them."

"Sir," I tried to interrupt, "Maria, she…"

"She knew she wasn't going to make it out of there," Shepherd said. "And somehow, she knew *you* would." He peered at me closely. "How did she know that?"

"I had less to die for." I hoped the answer didn't seem blithe. It was as honest as I could make it.

The old man grunted, whether in acknowledgement or skepticism, I couldn't guess.

"This city, you know why it's called Gennich?"

I blinked at the non sequitur. "No."

"It was my wife's family name." His lip curled in what might have been a smile. "I asked Hannah if she wanted me to name it after her, but she thought Gennich was a better name for it."

Shit. That was over a hundred years ago. He's older than I thought. Then, another thought on the heels of the first. *Hold on a second…*

"You founded this colony?"

"And you saved it. You and Maria and the others who…" He didn't finish. "I wanted to offer you something, something she would have offered if she were here. Something worth dying for. A home."

I felt my mouth hanging open and made an effort to close it.

"This war won't last forever," the old man pointed out, dark eyes locking with mine. "What are you gonna' do when they won't let you wear that armor anymore?"

"What would I do in a place like this?" I laughed sharply. "I grew up in a box; I can barely go outside."

"Boy, three days ago, you came an ass-hair from killin' yourself without blinking an eye." Shepherd's eyes flickered downward. "And you did your best to save Maria before you saved yourself. They told me they found her in the bunker with you trying to shield her." He took a long moment before he could go on. "I figure you can work your way through this, if you want to."

Shepherd pushed himself back to his feet, then paused to awkwardly pat me on the shoulder.

"I'll be around the hospital the next couple days. Let me know what you decide before they ship you out of here."

I nodded to Shepherd, hardly trusting myself to speak as the old man left the room, shutting the door behind him. I swung my legs off the side of the bed and carefully stood, still feeling a pins and needles sensation in my lower legs. The window was only a few steps away and I pulled the shades up, squinting into the afternoon light. The hospital was the tallest building in the city, and past the battered and battle-pocked structures at the edge of town, the plains where the Tahni base had been were visible.

A column of black smoke still rose over it, three days later, a kilometer across and billowing into the sky, a monument to the ones who'd died to save their home. No one had died to save Tijuana. They'd abandoned it to the cartels and the gangs and the violence, and anyone worth a damn just wanted to get away, to get somewhere safe, where the government would take care of them. I'd seen how well that worked out. Maybe a life out in the colonies wasn't such a bad idea, after all.

I was still staring at the smudge of blackness when the knock on the door shook me from my thoughts. I made myself a bet in the half-second before I turned. Fifty-fifty odds it was the medic again, and the same probability that it was a Fleet personnel functionary sent to correct my misidentification as Gunny McIntire. Poor bastard, buried somewhere in the wilderness, dead before he could fire a shot.

I would have lost the bet.

"Alvarez," Lt. Joyce Ackley said, smiling broadly. "It's good to see you in one piece."

"Ma'am!" I blurted, frozen in place between one step and another, for the second time today, sure I was seeing a ghost. "Holy shit, how come you're still alive?"

She chuckled, but there was a tug of pain in the lines beside her eyes, lines I didn't recall being there before. She stepped inside, moving a bit stiffly, as if she'd been hurt but not bad enough to be treated for it, and leaned against the wall, letting her head settle back.

"It was a near thing," she admitted. "The front end of the drop-ship held together a bit longer than the rear, just long enough for a few of us to make it to the ground without breaking every bone in our bodies."

"A few?" I stuttered out the words. I was afraid to ask and I looked away from the trauma playing out across her face.

"Ten," she elaborated, the words like broken glass. "Just ten of us lived through it, including you, and you were the only survivor from the rear of the bird. Me, four troopers from Third squad, Sandoval, Scotty Hayes…." I glanced up, finally hearing some good news, almost ashamed of the wash of relief I was feeling. "…and Cunningham."

I couldn't stop the snort of dark amusement.

"God loves idiots," she observed. "But he doesn't love them too much." Her expression was bleak. "Cunningham is stuck in a tank of biotic fluid up on the *Iwo Jima*, in a medically induced coma while they grow him a new spinal column."

I winced, flush with sudden shame at my thoughts about the man. Cunningham was an asshole, but that wasn't something I'd wish even on him.

"The rest are all pretty banged up to one degree or another, including me." She frowned. "I'm curious as to how the hell you wound up without a scratch and inside someone else's suit."

"My Vigilante went for a swim, ma'am," I confessed, giving her a brief run-down of what had happened. I didn't mention Maria, or her father's offer to come back here. I liked Lt. Ackley well enough, but we weren't exactly close.

Are you close with anyone?

"At least Third Platoon accomplished the mission," she reflected softly. Her gaze sharpened as she focused on me. "You know you're probably going to get a Bronze Star for this?"

"I hadn't thought about it, ma'am." I still wasn't. "Is Scotty here in the hospital or back upstairs on the *Iwo*?"

"He's here." Finally, a smile crossed her face. "I just found out you were here. They still had you listed as MIA until about an hour ago. He and Sandoval don't know you're alive yet."

I returned her grin with one of my own.

"If you don't mind, ma'am, I'm going to go take care of that myself."

———————

The hospital was small and old-fashioned, like something you would have found in Tijuana, but with fewer gunshot wounds. The rooms were numbered by floor, but the ones where Lt. Ackley had told me Hayes and Sandoval were staying were empty when I checked them out. I was wandering around the third floor, looking for a doctor or medical technician to ask about them, since there wasn't as much as a central data system terminal I could 'link into, even if I'd had a 'link to do it, when I found the break room.

It wasn't much, just a few pressed-wood tables and folding chairs gathered around as if in worship at the altar of an ancient coffeemaker, but there they were. Hayes was sitting in a wheelchair, his right leg extended out, wrapped in a bone-knitting sleeve, while Sandoval leaned against the table, looking pale and haggard but otherwise unencumbered by any portable medical equipment.

"Leave it to a couple Marines to find the coffeemaker," I said, leaning against the door frame to the break room.

They both stared at me, frozen, speechless, and for a half a second, I thought they weren't going to say a word. When the words came, they tumbled out and tripped over each other and Sandoval was rushing me as if it were unarmed combat training, and I almost went into a takedown defense. She swept me into a hug and I knew Hayes would have, as well, if he hadn't been confined to the chair.

Her embrace was strong enough to make my ribs creak and I returned it with equal enthusiasm, surprised at how glad I was to see both of them.

"Oh, Jesus Christ, Cam," Sandoval murmured in my ear, her breath warm against my face. "We thought for sure you were dead. Oh my God, how the hell did you get out?"

"It's a long story," I said, arms still around her. It felt indescribably good holding her. Beyond the fact she was an attractive woman who I'd been interested in for months, just the sheer warmth of human connection was almost overwhelming.

I wanted to say something, anything, but I couldn't speak. I was crying, the sobs racking my shoulders, crying for Betancourt and Rodriguez and Gunny Guerrero, crying for Maria and the gunner whose name I hadn't even known. Crying for Poppa and Anton, and for Momma. And for myself, for the youth I'd lost and the pain and the loneliness, for all the things I'd forced myself to endure without complaint because there was no one to listen to me whine, no one who would have cared.

Sandoval didn't let go and neither did I. She was saying something comforting, too low for me to hear, though I picked up the meaning. Hayes' hand was on my arm, squeezing support even though he was stuck in his chair, muttering agreement with whatever Sandoval said. I wondered if they'd already done their crying in private. I hadn't. I'd never trusted anyone enough to let myself cry in front of them, not even myself. Gradually, so slowly I thought it would never end, the sobs ebbed and I sucked in a breath, feeling empty and yet fulfilled all at once.

Sandoval pushed my face off her shoulder, reaching up and wiping at my cheeks with the sides of her hands, then taking my face between her palms and kissing me ever so softly on the lips. She pulled back and the surprise must have shown in my eyes, because she laughed.

"I think," she said, disentangling herself from me, "you can call me Vicky now."

"Hi, Vicky," I said, offering a hand. "I'm Cam."

"Nice to meet you, Cam," she said in utter seriousness, shaking my hand as solemnly as if we'd just concluded a business deal.

"I hope Cam's a nicer guy than that Alvarez dude," Scotty Hayes said, jabbing at my side, a mischievous glint in his eyes. "Because he could be a real prick."

26

THE CARGO HOLD OF THE COMMONWEALTH SPACE FLEET TRANSPORT *Iwo Jima* was depressingly roomy. A full company of Vigilante battlesuits had been packed into her confines three weeks ago, and now half of them were gone as if they'd never existed. Empty suit carriages yawned open like hollow graves and I tried to remind myself that not all the Marines who'd worn them were dead. A lot of suits had been wrecked in the mis-drops, a lot of people injured and trapped behind the lines, kept alive by the suit's medical systems until after the battle's end, like Lt. Ackley, Scotty Hayes, and Vicky Sandoval.

Hell, I'd lost *two* of the damned things in the space of three days.

I don't know why I'd come back down here. The hold was basically deserted during Transition, when the artificial gravity was activated. Why try to move around two-ton suits in one gravity when they could just wait until we popped back into realspace and take advantage of the microgravity?

But there were too many officers wandering around the crew areas looking for someone to comfort or recommend psych counseling to and I just wanted to be alone for a while.

"Gonna take a while to fill all those empty slots."

A few weeks ago, I might have jumped or sprang to attention at First Sergeant Campbell's voice, but instead, I just nodded to the woman.

"It sure is, Top." I looked at the gaping hole where Gunny Guerrero's suit had been stored. "I don't know how you're going to do it."

"Same way they do in any war, son," she said, her tone surprisingly casual, even friendly. I found it a little disconcerting, like I should be checking over my shoulder for an ambush. "We promote what's left and let them train the next group of newbies."

She was looking at me sidelong and I groaned as I realized what she meant.

"You gotta be kidding me, Top," I said, throwing up my hands. "I was just learning to be a damned team leader!"

"And now you're going to have to learn to be a squad leader," she said, irritatingly reasonable. "Just like Sergeant Hayes is going to have to learn how to be Gunny Hayes, platoon sergeant."

"Holy shit," I breathed the words, wondering how Hayes would react to that. "I guess it just hasn't sunk in yet."

"It won't for a while." She sounded as if she'd been where I was standing. "It hasn't quite for me, either. That's why I came down here, to convince myself they're really gone, give myself some time to deal with it."

"How long have you been a Marine, Top?" I asked her, finally taking a good, long look at the woman. At close range, I could finally see she had that aged yet ageless appearance of someone who'd been born on Earth or the inner colonies, and had the advantage of life-extending biotechnology.

The corner of her mouth turned up, as if she enjoyed the idea that someone had finally asked her.

"I enlisted as a private in the United States Marine Corps during the Sino-Russian War," she told me, and the hair stood at the back of my neck.

"Holy shit, Top!" I blurted. "That was…"

"Over a century ago," she finished for me. "Yes, I know." Her eyes clouded over, her shoulders sagging just slightly as if under the weight of memories. "And if you think this war is bad, pup, you should have tried watching your technological society that's been balanced on a razor's edge for decades finally collapse in on itself. We were all pretty sure it was the end of the world, you know?"

I didn't know. I couldn't even imagine. I'd seen the videos, the history documentaries showing the horrors of the nuclear war between China and Russia that had nearly brought an end to civilization, but I couldn't put myself in her shoes any more than someone born and raised as a Surface Dweller in Trans Angeles could imagine what it was like to live in Tijuana.

"The old cities burned," she said, her voice quiet, almost a whisper. "Los Angeles, New York, Chicago, Atlanta…and that was just in the United States. London, Paris, Rome…anywhere the food stopped coming, the riots started only days later. The police couldn't stop them, so they brought in the military and the streets ran red with blood. And when the world came up for air, nearly four billion people were dead, and the old world with it." She blew out a breath as if the words had exhausted her. "I stayed a US Marine until the Commonwealth took over all military duties, then I took my retirement. For all of thirty years. This was right about the time the life extension treatments became available. I had nothing else to spend all that money I'd saved on, and my veteran status put me near the front of the line. It was like starting over. Got a normal job, got married, raised three kids."

I didn't speak. This seemed unreal, the confessions of a ghost from another time, and I didn't dare interrupt for fear she'd fade into the shadows as if she'd never existed. Or, more likely, yell at me and give me extra duty for interrupting her.

"Got divorced," she went on, her shrug philosophical. "Retired from another career. And was looking for something meaningful to take up what looked like it could be a very, very long life. And then we found the wormholes and the Tahni along with them, and all of a sudden, the Commonwealth needed a Fleet, and the Fleet needed a Marine Corps." She smiled thinly. "And the Marine Corps needed me."

"How the hell aren't you a general by now?" I asked, honestly amazed. "Or Sergeant-Major of the Marine Corps?"

Top barked a laugh.

"Two reasons, kid. First, I'm far from the only old-timer in the Corps, and people who've been around as long as us tend not to quit. And two, and if I'm being honest most important to me, is that First Sergeant is the highest rank I can handle and still be on the front lines. I didn't join the Marines to sit behind a desk, and I don't think you did, either."

"I joined the Marines because I didn't have any other choice, First Sergeant," I admitted.

"I read your file, Alvarez. Don't flatter yourself," she added, "I read the files of all the newbies. You had a choice. You could have turned in your accomplice and gotten away with a slap on the wrist. You joined the Marines because you didn't want to be alone. You wanted a family, and the Marines will give you one. Just like any other family, you won't be able to stand some of them, and you'll spend as much time fighting each other as fighting the enemy, but in the end, love them or hate them, they'll have your back."

If anyone else had said it, I might have argued with them. When I'd said yes to the deal, I could have sworn I was joining up to get myself killed and get it over with. But I could have done that in the train station, if that was what I wanted.

"If you'll excuse me, Top," I said, making a decision…or perhaps merely giving in to a realization. "There's something I need to do."

Wade Cunningham looked like death warmed over. He was out of the Tank and back in a sick bay bed, which meant the nanite bath had done its job and finished regrowing his pulverized vertebrae and mending the gaps the fragmented bone had torn in his spinal cord, but you don't get that kind of thing for free. Especially not when you spent three days in a coma, with only the suit's medical systems to keep you alive. Where Cunningham had once been filled out, beefy, intimidating, he now seemed drained and skeletal.

He was asleep when I stepped into the compartment, and I thought long and hard about turning around and heading back. Then his eyes fluttered open and swam into gradual awareness, focused on me.

"Alvarez," he rasped, trying to scoot up in bed. I wouldn't have thought he had the strength, but somehow, he reached the button to raise the mattress up, then grabbed a cup of water from the bedside table and gulped it down. "What are you doing here?"

"I heard they had to grow you a backbone, Cunningham," I said, grinning a challenge. "About time, huh?"

Cunningham's expression twisted into a scowl for a second, firming up his sagging features for an instant, but then his head settled back into the pillow and he began chuckling, low and long.

"You're an asshole, Alvarez," he said, "but I guess I was a bigger one. And at least you came through." There was bitterness in his tone and in the set of his eyes. "All I managed to do was pound myself into the ground like a fucking tent stake."

I felt weird looming above him and I sat down on the edge of the hospital bed, instead, bringing us about level with each other.

"It was dumb luck I came down over that lake," I assured him. "Two seconds one direction or the other, and I'd either be dead or in the next bed over from you."

"I came down pretty close to the city," he corrected me. "If the Fleet had gone ahead and nuked the Tahni base, I would have been dead, and so would a bunch of the rest of us. You kept that from happening."

I shook my head, uncomfortable with approbation in general and in particular from Cunningham, someone who'd pretty much hated me before. It felt dishonest, somehow, as if he suddenly liked me for a situation which I hadn't been in control over instead of for who I was.

It doesn't matter. You don't have to love him, you just have to work with him.

"You'll have your own chance to be the hero, Wade," I told him, trying to mimic Gunny Guerrero, or Top, or the Skipper, because I was not any sort of leader. Maybe if I could imitate the Marines that I knew who were leaders, people wouldn't notice. "There's a lot of war left to fight."

I slid off the hospital bed and clapped him lightly on the shoulder.

"Hit me up when we're back on Inferno and I'll buy the first round at Myths and Legends. And maybe this time, I won't have to wake up in a jail cell."

"Sure thing." He raised his forearm and I bumped it. "Thanks for stopping by, Cam. And I just…" He trailed off and I thought for a second he was about to cry. "Just thanks."

"Any time, Wade." I tossed an offhanded wave as I left. "Get better."

I let the door shut behind me, pausing in the passageway to take in a breath. That had been so much more awkward and uncomfortable than I'd imagined, and I'd imagined it being pretty bad. How the hell did anyone do this for a living?

"Get better, son. There's work to do."

I glanced over at another of the sickbay compartments and saw the Skipper standing at the bed of one of the wounded, smiling down at the man, managing to look comforting and solicitous and so very confident, all at once. I didn't recognize the patient. I thought he might have been from Fourth Platoon. I knew he was a drop-trooper because not one of the Force Recon Marines had survived the ambush.

I stopped and watched Captain Covington, trying to memorize how he engaged with his people. When he finished up and headed out of the compartment, I thought about ducking away before he could see me, but it was too late.

"Visiting a friend, Alvarez?" Covington asked me. The question was innocent, casual, but I could see the canny understanding in his eyes. He knew exactly what compartment I'd come out of, who was in it, and what our history was.

"Visiting a fellow Marine, sir," I said.

He nodded, and I thought I saw approval in his look.

"Good job down there, by the way" he said. "I haven't had the chance to speak to you, but I wanted to let you know."

I felt my stomach constrict. I couldn't listen to anyone else going on about how good a job I'd done.

"It wasn't all me, sir. It wasn't even mostly me. The civilian resistance down there did the heavy lifting. They laid down their lives for their home. I just launched the missiles."

"You made sure the mission was accomplished," he said, brooking none of my argument. "The mission, the troops, and you. That's been the guidelines for every leader in every military since the Egyptians and the Babylonians." He grinned, a wry twist to the expression. "And no, I wasn't around for those wars, though First Sergeant Campbell may have been."

I guess that was supposed to be funny, but I only had a vague idea who the Egyptians and Babylonians were, except that they were a long time ago. I thought they had something to do with the Greeks and Romans, but I couldn't have sworn as to which one came first. I gave what I hoped was a polite chuckle, but it came out as even weaker than that.

"It's not the troops that's bothering you, though," Covington deduced, decades of wisdom behind his grey eyes. "It's the civilians, isn't it?"

"Yes, sir," I admitted. A medic tried to weave between us in the passageway and I squeezed against the bulkhead to make way for her. Covington didn't move, and I guess he didn't have to.

"It's something we've lost sight of," he mused. "On Earth, anyway. People back there hear about colonists being killed by the enemy, but it doesn't seem real. Wars don't touch Earth anymore, and the only people who die violent deaths are the gangbangers in the Underground who no one cares about."

My eyes narrowed, and I wondered if he was being sarcastic or simply trying to get under my skin. I decided on the former, since I didn't want to take a dislike for the man on incomplete information.

"But this is a war," he went on, all humor, dark or not, gone. "And civilians die in wars. For most of history, more civilians died than soldiers and sailors. Then things changed and the wars moved off Earth and so did the warriors, and all those pampered Earthers forgot the price. But people like you and I, we get to see it all, up close and personal."

"It's not the first time I've seen death up close," I reminded him. I was sure he knew already. "I saw my mother die in front of me. I hid in a broken-down car in the desert heat and heard the screams as bandits killed my father and my brother. And it still hurts, sir. It still hurts just as bad."

"I've seen quite a bit of death myself, son. It always hurts and it always will. If it didn't, you wouldn't be a Marine anymore, just a stone killer."

"They're recruiting us from the Underground," I reminded him. "From criminals heading for a century in hibernation. You can't tell me the Marines don't have any use for stone killers."

"We have a use for them," he admitted. "They make great mine detectors."

"Sir?" I asked, blinking in confusion.

"Sorry, old saying. They're cannon fodder, the people you point at the enemy and set them off to trigger ambushes. What they're not good for is making leaders, making trainers, making the Marines who'll actually win this war for us."

"You think I'm that?" I couldn't keep the skepticism out of my voice.

"I think," he told me, backing toward the lift banks, out of the sickbay, "that you're going to have the chance to find out."

EPILOGUE

THE CORRIDORS OF THE THIRD PLATOON AREA OF DELTA COMPANY Headquarters were depressingly crowded with baby-faced newbies, wandering around with wide eyes and confused looks, all afraid to ask anyone above lance corporal for directions.

Which left me out, thank God. That and the bump in pay were the only good things I could think of about the promotion to E-5, staff sergeant. Two months of an accelerated NCO Academy certainly hadn't been fun. Getting yelled at by pricks who'd never heard a shot fired in anger, having them tell me how to lead a squad in peacetime when we were in the middle of the biggest war in human history, having them teach me how to effectively yell at other people...none of that had been even remotely positive.

I thought of it as a ritual, like getting beaten into a gang, and made it through. Although getting beaten into a gang was one of the many things I'd sworn never to do when I left the group home.

At least this gang has the biggest guns.

The platoon sergeant's office was tiny, though at least he had one. The squad leaders had to share an office nearly as small, with four desks crammed into it. Fortunately, we rarely had the chance to use them. Maybe that was the other positive about being an E-5, though only in comparison to being an E-6.

I knocked.

"Come!"

Scotty Hayes looked very much at home behind the platoon sergeant's desk, though I noticed he still hadn't done anything to personalize the office. He'd been closer to Gunny Guerrero than I was, so I didn't give him any shit about it.

Standing in front of the generic, unadorned desk was a generic, unadorned PFC. He still had the shaved head of Armor School and the slight redness around his 'face jacks of someone who'd only had them implanted a few weeks ago. He shared the slightly lost, confused expression of the other newbies, but there was something in his eyes, an animal cunning you saw in the Underground on the true survivors, combined with the spark of real intelligence behind it.

"Hey, Cam," Hayes said. He nodded toward the PFC. "This is Private Thomas Henckel, one of our new Armor School graduates. I'm putting him in First squad to fill that hole in Alpha team. You want to take him back and show him around, get him settled into the barracks?"

"Sure," I said. I offered Henckel a hand and he shook it a bit hesitantly, as if the gesture was unfamiliar to him. "Nice to meet you, Henckel. I'm Sergeant Alvarez, your squad leader. You got your duffle out there somewhere?"

"At the front desk," he confirmed. His voice was strong, confident, despite being out of his element.

I waved at him to follow and pushed the door shut behind us, nodding to Hayes.

"Where you from, Henckel?" I asked him. "Do they call you Tom? Tommy?"

"I'm from Capital City, Sergeant," he said, grabbing his duffel and tossing it over his shoulder. It looked heavy, but he was a broad-shouldered, thick-chested and didn't seem to have a problem with it. "My Moms called me Tommy, but pretty much everyone else just calls me Henckel."

"What part of Capital City?" I knew already, I was just curious if they called it something different there.

"The Underground," he confirmed. "Jugghi Jhopri, the 3415." His eyes narrowed and he regarded me sidelong as we walked. "You?"

"Trans Angeles. But sort of all over."

He didn't seem satisfied with the answer, but it was the only one he'd get until I knew him better. We stepped out into the humid, dripping haze of late afternoon in Tartarus and I caught just a hint of discomfort in the way his mouth tightened.

"Don't like it outdoors?" I asked, and he glanced over at me with suspicion in his expression. I chuckled. "Welcome to the club,

Henckel. A lot of us are from the Underground. Did you ever even see the sun before you joined up?"

"I can handle it," he insisted, teeth clenched.

I said nothing. He either would or he wouldn't, but as long as he didn't wind up ditching his Vigilante in a lake, it wouldn't be a problem.

The barracks were nearly deserted this time of day. Everyone had gotten afternoon chow and settled into maintenance for the day and I knew exactly where the last available rack was in the last available room.

"Now the fun part," I told Henckel after he'd dropped his bag off on his bunk. "You get to link up to your Vigilante…and begin PMCS for the day."

"Joy," he murmured. He seemed about as awed and deferential as I'd been on my first day, which was not much. I wondered if he was actually that cool or if it was an act.

"Tell me something, Henckel," I said, pausing to salute a passing Second Lieutenant before he got all butt-hurt. "How's someone from the Capital City Underground come to join the Marines?"

He didn't answer immediately, again seeming as if he didn't quite trust my curiosity.

"You're from the Underground," he said, as if that explained it. "You know how it is there. Wouldn't you have done anything to get out?"

"Most people are happy," I countered, "with the free food, free housing, free entertainment, with never having to do a day of work in their life if they don't want to. I've seen them. They'd kill you if you tried to take it from them."

"Yeah, well, I didn't think I had much choice."

He frowned in disapproval when I laughed at that, stopping in the middle of the sidewalk heading to the suit storage bays.

"That'll only get you so far, Henckel," I warned him. "Sooner or later, you'll have to figure out why you're here."

"I can kill Tahni for you. Isn't that enough?"

"It's enough to make you a killer, not enough to make you the kind of leader who can win this war for us." I was stealing shamelessly. I didn't think the Skipper would mind.

"Is that what you think I am?" Henckel asked, boggling. "A leader?"

"I think," I told him, "that you're going to get the chance to find out."

———

The story continues in

KINETIC STRIKE

ABOUT
RICK PARTLOW

RICK PARTLOW is that rarest of species, a native Floridian. Born in Tampa, he attended Florida Southern College and graduated with a degree in History and a commission in the US Army as an Infantry officer.

His lifelong love of science fiction began with Have Space Suit- -Will Travel and the other Heinlein juveniles and traveled through Clifford Simak, Asimov, Clarke and on to William Gibson, Walter Jon Williams and Peter F Hamilton. And somewhere, submerged in the worlds of others, Rick began to create his own worlds.

He has written twenty-one books in six different series, and his short stories have been included in seven different anthologies.

He currently lives in central Florida with his wife, two children and a willful mutt of a dog. Besides writing and reading science fiction and fantasy, he enjoys outdoor photography, hiking and camping.

www.rickpartlow.com